MARILEE

Mary Francis Shura

SCHOLASTIC INC.
New York Toronto London Auckland Sydney Tokyo

ISBN 0-590-33433-6

12 11 10 9 8 7 6 5 4 3 2 1   2   5 6 7 8 9/8 0/9

MARILEE

A *SUNFIRE* Book

SUNFIRE

Chapter One

MARILEE Fordham released her hold on the ship's rail to brush a flying curl out of her eyes. When the young officer at her side reached out to steady her, she smiled up at him warmly.

The wind that blew in from the sea that January day in 1622 was a cold and bitter wind. It bloated the sails of the *Pryde of Gravesend* and bent the trees along the James River as it tugged Marilee's auburn hair from under the hood of her mantle.

"Virginia is not giving you the warmest welcome, I fear," Philip told her.

Marilee laughed softly. "I am not complaining," she reminded him.

Indeed, who among the passengers or crew aboard the *Pryde* would complain about any wind that buffeted them along the Virginia coast? Having survived four perilous months at sea, the very sight of land brought a surge of joy and relief.

1

Certainly Marilee was in no mood for complaining herself. On the contrary; when the first cry of "Land, ho" had been shouted by the excited lookout in the crow's nest, she had flown up from the cabin she shared with her aging maid to be the first one to watch at the rail.

She had not left that railing since, unless absolutely forced to. Except when he was off on ship's business, Philip had stayed at her side as they watched the land take shape. That slender, etched line on the horizon had deepened and gained color and form, until now the land lay close enough to smell the spicy scent of cedar trees and watch the smoke of hearth fires wend its way toward the clouds.

Until the day she boarded the *Pryde* for this passage, Marilee had spent the whole of her sixteen years on good English soil. Now, as she stared at the banks of the James, she had trouble remembering how it felt to step on firm land instead of balancing her slender weight against the swaying of the ship.

The wind gusted, loosening her hood to release more flying ringlets to whip about her face. She pursed her mouth and blew at them, only to have them tumble back, obscuring her view. With a sigh she shoved the curls back under the hood of her mantle and pulled its warmth tighter around herself.

Amused as always by her losing battle to keep that bright, abundant hair under control, Philip chuckled softly and leaned toward her with concern. "You would find it much warmer down in your cabin, Marilee," he advised her. "I shudder to think what your brother Matthew will do to me if I let this bitter wind blow you away."

She laughed up at him. "I can as easily imagine my brother behaving that violently as I can see myself frail enough to be felled by a breeze." Her hazel eyes were tender on the young officer's face. "I may be chilled, Philip, but I can't imagine being cold enough to miss my first sight of Virginia. After all, this will be my home from now on."

Although she had spoken the words bravely enough, she felt a sudden rush of tears to her eyes at the truth in her words. Even as she spoke she turned her head away, so that Philip could not see her face.

What had happened to her? She was not at all like the girl she used to be. She hated this business of being sad and fighting tears all the time. Before she had been happy without even trying. Her father had even teased her for being so well named. Marilee she had been named, and merrily she had gone through her childhood. She had been the first to see a joke, even if it was on herself. She had opened every dance and was the last to let the tired fiddler put down his bow. Even her childhood friends teased her about the way she could always see some bright side of any problem they had. "Life is entirely too important to be so heavy about," she had always claimed.

Yet, since her father's death, she seemed to have lost her hold on joy. The merest thing would fill her hazel eyes with tears, even as they were now.

Still she must not let Philip see that sad face again. Before meeting this young officer of the *Pryde,* she had only known of him as her brother Matthew's dearest friend and agent. She had been astonished to find him so young, a man in his mid-twenties, lean and graceful, with sandy hair and deeply set eyes, with a darkness that seemed bottomless in both their color and their expressiveness.

During this long sail he had become Marilee's own cherished friend. It was wonderful to have a new friend, and it was especially good to like Philip so well. Aside from a hundred acres of virgin land that Marilee would get for coming to Virginia and bringing her maid with her, all the property she owned lay in Philip's care. By the terms of her father's will, the money left by her mother would be managed and given to her by this remarkable young man.

And Philip *was* remarkable. She had learned how sensitive he was to a turn of phrase or a note of sadness in her voice. More than once on the voyage he had eased her grief with a perceptive word said in that deep and gentle voice of his.

She certainly didn't want Philip Soames ever to know how much she dreaded this new life she was facing in the wilderness of Virginia. It was no one's fault that she was unhappy. Every possible thing had been done to make this move easy and pleasant for her. Her brother was opening his home to her, and Philip himself had undertaken her welfare during this passage. How could she be so ungrateful?

Yet the grief that had come at her father's death had been joined by a growing fear, a formless, dark mass of pain that pressed against her heart, leaving her sleepless through the long nights of the passage.

Conscious of her companion's sympathetic silence, she forced her mouth to smile for him. "Besides," she reminded him in a teasing tone, "if I went down to my cabin I would be trapped there with Hannah groaning and howling of seasickness, as she has done the whole of this passage."

He laughed softly, showing a quick brightness of even teeth. "Poor Hannah. I hope that you are right in saying that she enjoys being sick. She certainly has had a king's portion of it during this trip."

"Nobody in the world enjoys worse health than Hannah," Marilee said, nodding briskly. "Even when I was very little and she was my nurse, I knew this. They say that my first words were groans of agony learned from Hannah's useless attempts to get out of doing what she was paid to do. My father used to say that even as a fish must have water to live, so Hannah must have her complaints."

Philip's face turned thoughtful. "While I realize that it would have been improper for

5

a young girl like you to make this long trip alone, I can't help wondering why you chose Hannah to be cooped up with all the way across the ocean. I am amazed that she even consented to come with you."

Marilee laughed. "You may not believe this, but she complained even more loudly at the thought of being left behind than she did about coming along."

His soft chuckle faded into silence. "No matter why she chose to come, it is still too bad that you couldn't have had a younger and livelier companion during these months. Someone like that would have made this a happier passage for you."

"Not possible," Marilee told him. "If I had been entertained by other company you would not have had to find the time to amuse me. I will always be grateful to you, Philip, for what you have shown and taught me. I will never see a gull floating on drafts of air without being reminded of you."

"The teacher learned more than the student," he told her. "Every growing thing will remind me of you, making me wonder if its leaves or bark hide the mystery of your healing art.

"Possibly," he went on, "it is just as well that you didn't bring some merry younger woman with you. You would be sure to lose her within a month of your landing at Jamestown. Some lovely Virginia planter would coax her to the altar as fast as the banns could be read. At least no one will steal your servant Hannah from you, not if they ever hear her chorus of groans."

Catching another wisp of that stubbornly flying hair, Marilee looked up at him. "All this talk of the scarcity of women in Virginia amazes me. After all, my brother found his wife here."

"Your brother Matthew Fordham is one of a kind," he told her. "Even as you are, Marilee."

Then, as if embarrassed by his own words, he returned to the subject of Hannah. "Poor old Hannah. Now she must even change the name of her ailment. One can't be seasick with the sea behind us and the water of the James River ruffling past our prow."

"The James River," Marilee echoed softly. She leaned eagerly against the rail to stare across the frothy water toward the land.

How wide the James River was. How swiftly it flowed as the tide swept in from the sea. How different it was from the rivers of her beloved England.

Without shutting her eyes she could see the Thames River winding its way through London, laced with bridges, mirroring the great towers and castles of that city. A sob caught at her throat.

"Not the same as London, is it?" Philip asked quietly, as if he could read her mind. Without waiting for a reply he went on. "When I first saw these banks, I had trouble believing them. Only in the King's parks does England have such trees. This country must

7

look as our England did in the past, before her forests were cut away. This is the England of yesterday, Marilee, and tomorrow."

"My tomorrows, anyway," she replied. "And I will love it," she promised, nodding as if to convince him as well as herself. "I will love Virginia because my brother Matthew is here, and because it was my father's wish that I come. But now," she went on brightly, "what is that darkness of logs set tightly against each other back among the trees?"

"That is Wolstenholme Towne. It has been there since 1619, and a considerable town it is. The palisades of the fort are made of logs. The stockade around Jamestown is made in the same way, as you'll soon see."

"I see the smoke of fires around that place," she told him.

"The planters have their homes and fields around the town, with every inch of earth set with tobacco plants. That whole area is known as Martin's Hundred." He took her arm. "But look there, a little up the river. That is the fort of Jamestown, where Matthew lives. The gates are already open wide to greet us. You can be sure that the first moment that our sail was sighted, some man leaped into his boat and rowed up to Jamestown to announce the news. Such arrivals are eagerly awaited."

Marilee couldn't restrain her steady flow of questions as the ship made its way upriver. Philip explained how the fortress of

Jamestown had been built in a great triangle, running a hundred and forty yards along the river at its longest side. "See where the corners meet?" He pointed them out to her. "The watchtowers there are armed with cannons."

Marilee was glad enough that as they drew near the fort, the increasing noise made it useless to try to talk. How long would it take her to get used to this constant talk of danger, of villages surrounded by stockades with guards and cannons against the world outside? She knew this must be necessary, having heard about the battles with the Indians, but being reminded of these perils chilled her more than the cold wind ever could.

The noise came from all directions, from above where the sailors shouted in the rigging and from around them on the deck, which teemed with activity. As the sails were trimmed for the dropping of the anchor, a swarm of small boats left the shore to swirl around the *Pryde*. Along the shore and the length of dock, crowds of people, some of them soldiers in scarlet pantaloons, jostled and waved, shouting greetings that the sailors returned.

"Surely Hannah will hear all this hubbub and come on deck," Philip said. "I believe your belongings are all packed and ready to be taken ashore."

Marilee nodded. Everything was ready but herself. How she envied Philip, who would spend only a few weeks in Virginia before sailing back to England. But then, Philip was different from herself. Philip had something to go back to: his work, his little flat that overlooked the river, and friends.

Marilee stole a glance at the tall, young officer at her side. How well she knew him. How close they had become. How many facets of his personality were apparent to her.

She had not exaggerated about how much Philip had taught her about the sea. He knew every bird that passed overhead by name. Gull, rake, and albatross were all familiar to him, as were the great creatures of the sea.

More than that, once he discovered what a thrill she got from seeing new sights, he went out of his way to show them to her. Whenever strange sea creatures came within sight of the ship, he would call her from her cabin to come and see. How many hours had she stood with his hand steadying the spyglass as she watched dolphins play on the horizon or studied the wheeling restlessness of sharks?

At first she had felt that she had little to offer this man in return. What could she, a simple girl of sixteen, know that would interest such a man of the world? She had underestimated him. When, a few days out of Gravesend, a young cabin boy had fallen ill, Marilee had suggested a remedy of rice water for his ailment. When the boy's condition improved as if by magic, Philip was impressed.

"How did you come by such a store of

knowledge?" he asked, looking at her in amazement.

She had shrugged and tried to laugh it off. "My mother knew about healing," she told him. "Her garden was as rich in herbs and spices as it was in turnips and peas. What she didn't grow, we gathered in the meadows and dried for the winter."

He nodded. "How fortunate you were to have a mother who could teach you this." Then he looked out to sea thoughtfully. "I wonder if you will find your healing herbs in Virginia. God knows there is sickness enough here and need of healing."

"I have wondered about that, too," she admitted. "In fact, I had so little faith about finding things I might need that my trunks are crammed with seeds and slips and bags of chalomel."

He had laughed warmly. "That is what I want to see, a flaming beauty like yourself grubbing in the Virginia dirt."

"Then stay for the first warm earth of spring," she told him. "I will be the one down on her knees coaxing seedlings to life."

From the first she had wondered that a man so sensitive and attractive in every way had neither a wife nor family. Then, one magical night when even the ship seemed to be sleeping, he had come and whispered through her lock until she woke up, left her bed, and came up on board with him.

The moon had been a full, glowing orb that laid a path of light to the end of the world.

Through it a school of giant whales was moving, churning the water to frothy lace, lifting fountains of light into the air with their great, gasping exhalations.

When those giants had passed, leaving the sea still again, he had talked to her about the loneliness of his life.

"I have thought of marriage," he had told her, carefully avoiding her eyes. "Each time my ship nears harbor I see the anticipation of the men around me and think of what a joy it would be to have some loving wife waiting for me, too." Then he shook his head. "But even if the woman lived who could fulfill my unreasonable dreams, I doubt if I would have the courage to ask her to marry me. The wife of a seafaring man has no life to envy. All those months of prayer and fear and waiting." He fell silent for a moment before adding, "I remember too well my mother's grief and my own."

Then he had turned to joking because, like herself, he was not a person who liked to spend words on solemn talk. "Can a man who is not at home enough to keep a cat expect to satisfy a wife?"

She pressed her eyelids tightly shut to hold back the tears. All that lay in England for her lay underground: her mother, dead these many years; and now her father, so recently lost that the fragrance of the flowers on his grave had still lingered in her head when she had boarded the *Pryde* for this journey.

Chapter Two

PHILIP was called away from Marilee's side on ship's business. During the brief time he was gone, the beach between the river's edge and the open gates of the fort became completely covered with people who pressed together, shouting and waving at the crew and passengers on board the ship. Marilee wished they would hold still instead of moving around so much. She knew that Matthew would be there, but she had seen no one who possibly could be him.

By the time Philip returned she had been struck by a sudden panic. She seized his arm almost frantically. "I've just had the most frightening idea," she told Philip. "Will I recognize Matthew? How will I pick him out from all that crowd? I'm not even sure I know what he looks like."

"How could you forget Matthew?" Philip asked in disbelief.

"I was only a child of ten when he left for America," she reminded him. "I know exactly how he looked when he left home, but he could have changed a great deal since then. Six years is a long time."

"He must have been twenty then," Philip said thoughtfully. "A man at twenty is fully grown and looks as he will for a long time. As a matter of fact, *he* will have changed a whole lot less than *you* have." He laughed at the thought. "What a shock he is in for. He will never expect a half-grown girl to have flowered into such a beauty. He will probably look right past you and deny that anyone so lovely as you could be joining his household."

"Beauty indeed," she said, smiling over at him. "Perhaps he will have a clearer eye than his friend Philip." Her tone was teasing, but her heart had fallen at his words. Matthew's household. "I don't know Abigail, his wife, either," she reminded Philip. "He married her here, you know, and I've never seen even so much as a drawing of her."

Marilee was conscious of his glance at her face and felt the comforting pressure of his hand on her arm. Still, his tone was one of surprise. "You really are concerned about this, aren't you?" he asked.

Before she could reply, he went on heartily. "There's no need to worry. I will help you.

Study the faces in the crowd. The most hand-some man you see there will be your brother and my friend, Matthew Fordham."

Hannah had come grumbling from the cabin below decks to join them at the ship's railing. She didn't seem to be any happier above deck than she had been below. "If this is the weather of Virginia, we have an ill time coming," she warned. "Such a wind as this can freeze the bones. A body can die of such a chill."

"Come, Hannah," Marilee coaxed, turning with a smile to the old woman. "Think only that good, solid earth will be beneath your feet within the hour and that a warm fire waits for us at Matthew's home."

"Home, is it?" Hannah sniffed, staring at the fort on the shore. "I see nothing but thatched cottages and a quantity of dogs that look like they are only waiting for the legs of strangers to sink their teeth into."

Marilee smothered a giggle. "Come, now, Hannah. Stop complaining and try to find my brother Matthew in that crowd."

The amazing thing about the crowd on the shore was how young the people looked. Marilee did not see a gray head, nor any woman even close to Hannah in age. But then, she thought, young countries are for young settlers. The King and his parliament had made many appeals to Englishmen to come to this new country and grow a great popula-tion here. Perhaps the growing of a colony was like that of a garden; the younger the sapling, the easier it transplanted to new soil.

Still searching for Matthew's face, her attention was caught by a young man who was moving through the crowd, working his way toward the dock. "The most handsome man you see," Philip had said. Surely there was no man under the Virginia sky more handsome than this gentleman, who smiled as he walked among the people on shore. She was not even sure that she had seen anyone more appealing in all of England.

He too was young, not looking a day over twenty, if that. Even from this distance she could catch the brightness of his smile as he spoke to people he passed. His mouth was wide and warm with humor, under eyes that seemed to hold glints of aloof laughter. Never, except on a child, had she seen such fair hair or curls that fell so gracefully upon a spotless linen collar.

He was as slender and elegant in dark silks, with an explosion of white ruffles under his cleft chin. The gilt of his shoe buckles caught the light, and his firm legs were well formed in pale white stockings.

He couldn't be Matthew, of course, since all the Fordham family shared the same rich auburn hair. But he was so wonderful to look at that she kept watching him as he drew nearer. Although she said nothing about him, she might as well have commented on him. Philip Soames followed her glance, stiffened at her side, and made an astonishing sound in his throat, almost like an animal's growl of anger.

Then, as if growling were not enough, he almost barked at her. "You have forgotten much," he said crossly, "if you would confuse a fine man like your brother with Michael Braden."

She stared at Philip, amused. It wasn't like him to turn so angry all of a sudden. "You can't deny he is handsome," Marilee said, put off a little by this unexpected rebuke.

"Braden might appear handsome at first glance," Philip agreed in a surly way. "Only look again and the truth will be clear to you."

Marilee realized that he was serious. Even though she was still annoyed by his surliness, she took his arm and teased him. "Is that another warning, Philip Soames? If so, I will file it among the many others you have given me. You are very lucky that I am not a coward, you know. If I were, you might have to drag me kicking and screaming off this boat. First you regaled me with the dangers of the American Indians. Then you listed all the dreaded fevers that have carried Virginians off to early graves. As for the wild animals . . . well, I, who have never seen any creature more terrifying than a rabbit in a hedge, have been given nightmares by your accounts of wolves and wild bears. Now you add handsome men to this list of local perils. Tell me, Philip, do I dare to put my foot on Virginia soil?"

After a startled stare Philip put his head back and laughed. "You dare, Marilee," he assured her. "I had no idea that I had told you of so many frightening things." Then, his face suddenly sobering, he took both her hands. "All those warnings came from one source only, my heartfelt wish for your safety and happiness. You do know that?"

She nodded, her eyes suddenly moist with tears. "I know your friendly concern for me, Philip."

"I speak from more than concern," he began. "What began as concern for you is now something rich and strange."

At that moment Marilee, glancing toward shore, interrupted him with a glad cry.

Hannah had seen him, too. The tall young man emerging from the gate of the fort would have been hard to miss. He was taller by half a head than most of the men he passed. He was slender and strode across the stony beach toward the dock. The sun glistened on his dark, reddish hair. His smile was excited and warm as he stared upward at the ship's rail.

Before Marilee could catch her breath, the air was rent with a wail. Hannah, her hands before her face, began to cry helplessly, muttering prayers between her sobs. "It's him," she wailed. "The master himself in life in that boy."

Marilee knew that she should turn to the old woman with comfort. She knew that she must make Hannah stop wailing before

Matthew drew near enough to hear her. She knew all this, but she stood frozen. Her own tears flowed unheeded, chilling her cheeks and falling on the wool of her cloak.

Her father in life. Marilee's heart went out to this brother who was so like her dead father. His walk was the same, careless and free. His smile crooked at the same wonderful angle. Even Matthew's hair, given a toss of gray at the temple, was the same rich auburn that her father had worn to his grave.

Through that haze of tears Marilee felt an eerie coldness grip at her heart. Even as he moved toward her, Matthew grew hazy, his outline becoming unclear. It was as if he, like their father, was fading into death before her very eyes.

"Matthew," she whispered over and over, gripping at the rail, feeling her knees shake.

Philip caught her by the arms and supported her. His voice, filled with tender concern, seemed to come from a long way off. "Marilee," he said urgently, "are you all right? What is wrong?"

She forced herself from that faint, dizzy place and struggled to make her voice firm and reassuring. As her eyes cleared of that hideous fuzziness, she looked up into Philip's face.

"The shock," she tried to explain. She didn't dare tell Philip or anyone what a dreadful fantasy had filled her mind. Simply to tell of such a thought might give it power.

"I-it was the joyful shock of seeing Matthew again," she stammered, "after so long a time."

While Philip did not take his supporting arm away, he did seem to accept her explanation. "My dear," he said softly.

The long boats were let down and set afloat in the choppy tide, and the trunks and cases were lowered into them. Soon Marilee herself was rocking in that slim craft with Hannah, silent at last from terror, in the seat behind her.

Matthew did not even wait for his sister's boat to be tied. As it scraped against the dock he leaned and lifted Marilee into his arms, as if she were a doll. How tightly he held her, so tightly that she would not have been able to draw a breath if she had one to draw. His hair smelled of sunshine, and his cheek against her own was rough in that same manly way that her father's had been. His voice, whispering her name over and over, might have been her father's voice.

When he set her on her feet on the dock, he smiled into her face. How rich with life he was: smooth skin, shining hair, eyes glistening on her own. How could her mind have tricked her into such a vision of death?

"Welcome, beloved Marilee," he said warmly. "Welcome home."

Chapter Three

EVEN after the first crush of his greeting was past, Matthew clung to Marilee, looping his arm around her shoulders and smiling down at her once in a while with undisguised delight. Marilee's cheeks still tingled from the embarrassment of his praise of her. It was always nice to be told that you were pretty, she thought, especially if you were sure that the person saying it was really sincere. But Matthew's words had struck a deeper chord in her than idle flattery ever could. He kept mentioning not only her beauty, but also her haunting resemblance to their mother. How many times had she stared into a mirror and wished she could resemble, even a little bit, the beautiful woman who had raised her? Matthew even once claimed to see their father's smile behind her own. This was coming home, to have him near like this.

Marilee fought back tears of joy as she looked up at him. How warm and safe she felt. How much she had missed such tender contact in the months since her father's death. Like Marilee and Matthew, their father had been an affectionate and demonstrative man. In the months since his death, Marilee had missed the warmth of his nearness as much as she had missed his voice and his smile. Through all that time she had been surrounded only by servants, distant relatives, and the lawyers who had taken charge of her father's estate. After so long without the touch of another human, she had almost forgotten what joy lay in contact with someone loved.

With his arm still around her, Matthew Fordham asked his friend Philip Soames a dozen questions about the state of England and the mood of the people there.

Marilee had listened to more political talk during the passage than she had heard in her entire life. She was tired of it and turned her attention to the crowd milling about on the beach. It was far more fun to watch the reunion of friends and families than to listen to talk of kings and parliaments.

While the men talked, the cargo continued to be lowered from the ship into long boats and brought to shore. She recognized her own boxes and trunks as they were unloaded from the boats and set on the rough sand of the beach.

"That was certainly a slow enough passage," Matthew commented to Philip. "With every week that passed without your coming, I thought up some new awful thing that had happened to you. I really wished I didn't know all the things that could go wrong with a winter passage, because every one of them happened to you in my head."

Philip laughed. "Thank goodness those problems existed only in your mind. Naturally I'm sorry you put yourself through all that worrying, but I would be a lot sorrier if your fears had been better founded. Not only have we arrived in safety, but this was a good voyage."

Good! Marilee stared at him in astonishment. What did it take to make this man think ill of a crossing? Would she ever be able to forget the violent storm that had snarled out of the north to send the *Pryde* diving and reeling until each thread of her sails dripped with icy salt water? What of their slow and tortuous passage through those drifting mountains of ice that threatened to slice the ship's hull with their sword-sharp pinnacles? And the calm that had turned the ship to a wooden toy, drifting idly on a sea that mirrored the swaying gulls floating overhead?

"The passage was not without its bad moments," she reminded Philip, trying to keep her voice only mildly reproachful.

Someone chuckled at her words. Marilee frowned at the sound. Who had the nerve to judge whether a moment was bad or not unless he was there to experience it? She glanced around to see who had been so easily amused. Had Matthew laughed at her? That didn't seem likely. It certainly had not been Hannah. The maid was standing like a great, flowered stump with her head back, staring upward at the giant trees that surrounded the clearing where the fort had been built.

There were plenty of other people around, but they were strangers, deep in conversation with their own friends. Marilee looked carefully at the young man loading her possessions into a rude wooden cart. Surely he hadn't done such an impudent thing. Anyway, he appeared to be too intent on his work even to know they were there, much less to have eavesdropped on their conversation and laughed at her.

How powerful this young servant looked. His loose blue smock, faded by the sun and belted at the waist with a thong of leather, could not conceal the width of his shoulders or the power in his sun-browned arms. She knew what was in that trunk he held. She had packed into it the heaviest things she owned: the great Bible from her father's house and a good number of her favorite books besides. Yet he had lifted the trunk as if it held nothing of greater weight or consequence than ribbons and frills. How strange that a man of such great strength should have a shining head of loose, dark curls.

Matthew's arm tightening around her brought her attention back to his conversation. "That phrase Philip used is typical of a man of the sea, Marilee. He will call any crossing that spares the lives of all aboard a good passage, no matter what inconvenience or discomfort may have been suffered."

"We lived," Philip agreed brightly, smiling into her eyes. "We all lived to put our feet on solid ground again, and therefore it was a good passage."

As the men's talk turned to the particulars of the tobacco crop and Matthew's expectation of income from his, Marilee glanced again at the young man loading the cart. She gasped to see that he was holding her blue trunk in a careless manner, as if he meant to toss it into the cart without a second thought.

"Watch out," she cried to him. "There are breakable things in that trunk: crystal and my mother's china."

The moment he stopped the blue trunk in midair and raised his eyes to her, she knew without a doubt that it had been his laugh she had heard. His face was strongly formed, a well-shaped nose and cheekbones of an almost aristocratic strength. His lips met in a careful line as if to restrain a hearty laugh, but his eyes made no such attempt. These eyes were a strange color, like dark smoke against a summer sky. They were fringed with lashes as dense and curly as his hair. None of that really mattered. What was important was that as he looked at her, his eyes glistened with amusement as plainly as if he had shouted with laughter.

She felt herself flush at the impudence in his gaze and would have looked away swiftly if he had not spoken to her, his voice soft and mocking.

"Indeed I will watch, Mistress Marilee," he told her softly, "even as I watched for, but never saw, the pixies in the hedge or the ghost horses charging along the lanes."

Marilee stared at him. The voice was the same, only deepened with time and maturity. Reeves, Timothy Reeves. This was the son of the man who kept her father's stables so long ago.

She saw herself as a child — six, perhaps seven — standing at the stable gate watching this boy lead out horses for exercise. He had been thin then, small and frail, and those masses of fine, dark curls had been paler in color and even longer, making his eyes seem enormously large in his thin boy's face.

What a tease he had been in those days. He had never missed an opportunity to play a trick on her or mimic her efforts to do things as well as her brother did.

She felt her face turn scarlet under his smile as she realized what he was referring to. How strange that she should have forgotten and he had remembered. From her room high in the house she had watched dark movement stirring the leaves of the hedge that bordered the garden. All the whispered stories of the servants had rushed back to terrify her days and freeze her sleepless in her bed. In those days she had been certain in her heart that evil pixies lived in those hedges, and she was silly enough to warn him to look out for them.

As for the swift horse's hooves that drummed by in the lane at midnight, she was not the only one who heard them and believed them to be the phantom horses of the dead passing the family gate, driven by a headless coachman.

When Timothy Reeves had teased her then, she had even halfway liked being made fun of. She felt her body stiffen. Somehow this wasn't funny anymore. This was a different time. They were no longer children together. She was a grown-up in a new life in this new country.

"I didn't know you were here, Timothy Reeves," she said lamely, not wanting to reveal her displeasure. This Timothy was different in more than size. Size alone never gave a man the look of substance. Yet Timothy Reeves, smiling down at her with those smoky eyes, looked less like a servant than a substantial man parading as one.

"I go wherever Master Matthew Fordham goes," he said. This was not a matter-of-fact statement but a proud one. Even though there was no logical response for Marilee to make to this statement, Timothy remained there with the blue trunk lightly in his hands, studying her, as if he were waiting.

When she remained mute, he nodded and asked, a little wistfully, "Is our village back home the same?"

When Marilee told him that it was, with Goody Powers still bullying the children and the churchyard still overgrown with thistles, he nodded. "Well, it is alone then. For you, Mistress Marilee, are wondrously changed."

His words flustered her. She was accustomed to the flattery of men. Even Philip Soames, for all his open friendship with her, once in a while lapsed into that artificial kind of talk that presumed that every woman wanted to be told how beautiful she was every minute of every day.

But had Timothy's words been a compliment at all? If a woman were to grow an extra nose or gain weight, she would be still be "wondrously changed," as he had put it.

Hannah saved her from having to respond to this remarkable observation. Seeing Timothy for the first time, Hannah let out one of those great cries of hers that stopped all other conversation within shouting distance.

"Reeves," Hannah shouted. "As I live, it is Timothy Reeves in the flesh."

Marilee would have been incensed to have so much attention called to herself. Timothy took it in easy stride, nodding at Hannah with that smile still lurking around his mouth. "Mistress Hannah! How did you do on the crossing?"

"Do?" Hannah echoed. "Such pain, such terror."

She launched at once into the tale of her great anguish while Timothy, constantly nodding, finished loading the cart. Just as Timothy knelt to lift the shafts of the cart to wheel it toward the open gate of the fort, Matthew turned to him.

"Timothy," he called. "There is a problem with the shipment that Mr. Soames brought out from London. Rather than let it wait overnight, I'll go aboard with him. You will watch out for my sister and Hannah, won't you?"

"Aye." Timothy nodded, setting the handles of the cart back down with a genial expression.

Hannah, having a fresh, captive audience, began a long recital of the ills and sorrows of everyone in the village back home. Marilee, ill at ease with this morbid talk, walked apart a little way, looking back at the ship she had just left. Suddenly she heard a voice at her elbow. Turning, she found herself face-to-face with the remarkably handsome young man she had seen from the ship.

The distance had done Michael Braden a disservice. Face-to-face, as they now were, Marilee found him even more appealing than he had seemed from afar.

After the mocking amusement with which Timothy Reeves had viewed her, Marilee found Michael Braden's expression singularly attractive. She thought she might define his look as one of admiration and concern. Charming, that's how Michael Braden seemed at that moment — charming.

"Forgive my boldness," he said, his eyes

intent on hers. "I would wager a king's ransom that you are the sister that Matthew Fordham has so eagerly been waiting for. May I introduce myself? I am Michael Braden. Since your brother Matthew and I are great friends and spend much time talking, I've known of your travels here and have awaited your arrival with anticipation. Welcome to our shores."

"Thank you, Mr. Braden," Marilee said, nodding. "I am delighted to meet Matthew's friend."

"I would lay odds that no man in Virginia has more friends than Matthew Fordham," he told her. "Nor is any man more deserving of them."

"That is good to hear," she replied, keeping herself from a giggle only by concentrating. How strangely this Michael Braden talked. In the space of a minute he had the same as made two bets. Was this handsome man nothing but a gambler? She forced her mind back to his words.

"I must admit that I am astonished to discover how modest Matthew is. That is not a trait I ever connected with him."

She frowned a little, not understanding what he meant.

Michael Braden smiled, flashing white teeth. "He dwelt on your wit and humor when he spoke of you. He also talked at great length of how you had inherited and developed your mother's skill in healing and knowledge of herbs. If I'd known that your beauty was as overwhelming as your talents, I should have been even more eager to see the *Pryde of Gravesend* bring you safely to our shores."

She smiled, fighting that rise of color that always came to her cheeks when men were extravagant with their praise.

"Thank you, Mister Braden," she told him. "It's always pleasant to be made welcome."

As she spoke she looked back at the ship to see if Matthew and Philip had come back on deck yet. Following her eyes, Michael Braden chuckled softly. "It is perfectly safe, knowing that pair, to bet that they will spend at least an hour at their accounting."

This time she didn't even try to conceal a smile or the soft laugh that came with it.

He looked startled. "Am I amusing?" he asked.

"I'm sorry," she said. "I didn't mean to laugh at you, but you do have a remarkable habit of mentioning betting. I am just not used to that, and it struck me as amusing."

He laughed softly. "You have a quick ear. I can't claim to be less than a dedicated gambler."

She was astounded to hear him admit this. Gambling had been considered a curse back in her father's village. Women and children had suffered when men were controlled by this passion. Her own father had lost a dear friend to gambling. Having lost all his estate, he was thrown into debtor's prison where he died of jail fever at a young age.

"I must admit at once that I don't have a high opinion of gamblers," she told him, wishing suddenly that Matthew and Philip would finish their business and come to get her.

His smile was gentle, and he showed no sign of being insulted by her remark. "Then why are you here?" he asked. "What greater chance can one take than to cross that great ocean to try to make his way in a new and wild country? We all risked much in coming, and risk more with every sunrise. Virginians are by their nature gamblers, willing to bet on their luck against all odds, or they wouldn't be here."

She studied him thoughtfully a moment and then nodded. "That's an interesting way to think about it. Seen that way, perhaps being a gambler isn't the worst thing in the world."

"It's certainly better than horse stealing," he suggested in an equally sober tone.

She laughed at his tone, and he reached out for her hand.

"Would you like me to withdraw my bet and simply suggest that the men might take a long time with their accounting? I was going to add that you must have become tired of that small ship during those months. I might even have added a small side bet that you would enjoy a walk along the beach while you waited for your brother."

This time she laughed out loud. He was

marvelously deft at teasing her about her lecture. How wonderful it felt to be laughing again with this handsome stranger. How wonderful it felt to have the firm earth under her feet instead of constantly bracing herself against the rolling of the ship. And after all, this man, gambler though he might be, was Matthew's friend.

"I would like that very much," she told him.

They had taken only a few steps when she heard a creaking sound behind her. Looking around, she saw Timothy Reeves, accompanied by Hannah chattering away, pushing that great overloaded cart along behind them.

"Timothy," she said quietly, "Mr. Braden and I are taking a little walk along the beach while I wait for my brother. Please don't feel that it's necessary to follow us with that cart."

The wonderful glitter of humor that had brightened his face earlier was totally gone. The smoke of his eyes had cooled to hard lead, and his mouth was a thin line in that browned face. "I have orders from my master," he replied, not setting down the shafts of the cart.

"But this is ridiculous," Marilee told him. "I will not be dog-tailed about by that great, lumbering cart." As she stepped away Timothy rolled the cart to follow.

Michael Braden, who had silently listened to their exchange, moved in and spoke sternly to Timothy. "Now listen," he said firmly. "No harm can come to Mistress Fordham when she is with me. Just stand where you are."

"I have orders from my master," Timothy repeated.

"Fools," Michael Braden said to Marilee angrily, glaring at Timothy. "These peasants are all fools."

Marilee winced. This was the kind of talk that her father would not permit. Yet, in truth, if she had ever seen a man behave in a cloddish manner, it was Timothy Reeves at this moment. And he was clearly an angry clod with fire in his eyes.

Marilee stepped back a pace to speak to Timothy. She struggled to keep her tone conciliatory. "I heard what order my brother gave to you, Timothy," she reminded him. "He clearly said, 'You will watch out for my sister and Hannah.' Watching is not the same as staying so close that Mr. Braden and I cannot exchange a private word."

"Mistress Marilee, I don't think you should —" Hannah broke in.

Now it was Michael Braden's turn to look amused, and Marilee's time to flare with anger. This was ridiculous. Here she was, a grown woman in a new place, being humiliated on all sides by servants, as if she were a bone being fought over by two hungry dogs.

"Hannah," she said in a severe tone, "I will handle this."

Turning again to Timothy, she said coldly, "Mr. Braden and I will walk along the beach here in full view of you and Hannah. You will not drag that cart along behind me."

Timothy Reeves flushed a deep red beneath his tan and nodded without lowering his eyes.

Only when they were well beyond Timothy's hearing did Michael let himself break into a soft laugh. "Now *that* was a performance. I wager that there are not two women in Jamestown who would take on young Timothy Reeves and set him down such a notch. And he has ached for such taking down for a long time."

"I'm sorry to have to do it," Marilee admitted, longing to look back at him and Hannah but not trusting herself if she did. "I know he and Matthew are close, and he is loyal and trustworthy, but that ridiculous cart!"

Glancing up at Michael, she felt the warmth of his smile bring that quick flush of color to her face again.

As if on cue, they both broke into soft laughter and turned to walk a few steps in the other direction.

"Now that we have this bit of privacy at the cost of Timothy's everlasting hatred, what shall we talk about?" Michael asked.

"The weather, if you please," Marilee said lightly. "The point is *having* privacy, not *using* it."

"Perhaps you would like to tell me about the horrors of your crossing at sea," he suggested. "That is always the new arrival's favorite story." She sensed a teasing in his tone but felt none of the offense that had come from Timothy's jesting.

With Philip's words fresh in her mind she quoted them glibly. "In all, it was a good voyage."

He smiled at her. "What? Where are the dramatic accounts of all that you suffered and what great anguish you underwent? Were there no storms at sea? No calm in which the water supply ran short and all prayed for fear of their lives? Did not God personally intervene to bring you safely to harbor?"

Although she was a little shocked at his light treatment of the deity's name, she was tempted to giggle. And, having assumed Philip's pose, she felt obliged to continue in that position. This time the words were Matthew's. "Any passage that spares the lives of all aboard is a good passage," she said lightly, "no matter what inconvenience or discomfort has been suffered."

Michael Braden whistled softly. "Your brother was too modest in his praise of you. Were you my sister, I would hide you in some secret place for fear an army of suitors would batter down my door."

Reminded of Matthew by his words, Marilee glanced toward the ship. At that moment Philip and Matthew, still deep in conversation, where stepping into a small boat to return to shore.

She turned and offered her hand to Michael Braden in farewell.

"I see that my brother is returning," she explained. "I've enjoyed our walk, but would you excuse me now?" Because of Philip Soames's flare of anger over Michael Braden earlier, she was not eager to have him see her in the man's company. She was far too fond of Philip to want to trigger two such outbursts in a single afternoon.

Michael's smile was sudden and blinding. "For now," he agreed, bending, his lips brushing her hand.

She was glad that she had to turn away to rejoin Matthew and Philip. That hateful flush had risen in her cheeks again at his words and his touch.

How could a man repeat a single word such as *now* and make it sound as if the two of them might be spending a great deal of time together on another day?

Chapter Four

PHILIP Soames smiled as he turned to Marilee. "I must tell you how much it grieves me to abandon you to such miserable company as this Matthew Fordham person," he said soberly. "However, if I do not get myself back onto that ship and attend to my duties there, I might find myself in even more miserable company than this."

Matthew laughed at his words. "I shall forgive your insults and expect you at my house when you are through," Matthew told him. "We will wait for you for supper. My wife always looks forward eagerly to your visits. She'll be as delighted as Marilee and I will be to have your company."

As he spoke he smiled down at Marilee with a delighted expression, as if he could not yet believe his good fortune in finally having his sister at his side.

Philip smiled, dropping his teasing tone. "That is really kind of you, Matthew, but perhaps you should speak privately with your sister before condemning her to another evening in my company. It is possible that Marilee has seen more than enough of me these months past."

"Not possible at all," Matthew said, shaking his head. "We will expect you."

Philip walked away briskly, Marilee's gaze following him.

"I hope I was safe in presuming that you and Philip had become fast friends during that long passage," Matthew remarked quietly.

"Oh, yes," Marilee told him swiftly. "He is a wonderful man, wise and patient. I can't imagine how dreary that passage might have been without his company. I was astonished at how many interests we have in common."

Matthew nodded. "There is some mystery in Philip's past. I understand from others that he was at Cambridge, only abandoning his studies to go to sea when some tragedy struck his family."

With the cart rumbling ahead of them under Timothy's adroit guidance, Marilee and Matthew climbed the small, hilly beach and entered the gate of the fort of Jamestown. Inside the walls, smoke from cooking fires perfumed the air. Marilee recognized the scent of roasting chicken, rich with the fragrance of sage and onion. Comfortable domestic sounds replaced the shouts of the sailors and the slap of the river tide against the dock.

Marilee caught her brother's arm. "How like our village at home."

"Yet how unlike," Matthew reminded her.

Although the houses, built quite close together along the line of the stockade wall, were topped by thatched roofs like the village cottages at home, their construction was clearly different. The houses were set close to each other in that enclosure. Among them ran a tangled web of paths leading here and there in a random way. Marilee saw no sign of a church, but a rude chapel stood in the center of the village near the guardhouse, and open stables held horses and cattle bedding down for the night. A milkmaid passed, bearing a steaming pail of frothy milk. A calf bawled forlornly from somewhere in the compound.

Marilee suddenly said to her brother, "Philip has little fondness for your friend Michael Braden."

Matthew turned to stare at her in surprise before smiling at her and tightening his hand on her arm for a moment. "I should have known that Michael Braden would have introduced himself to you at once. He does have an eye for beauty, and yours is rare in any country." Then he frowned. "It's true there is no love lost between Philip and Michael. That is too bad, really."

"I can't imagine Philip turning against

anyone except for a good reason," Marilee told him, defending her friend.

"Your loyalty to Philip is admirable," Matthew told her, "but as you will soon learn, the world is different here. There are so few of us, and the country is so big. So many perils threaten us that we must avoid making enemies among ourselves. We must forgive much in each other if we are all to survive. And, like all other men, Michael has had his share of grief."

Marilee dropped the subject of Michael Braden. It was enough to know that he was extraordinarily good-looking and that she had enjoyed a pleasant walk with him. She tightened her hold on Matthew's arm and whispered, "I love you, my brother."

"And I, you," he replied, his voice suddenly hoarse.

Hannah and Timothy Reeves had disappeared by the time Matthew guided Marilee to the front of a thatched cottage whose blue smoke fanned lazily into the darkening sky. A stable stood to the left of the house and, above it, a small loft with a single window. Matthew turned and smiled at her as he opened the door with a flourish.

"Welcome, Marilee," he said gently. "Welcome home."

Even though dusk was falling in the street outside, the darkness of the interior of the house confused Marilee for a moment. A tall candle on a table to her left fluttered wildly in the breeze from the door. In quick steps a young woman approached them from the back of the house.

Matthew's wife came forward briskly and slid her hand in under her husband's arm. She stood very close to him and smiled up into his face before even acknowledging that anyone had entered with him. She might as well have shouted that this man was hers and no other soul had a claim on him.

Only then did she look directly at Marilee. As the flame of the candle calmed, Marilee saw a girl who looked no older than herself. Fair yellow hair, gleaming golden in the candlelight, was frizzed around Abigail's temples, framing blue eyes that were set a little too near each other for total beauty. But Marilee could plainly see what had led Matthew, in his letters home, to describe his wife as a notable beauty. A wonderful dimple punctuated Abigail's left cheek, and her mouth was as round and rosy as a strawberry above her creamy throat.

"This then is your sister," Abigail said, extending a soft, well-formed hand.

Marilee nodded and smiled. If there had been a word of welcome, she could have thanked Abigail for it. What did one say to simply being defined as a relative? "I am delighted to meet you," was all she could think of.

Without returning the compliment Abigail turned to Matthew. "Perhaps your sister would like to see the room where she will stay. Her maid went ahead with her trunks."

Marilee trailed after Matthew along a dark passage to a wooden door that stood ajar. Through it came Hannah's voice, still chattering away.

"Ah, Timothy," Matthew said as they entered. Hannah, still wearing her bonnet, sat on one of the two beds in the room, bracing her broad body with both hands as she watched Timothy Reeves unpack one of Marilee's trunks. The young man's bulk seemed to absorb most of the space in the room as he knelt to this task. Marilee felt her face redden as she realized that the froth of white in the young man's hands was one of her ruffled underskirts.

"Hannah," Marilee cried in rebuke. "What are you doing? This is not work for my brother's servant. Leave the things be," she said to Timothy. "Hannah and I will attend to them later."

Timothy straightened and smiled at her in that mocking way. "The master said to offer you every service."

"That's right, Marilee," he brother put in swiftly. "Timothy is here to serve you, even as Abigail and I are. I do hope that you will find these tight quarters comfortable."

"Perfectly," Marilee said as gently as she could while eyeing Hannah, who already had her mouth open to protest.

After exchanging a glance with Matthew, Timothy joined him at the door.

"Again, my welcome," Matthew said. "We will see you for supper then."

Marilee turned from the door to find Hannah staring at her angrily.

"It was uncivil of you to rebuke me in front of the Reeves boy."

Marilee caught her lips between her teeth to hold her tongue from a sharp retort. Nothing would be served by her falling into a shouting match with Hannah now. The months of idleness at sea had clearly gone to Hannah's head, making her forget why she was here.

Marilee sighed. She felt strange as she leaned against the door of that cramped, dark room. Nothing seemed real or solid. There was an airiness in her lungs, as if she had run a long way without rest. Instead of feeling tired and weighted down by the burden of this change, she felt as if she had been cut loose from the real world to drift without control.

Perhaps her imagination was out of control, too. Perhaps she had imagined a great coolness in her sister-in-law's welcome. Was it unfair to have judged the girl from that first moment? She only knew that if she had met Abigail Fordham at a party or in the drawing room of a friend, she would have classified her at once as a giddy, vain girl with fewer manners than a lady required.

And though she did not want to start this evening with a fight, Hannah, who had been nurse before she was maid, must be brought into line for this new life to work. Marilee drew a deep breath and sat down across from the glaring old woman.

"Listen to me, Hannah," she said quietly. "This is not a great house in England with a staff to fill your every need. I suspect that a kitchen girl and the Reeves boy are all the help in this household. I am willing to carry my share of the duties and you must be, too."

Hannah's wail was at least soft enough not to be heard beyond the door. "Oh, that an old woman should be brought to this, an old, sick woman with years of loving service behind her, to suffer this wild country."

Marilee lifted her fingertips to cool her forehead. "Hannah," she said firmly, "stop that noise and listen to me. You had the choice. You could have remained in England to live with your own sister. Don't bother to tell me again what a fool your sister is. Only remember that this immigration was your choice. You will now make the best of it, no matter how you feel."

Hannah was gifted, Marilee decided as she rose and turned away. Hannah could produce an instant flow of tears at a moment's notice. They came now, reddening her eyes and bringing a great attack of sniffles.

"That I should have raised you to be the heartless creature that you are, Marilee Fordham, to speak to me like that."

Warm water waited in a covered pitcher. Marilee poured some onto a folded cloth and handed it to Hannah.

"Very well," she said quietly. "Wipe your

eyes and freshen yourself for supper. Mr. Soames will be here this evening. I will make arrangements with him for your return passage to England. I will arrange with my agent for your travel to Sussex where your sister lives. What I will *not* do is start this new life with you weeping and accusing me at every turn."

Even as Hannah gasped for a reply, Marilee opened the door and let herself out of the room. "I'll see you at supper," she said firmly. "Leave the rest of the packing until morning."

Once in the dark hall, Marilee leaned against the outside of the door and held herself tightly for a long moment. By closing her eyes she could see her father's face during those last hours of his life. She could feel the dry flesh of his wasted hand on her own. "Be strong, my Marilee," he had whispered. "Draw on that river of strength that is your Fordham blood. Go forth with Matthew into that new land and be strong."

Beyond, in the next room, she heard her brother in conversation with his wife. Vague clatterings and the fragrance of cooking meat signalled the nearness of dinner. "Strong," she repeated to herself. Then remembering the possessive way Abigail had pulled her husband to her side, "Strong alone," she added to herself.

Lifting her chin and forcing a smile to her lips, she went down the hall to join her brother and his wife.

* * *

Philip Soames came with gifts. After the barest of greetings he handed Abigail Fordham a fair-sized square box. "Easy," he said, as he put it into her hands. "It's heavy."

Abigail dimpled and tightened that ripe mouth into an astonished *O* as she took the package, pretending that its weight almost dragged her to the floor.

"Now what can that be?" Matthew asked, laughing.

"Let's say that it is a significant gift, not in size or cost but certainly in meaning," Philip said, winking slyly at Marilee as he spoke.

"You really shouldn't, you know," Matthew said as Abigail fumbled at the wrappings. "We welcome you for your good company alone, Philip."

"Protest your own gifts," Abigail told her husband archly. "Philip knows what he's doing."

"You suggest that I should turn down this wonderful brandy that I look forward to from one of Philip's visits to the next? Not on your life. He might make the mistake of believing me and not bring it the next trip."

Marilee felt very much a stranger during this banter. This was clearly a scene that had often been replayed among them. For, as Abigail removed the last of the wrapping from her gift to reveal a large, lovely loaf of pure, white sugar, both men cried at once, "Sweets to the sweet," and all three of them laughed together.

Abigail rose and started toward the kitchen, carrying the sugar loaf in both hands. As she passed Philip she paused and dropped a coquettish kiss on his forehead, saying, "Thank you, Philip. I shall enjoy this with sweet thoughts of you."

Philip smiled at her, then turned to Marilee. His expression was suddenly boyish and shy, totally unlike his usually dignified manner. "For you, Marilee, I have so strange a gift that I am embarrassed to show it to you."

"Oh, come, Philip," Matthew said. "How strange can a gift be that comes from love and friendship?"

Philip shrugged. "Let us say that I shall hold my breath until she has looked at it."

Abigail had returned to stand beside Matthew with her hand lightly on his shoulder. She watched silently as Philip took a tiny, wrapped package from his breast pocket.

When Marilee met his eyes, she felt a sudden tug of something like dread. There was more in his eyes than the friendship they had shared for the past months. From the combined eagerness and fear that she read in his expression, she knew that whatever he handed to her was more important to him than it should be.

She felt something small and round inside the carefully folded parchment. With the paper off, the object in her hand looked like . . . it really was — the tooth of some sea creature.

Matthew cried, leaning toward it, "I've

never seen a whale's tooth so small. Where did you find such a treasure, Philip? Such perfect ivory without flaw."

"I've kept it many years," Philip replied quietly. Marilee felt his eyes steady on her face.

"What fine lines have been drawn on it," Matthew said, lifting the candle nearer to see better.

"I think Marilee will recognize the scene," Philip suggested.

Holding the tiny tooth between her fingers, Marilee leaned so near the light of the candle that she could feel its warmth glowing on her face. Then she gasped. "London," she said. "The towers of London." The city was all there, suggested by marvelously delicate lines, the curve of the River Thames, the arching bridges. When she raised her eyes to Philip, revealing her delight in this marvelous, tiny gift, she could see the anxiety drain from his face.

"Oh, Philip," she said softly, "what a wonderful present." She closed her hand around it, feeling its firmness warming to her touch. "I shall treasure it always."

"I don't understand," Abigail said bluntly from behind Matthew. "The city of London?"

"Alone among women, Marilee deserves to hold that queen of all cities in the palm of her hand." Philip said quietly. "All these years I have kept that trinket, knowing that one day I would meet a woman who should own it."

From that moment the mood of the evening changed. Abigail turned and left the room, as if something urgent had silently called her to the kitchen. Within a few moments the meal was served by the quiet kitchen girl whom Marilee had only caught a glimpse of before that moment.

The table was set with polished pewter that mirrored the glow from the candles with a festive glitter. The food was delicious, a tender roast of venison with browned gravy and a fried bread in accompaniment. Still, the food caught in Marilee's throat, refusing to go down because of her hostess.

Abigail had returned from the kitchen with her fine head tilted at a haughty angle. She did not exactly pout, not so distinctly that you could accuse her of it, but the effect was the same. When asked a question, she responded with a distant monosyllable. When not engaged in the conversation, which she refused to be, she gazed fixedly at an empty corner of the room, as if she had removed herself from them in every way except physically.

Matthew, embarrassed by his wife's withdrawal, tried to make up for her silence. He talked rapidly and freely, leaping from subject to subject in a way that clearly revealed how far his mind was from his words. Philip Soames, with sudden frown lines between his fine eyes, did his best to keep up with Matthew's conversation as he glanced thoughtfully now and then at Abigail.

Marilee had a sinking feeling that this dreadful meal was going to last forever, that she would sit there with her throat closed against food until her hair turned gray and her back bent with age.

Finally, when they were through, Marilee leaped to her feet in relief and offered her services to Abigail in clearing the table. Abigail shook her head coldly. "There are hands enough without yours," she said.

Marilee had laid the small, perfect tooth with its etched silhouette of London beside her plate. As she rose she picked it up and held it again in her hand. As she did so, she felt Philip's eyes on her. Smiling back at him, Marilee felt a tug of pain. How easy and happy they had been on the ship together. How sad that this first night ashore should be so tense and miserable. She hoped he knew that she was not going to let Abigail's moodiness spoil her joy in his gift. She smiled and closed her hand around the piece of ivory to show him how much she liked it.

Chapter
Five

THE *Pryde of Gravesend* had been a cradle. The ebb and flow of the great ocean's waves had been a lullaby. All this Marilee realized as she lay in the slender bed across the room from Hannah and tried to find sleep in her brother's house.

For a long time after she lay down on the bed she could hear the hum of conversation beyond the wall: Matthew's deep, rumbling voice and Abigail's higher tones. The wind in the giant trees around the fort keened as if in sorrow. Night birds called dolefully. From somewhere far off, some animal howled at the moon. Then, just as Marilee's eyelids would close in sleep, the guards would march by on their hourly patrol of the fort, startling her awake once more.

What sleep finally came was fitful and swiftly banished by the first birds of morning. Marilee lay and laughed quietly to herself at their raucous singing. The birds of the new world, she decided, were convinced that all their fellow creatures had been struck with deafness and would only hear what they trilled at the top of their lungs.

Oh, for an English wren, swift and brown, piping quietly in a flowery hedge.

Pulling her comforter around her, Marilee sat up in bed to watch the daylight leak slowly through the strips of the shutters on the window.

As ready as Marilee was for the day to come, she dreaded facing her sister-in-law Abigail again. Had she done something offensive during that delicious supper? If not she, then who had offended Matthew's wife and sent her into that rude and uncivil pout? And having gone to bed in such a vicious mood, how would Abigail waken?

The answer to this last question came in a pleasant clattering of pans and scraps of song trilled carelessly, as if they were only punctuation points between someone's happy thoughts. A rooster crowed and then another, making morning suddenly official.

With her face splashed with icy water from the pitcher, and her hair caught into some kind of shape, Marilee crept from the room, holding the wooden door with both hands for fear of rousing Hannah, who still snored heavily across the room.

She was making her way to the kitchen through the unfamiliar rooms when Abigail appeared in the doorway, her song dying on her lips.

"You startled me," she said, smiling at Marilee.

Could this girl have any idea how startling her own friendly smile was?

"What a glorious thing it must be to awaken singing," Marilee told her, weak with relief at Abigail's cordial manner.

Abigail made a little face that was absolutely charming. "I do love morning," she said, "and quite forget that not all people do."

"Oh, but I do, too," Marilee breathed. "Is there something I can do to help?" The hearth was glowing with a fresh log, and a kettle already steamed there.

Abigail frowned around the room and shook her head. "If you are good at slicing bread you might do that," she suggested. "I make it go off at a such a crazy angle that it must be straightened every other slice. Matthew likes a lot of buttered bread with cold meat and mustard in the morning." She made that face again. "For myself I have jam with my bread and hot milk with a little sugar and cinnamon."

No wonder Philip's gift of the sugar loaf had been so welcome, Marilee thought. Back in England she had been told that no foodstuff was as hard come by in America as sugar and fine, white flour.

"The girl is not here then?" Marilee asked. "The one who cleared the kitchen last night?"

Abigail shook her head. "Her name is

Sukie. She comes after the milking and only stays for the day." Abigail smiled, flashing that wonderful dimple. "I'm no better at making butter and cheese than I am at baking bread or slicing it. Usually Sukie's bread is quite good. Is that loaf all right?" She peered at the loaf under Marilee's hand with a worried look.

"It looks beautiful," Marilee told her. "Finer and lighter than mine by a good deal."

Within minutes Matthew joined them. His bulk made the room seem suddenly small. His well-shaped face was tanned from the sun, and his hair shone in the morning light. Marilee dropped her eyes to hide the pride she felt in the handsome man who was her brother.

Matthew's high spirits and Abigail's continued warmth made breakfast delightful, since Hannah did not bring in her complaints until they were nearly through eating. Nothing was said about the unpleasantness of the night before. In fact, Matthew spoke only of the coming day.

"You must have plans for your first day in Virginia?" he asked Marilee.

"I should unpack, of course," she admitted, "but I am terribly excited about exploring your village."

Abigail giggled, a sound as delicious as her scraps of song had been. "Don't let anyone hear you call this a village. They think of it as a city. James City, they call it."

Marilee's eyes sought her brother's, and he laughed, too, then nodded. "By all means you should take the time to look around. Hannah can unpack the trunks." At Hannah's groan of obvious pain he added hastily, "Or they can wait."

"You could walk with Matthew when he leaves," Abigail suggested. "There is nothing to do here that Sukie won't get to."

The sunshine was glorious in the crisp, cold air. Marilee watched Timothy Reeves lead out her brother's saddled horse. Matthew dropped a swift kiss on her hair before he swung into his saddle.

"Remember that you must not go outside the gates of the fort," he told her. Strangely, he seemed to be speaking to Timothy Reeves as much he was to her as he said this. But at least Timothy seemed to be in no mood to mock her this morning. Instead his handsome face was dark, as if with anger, and his lips were held in a tight, closed line as he handed his master the horse's reins. Perhaps his moods were the reverse of his mistress's, as if she cared.

Marilee felt curious glances following her, but for the most part, the people in the streets were busy on their own errands and gave her only a duck of a nod and a mumbled "G'morning." She watched a stout girl milking a brindle cow and chuckled at a flock of chickens who left a pile of corn to chase a hen.

She was startled to see several Indians among the people on the street. She tried very hard not to stare but found herself glancing at them again and again. She had never seen any Indian in real life, only a picture of the Princess Pocahontas. She was amazed to find them such handsome people, tall with swarthy skin and fine, clear eyes. Unlike the princess, who had been shown wearing a proper hat and a broad ruff in the style of Queen Elizabeth, these people dressed in tanned leather with more of their flesh bare than she could look at without an embarrassed glance away.

She had walked the length of the fort and was turning back when a small, sturdy figure darted out of nowhere. He could not have been more than three or four years old. He was running without shoes in a short, full smock and weaving this way and that as if demons were behind him.

Someone was shouting at him. "Willie," she heard. Then, "Willie, come back here." Then a clear cry for help: "Catch him!"

At this, Marilee leaned over and snagged the little creature as he flew past her. He did not so much as look up to see who had him. Instead, he continued to run there in the air, his soiled stocking feet pumping a wild circle as his fists pummeled at her to set him free.

The woman who had called out heaved to a stop beside Marilee, panting and gasping for breath. She was the grown-up, womanly model of the child that Marilee was holding gingerly at arm's length. Her broad face, tawny hair, and splatter of freckles across a turned-up nose made her quite the happiest-looking girl Marilee had ever seen. She was as awkward as the boy was agile, as she was obviously expecting another child. She leaned over her billowing apron to take the boy from Marilee's grasp.

Then, letting him dangle in her grip, she smiled broadly at Marilee from a face scarlet from running. Even so, the smile she gave Marilee was like sunshine on a fresh garden.

"You have to be Matthew's sister," she announced. "You can be no other." She shifted the child from her right hand to her left and wiped her palm on her apron before offering it to Marilee.

"Deborah Yarrow, that's me. My goodness, but you were a long time coming. Matthew has blinded himself watching for your sail upon the river. Did you go by the Indies?"

Marilee laughed. "Just around a few icebergs. It is good to be here, and I'm happy to meet you, Mistress Yarrow."

"Deborah," the woman corrected her. "And this is Willie, for all the good it does the world." She smiled as she spoke to soften the harshness of that judgment. "Barefoot Willie," she added, looking down at him. Then her face turned suddenly wistful. "How good it is to meet you after all this time. If you've no other plans I'd be happy if you would come and sit with Willie and me. I could offer you a biscuit and some cider."

Marilee felt something leap within her. Was it possible that she would find a friend here so swiftly, someone near her own age that she could be comfortable with, as she had been with her good friends back in England? Deborah Yarrow's face, as she smiled at Marilee, was so promising of quick, dancing words and laughter that Marilee leaped to the suggestion.

"I'm fresh from breakfast," Marilee admitted, "but yes, I'd love to come."

Deborah's house was as unlike Matthew's on the inside as it was identical on the outside. No polished pewter shone from the shelves, nor did the rushes on the floor breathe perfume. Instead, this house shouted "family" from the rude gun rack inside the door to the ball and playthings scattered on the rushes of the kitchen floor. A round, yellow cat sleeping in a sunny window turned and stared at Marilee for only a moment before tucking back into sleep.

"I have no tea, given its price," Deborah told Marilee. "Willum and I make do with sassafras. Have you tried it?"

When Marilee shook her head, Deborah poured them each a mug and set a tray of sweet biscuits between them.

Marilee was savoring the rich perfume that rose in the steam from her cup when a knock came at the door.

Deborah groaned as she labored to her feet. "I don't mind eating for two," she told Marilee as she moved toward the door. "It's moving for two that keeps me panting."

From where she sat, Marilee could see the sunlight beyond the door. In it, towering over Deborah with his dark curls shining, stood Timothy Reeves. Marilee looked away quickly, hoping that he wouldn't see her, and that whatever brought him to the door would not disturb this wonderful chance to get to know Deborah.

Her hope seemed justified when Deborah came back at once and let herself down onto the bench with a groan. "You had the young man worried, disappearing like that," she told Marilee. "But someone reported seeing you wrestling with young Willie there."

Marilee stared at her in amazement. "What does he think he is, my nursemaid?" she asked.

Deborah shrugged. "He will do only what Matthew tells him. Your brother is probably concerned for you until you learn what dangers there are."

"Dangers," Marilee repeated, smiling. "That's all I have had poured into my ears about this place. An officer aboard our ship, Philip —"

Deborah did not even let her finish but leaned toward Marilee with a wide smile. "Philip Soames. Of course. I heard he was on the *Pryde of Gravesend* and had forgotten. How is Philip? In good health, I hope, and in fine spirit?"

"Well and in good spirit," Marilee assured her. "My goodness, I think that everyone knows everyone else in this place."

Deborah laughed and pushed the tray of cookies away from young Willie's hand, which was groping blindly for them from the edge of the table. "Philip was on the *Marmaduke*, you know, the ship on which I made the crossing. I and the other women, like your own brother's wife, were paid for by the Earl of Southampton."

"I really don't know anything about all that," Marilee admitted. "Then you and Abigail came over here together?"

Deborah nodded. "An even dozen of us, like fine eggs, one widow and the rest of us unmarried. We were all young and lively, with husbands to choose like buying a ribbon at a fair. But during that passage, come foul weather or fair, Philip Soames was friend and comfort."

Even as he was to me on the *Pryde*, Marilee thought to herself.

A moment of carelessness on Deborah's part had netted young Willie a handful of cookies from the overturned plate. He sped to the corner of the room with his treasure and settled to devouring them with a watchful eye on his mother.

He need not have worried. Deborah, drawn out by Marilee's honest interest, gazed off unseeing as she described her own trip to Virginia.

"God only knows what would have come of me if the earl had not decided to put up the money for the lot of us. With my mother and father dead of the fever, there was no one who wanted me. They inspected us, you know. We had to be healthy, of good character, and have reasonable education. Of course, the good earl got his money back in the end. For each of us the husband had to pay one hundred and twenty pounds of first-quality tobacco." She flashed a smile at Marilee. "Sometimes I tease my William and ask how good a bargain I was at such a price. He has yet to ask for that tobacco back."

"But when you got here, what happened?" Marilee pressed. "Did they just pass you around like . . . like a plate of biscuits?"

"Oh, no," Deborah said, shocked at the idea. "We went into the homes of married planters and were treated like their daughters while we were courted and won. We could turn down any suitor we pleased for whatever reason we had. I turned down no one. One look at Willum and I knew why I had come."

It was then that Deborah said something that caught strangely in Marilee's mind, so strangely that she did not even pursue the subject anymore.

"I am eager to meet this Willum of yours, Deborah," she told her new friend.

"He will want to meet you, too, Marilee." Deborah paused. "But as a matter of fact, it will be better if you are a here awhile before the two of you meet. Willum is not the man I would have chosen if I had stayed in Sussex. Nor is he the man I would have wed if I lived in London. But I knew where I was, thank God, and chose a husband for Virginia and no other life. It was me who got the bargain for that load of fine tobacco."

Marilee yearned to ask her new friend about Abigail, if she had turned down many suitors before choosing Matthew, or if, like Deborah and Willum, theirs had been love at first sight. But not only did Marilee not want to be branded as a disloyal gossip on her first day, but also she sensed some hesitation in Deborah where Abigail was concerned. After all, she had not even called her by name but referred to her only as "your brother's wife." Yet she had called Philip Soames by his first name in that relaxed, familiar way that Marilee herself had begun to do at once.

"That's a fascinating story," Marilee told her, rising. "I feel as if I'm wasting your day. I can't thank you enough."

"I should be the one to say thanks," Deborah told her, rising to lay an affectionate hand on Marilee's arm. "I have been to London and back in my mind as we talked." She smiled at Marilee. "I was even young and fair there in my mind for those few minutes. My whole day will go happily."

London Town. Marilee slid her hand into her apron pocket and felt the glowing surface of the scrimshaw tooth Philip had given her. "Let me show you something beautiful," she told Deborah, pulling it out.

Deborah squinted at the fine etching before taking it to the window where there was full light. She shook her head, held the smooth, ivory trinket in her palm, and turned back to Marilee. "What a wonder, to hold that great city in your hand. Where did you get such a treasure?"

"Philip Soames brought it to me last night," Marilee explained.

Deborah's eyes narrowed, and she frowned. "And what did Matthew's wife say to this?"

Marilee could not meet her hostess's eyes. "Very little, I think," she replied.

Little Willie came flying across the room the moment they walked toward the door. Deborah made a gate of her legs at the door to prevent him from escaping into the busy street again. They made promises to meet again soon, before Marilee stepped into the sun to go back to her brother's house. She had taken only a few steps before she saw a tall figure come from a nearby doorway and fall into step a few paces behind her.

Timothy Reeves.

When she stopped in her tracks, he did, too. Then, whirling, she marched back to where he stood watching her approach with an expressionless face.

"Don't tell me that my brother has no better use for your services than to have you tag after me," she said.

A fleeting anger darkened his face, but his voice came softly. "Very well, I won't."

"Then stop doing it," she told him.

His laugh was easy and comfortable. "My dear Mistress Marilee. I didn't say that Master Matthew gave no such orders. I was simply obeying your request that I not report on how much more useful I could be to my master in some other activity."

She stared at him. This was no fool as Michael Braden had said. If anything, he was quite too glib for his own good. And to be honest about it, he was funny. She chuckled in spite of herself. "If we were sparring, I think you would have gained that round," she told him.

When she began to walk again, he called after her. "Shall we go together, or do you prefer me to tag along?"

That had been a bad way to express what she felt. She sighed. "You are a most exasperating man, Timothy Reeves," she told him. "Come and walk with me this one time, but I intend to have a talk with Matthew about all this."

The morning was more than half-gone. The full sun warmed Marilee's head as she laid back the hood of her mantle. A spicy sweetness like the breath of the sea moved in the air, and the birds beyond the fort had tired of their shouting and settled into song.

"Is one hundred and twenty pounds of tobacco worth a good deal of money?" she asked him after a while.

She felt his glance but didn't look up. "Tobacco is the money of Virginia," he told her. "One hundred and twenty pounds of first-rate tobacco is a small fortune. Small, but a fortune, nonetheless. Why do you ask?"

"Mistress Yarrow was telling me about

the women brought over by the Earl of Southampton, and I wondered. It seems a strange price for a wife."

"Some of them were strange wives," he said quietly. Since there was clearly more meaning in his words than his tone revealed, she glanced up at him. He had assumed an expression of comic innocence that almost brought another chuckle from her lips. She swallowed it hastily.

"The Virginia air has an ill effect on those who live here," she decided aloud. "They are surly one moment and friendly the next, so that a person never knows what to expect."

He nodded amiably. "It affects those who are strangers the same way, turning them from pleasant human beings to haughty beasts in a breath. Perhaps one should always expect the worst."

They were at her brother's door. She turned at his words. Had he dared to call her a haughty beast? That bland, pleasant expression somehow triggered her sudden anger. Clearly he was laughing at her, those smoky eyes full on her face.

All the things that came to her mind would be most unladylike to say. She refused to drop to his level of rudeness. She turned away angrily and slammed the door hard behind her.

But not quickly enough. His mocking laughter followed her into the room.

Abigail appeared in the doorway, startled by the sound. That soft, joyous look of the morning was gone from her face. Her voice as she spoke was harsh with displeasure. "What on earth made you do that?"

"Nothing really," Marilee told her, startled by the change in Abigail's manner since they'd parted at breakfast.

At her reply Abigail walked to the window and looked out. Then she shrugged, turning away. "That Timothy Reeves! Never mind, he has ached for some putting down for a long time. Believe me, he will get it."

Abigail turned and switched away toward the back of the house. Marilee stared after her thoughtfully. She had heard practically the same words said before about Timothy Reeves. Before she could remember the circumstances, she heard Hannah calling plaintively from the bedroom they shared.

Marilee groaned. After being seasick for an entire four months, was it possible that the woman was now landsick?

Chapter Six

THE *Pryde of Gravesend* was to hang at anchor in the Jamestown harbor for a full fortnight. Measured in days, two weeks did not sound like a very long time. In fact, because the departure of the ship would take away her friend Philip Soames, Marilee had first viewed those fourteen days as a painfully brief period. Yet the conditions in her brother's house were so uncomfortable that Marilee began to feel that she was living these days an hour at a time, with each hour managing to add an extra weight to the heaviness of her heart.

Hannah's endless complaints had been parlayed into a mysterious illness that made her a hopeless burden on Marilee and the household. After snoring through the night like some great beast on a rampage, Hannah would rise and report to Abigail that she had not "closed my eyes for more than a minute, given such pain."

When Marilee mildly protested this exaggeration, she was labeled a cruel and heartless girl.

Since Hannah spent the whole of the day drinking tea and groaning, the unpacking remained untouched except for the clothes that Marilee needed and unpacked herself to store in the wall cabinet. Since two extra people obviously added to the household tasks, it was Marilee who swept, labored over the butter churn to free Sukie for other tasks, and did the marketing.

Marilee welcomed this last duty because it took her out of the house into the fresh morning air. When she put on her bonnet and hooked a basket over her arm, she could at least escape Hannah's wailing and Abigail's surly silences. Letting herself into the busy streets of the little village always brought a lift to her spirits. Within only a couple of days she had become known enough to be greeted warmly by all the regulars of the town, and had begun to recognize certain planters and their wives who came to the fort from their outlying plantations.

Marilee had her favorites. The woman who ran the dairy was a sharp-eyed girl in her late twenties named Maggie. Maggie had the clear, unblemished skin of a milkmaid and a head of hair like tangled straw.

The first time Marilee paused to smile at her, Maggie had fixed her with a baleful stare. Since the woman had no cause for this rudeness, Marilee returned her gaze boldly and said, "Good morning, Mistress Maggie."

The milkmaid snorted. "It's well enough for you to call it a good morning. For myself all mornings are the same, light in the east and milk in the pail."

Maggie chuckled in spite of herself. "I cannot argue that things could be worse. The light could come from the west and the pail stand empty."

The girl looked at her sharply. "Then at least I would be free to wander around the streets leading a parade of idle men, like some women I know."

"Idle men," Marilee repeated, looking around. Sure enough, a few yards behind her, Timothy Reeves, his face dark with a scowl, watched as Michael Braden strode briskly toward the stable where Marilee stood.

"Perhaps he comes to see you," Marilee suggested softly.

Maggie glanced up. Her face split in a wide grin, and she laughed heartily. "Not that one," she said like a promise. "We have already dueled with our tongues, and he carries scars." Then she turned back to her work, sending fresh, singing streams of milk into the pail.

As always, Marilee was startled by Michael's astounding good looks. His vest of sea-green silk changed to shades of blue as he moved. The linen at his throat was the color of a pearl, and his fair hair seemed the same shade in the sunlight.

"Ah, Mistress Marilee," he said, amazingly able to ignore the great cow and the girl on the stool, as if they were not there. "I came to look for you. The fishermen have brought in a giant of a sturgeon on the beach. I thought you might relish seeing such a wonder."

Before she could reply, Timothy Reeves stepped forward. "Mistress Marilee is not to leave the fort."

Michael Braden sighed, staring at Timothy. "Must we repeat this ridiculous drill every time I speak to your mistress?" he asked tiredly. "Go about your idleness somewhere else and leave us in peace. You don't see other great louts like yourself doing nothing more than leaning against fences, do you?"

Marilee knew she should speak up quickly and try to prevent another explosion between Matthew's servant and his friend. She was not quick enough. Timothy's voice was soft with mock respect.

"Only yourself, sir," he replied.

The stream of milk stopped. Maggie sat perfectly still for a moment, before collapsing into roaring laughter. The cow, confused by this, turned to stare at Michael and Timothy with bulging brown eyes.

Michael did not show his fury like ordinary men. He paled instead of reddening, and his eyes narrowed to slender lines rimmed by dark lashes. Although he made no move toward Timothy, the very straightness of his back was threatening.

"Timothy Reeves," he warned quietly, "your day is coming."

Maggie, who was wiping the tears of laughter from her eyes, nodded vigorously. "That will be the day that the sun dawns in the west, Mistress," she told Marilee, gasping for breath from her outburst.

Michael Braden turned his eyes to Marilee and spoke calmly. "I clearly need to straighten this all out with your brother. In the meantime, surely there is somewhere I can escort you where the company is more suitable to your station."

Since this situation could only get worse, Marilee nodded. "I was thinking of stopping to see my friend Deborah Yarrow," she told him.

He nodded, offered her his arm, and they set off.

He said nothing of the scene just past. Instead, like a gentleman at a weekend party in England, he made casual conversation, asking her opinion on various questions, turning to study her eyes again and again, always with a gentle admiration in his glance.

At Deborah's door he paused. "Dear Mistress Marilee," he said, "while it seems our fate to have unpleasantness spring up around us, still I would not give up my moments with you even at that price. You have grown dear to me very swiftly."

Marilee felt herself flush, and she struggled to find some response to this astonishing statement. It was not necessary. Even as Deborah, who had seen her coming through the window, opened the door to her, Michael had turned and was gone.

Although it weighed heavily on her mind, Marilee did not tell Deborah of the scene between Michael and Timothy. Instead she spoke of Maggie and what an interesting girl she was.

"Interesting," Deborah said, laughing. "That is a mild word. Dear Maggie has a tongue like a coachman's whip. No man in the village dares cross her for fear of what she might shout at him. Yet, when left with her animals, she is as genial as a child. I have heard her sing softly to those beasts in a voice that the birds in the trees might envy."

"Has she no husband?" Marilee asked.

"Widowed," Deborah told her, setting a steaming cup of sassafras tea before her guest. "Her Jonathan died of summer fever their first year, leaving her three things: those two cows and a broken heart."

"It's a wonder she hasn't married again," Marilee mused.

"Many men have sought her in vain. She is that rare woman whose love survived death."

While there were no more great scenes between Michael and Timothy, it was a rare day that Marilee did not encounter Michael

73

in the village street and fall into conversation with him. She looked forward to these times, even though, as they talked, Timothy always stood a few paces away, watching with that angry face.

Yet when she and Timothy actually talked, she found herself liking him more than she meant to. He was clever and made wonderfully funny remarks that brought back that instant laughter of her old days. He knew everyone and was wiser about the colony than anyone she knew.

It was Timothy who pointed out to her the young Indian man named Chanco, who was often in the village and seemed a favorite with everyone.

"He is the living proof of how it should be between our people and his," Timothy told her. "While he is the servant of a man named Mr. Perry, he has been befriended by Mr. Pace. Chanco is our friend, and we are his."

Yet in spite of how much she sometimes enjoyed Timothy's company, having him follow her everywhere made her feel like either a helpless child or a thief.

Even the nature of Virginia society warred against her. From the first day of her arrival she had been sought after by every wife-hunting planter along the river. Matthew, to whom she might have turned with her distress, was gone from dawn to dark in the neighborly service of building a house and barns for a newly married friend. When he was at home, Abigail was always hanging on to him so that Marilee could never exchange a private word with him.

Philip was there one Sunday, and that time brought about such a wonderful experience that it stood out like a beacon in Marilee's mind. The suggestion had come from Philip during a Saturday night card game.

"Have you see your own Virginia land yet?" Philip asked Marilee.

Matthew spoke up as she shook her head. "I feel dreadful about that, Philip, but there simply hasn't been time. As soon as I finish this work I am doing at Martin's Hundred, I will make that trip with Marilee." He smiled. "It is such a fine stretch of land, too. I'm proud of my choice for her."

Philip stared unseeing at his cards, then looked up. "I have it. A great idea. Surely you don't plan to work on the Sabbath. I could put together a lunch from the ship's stores, meat and bread and some ale to chill in the river. We could take a boat and have a first meal on Marilee's own plantation."

"What a wonderful idea!" Matthew said. "We could leave after chapel and be home by dusk. Doesn't that sound great, love?"

Abigail dimpled at him from behind her cards, which were fanned in front of her face. "Matthew, for heaven's sake. Have you forgotten that I am the girl who does not like the wind messing her hair, nor the filthy river water soiling her clothes? But go and have your unpleasant excursion. Hannah and I will be comfortable here while you are gone."

"Oh," Philip said, instantly contrite. "I have no intention of taking your husband from you. It wasn't a good idea after all."

"Of course it was," she replied. Then, smiling at Matthew, she added, "As for taking my husband from me, no one could do that. But you may borrow him for the day."

And such a day it was, crisp and cool but with enough sun to cast great tree shadows on the face of the river. The four of them rowed upstream, laughing and singing like children on a holiday. Matthew and Timothy Reeves worked the oars, insisting that Philip, being an ocean man and not a river man, would not be able to handle the work.

There were few buildings to be seen from the river. These were hidden behind wooden palisades but always had a beaten path that led to a dock or a crude tying post at the edge of the river.

"The James is Virginia's high road," Matthew commented. "Sometimes I wonder if there will ever be such a busy road running up the land."

"If it comes it will only pass the back doors of houses." Philip laughed. "Or like the houses along the Thames, the designers will have to plan two views, a river view and a land view."

Timothy poled the boat ashore at a spot that looked no different from all the woods they had passed. Yet the moment Marilee stepped onto the narrow beach, she felt a wonderful shiver of excitement. Her land. This was her very own land to till and harvest and cherish.

Matthew had been watching her face. "Nothing like that, is there, Marilee?" he asked. "I will never forget the thrill of feeling my own land under my feet for the first time. But, come, let me show you what has been done here."

There was no sign of a building from the river view. They followed a path that had been hacked through the woods up a small hill. A band of hogs rooting in the mulch under an oak tree were startled by their coming, and ran squealing and grunting off into the woods.

"Yours," Matthew told Marilee smiling. "It's required that a habitation be built and the land be stocked. Thanks to the richness of the acorn crop and the abundance of water, hogs provide their own care."

At a bend in the path he raised his hand. "Now listen."

In the stillness came the faint musical sound of falling water. He stepped to the left and motioned Marilee to follow.

The house was nothing, a single room with a chimney of rude clay. But from this spot, a break in the trees gave a view of the river. To the right of the cabin a small stream tumbled over gray rocks downhill toward the river.

Marilee was delighted past words. "Beautiful, oh, beautiful," was all she could say.

When they drifted back downriver after their lunch, Marilee felt that she moved in a dream, the song of that stream musical in her mind. How grateful she was to Philip for his wonderful idea. How grateful she was to Matthew for finding and securing such a place of beauty for her.

Unfortunately, having seen her beautiful land, Marilee was even more disgusted with the eagerness of the suitors who continued to come and try to woo her. When one of these suitors, a thick-bodied widower with a house full of young children, asked Matthew's permission to court her in marriage, Marilee told him no with a great deal of emphasis. Since she never got a real chance to talk to Matthew, she exploded to Deborah about this ridiculous suitor.

"The man doesn't know me. Why would he court a woman he knows nothing about? I could be a shrew with a lively temper. I could be lazy or know nothing about housekeeping. He would be buying, as the old saying goes, 'a pig in a poke.' "

Deborah laughed. "Perhaps the love he has for you is tobacco fever. You must realize that upon coming here you got two head rights of land, one for yourself and one for bringing Hannah. He does not see your sparkling eyes and glowing hair, my dear. He sees neat rows of tobacco growing money on your land and a housekeeper to tend that small army of children."

"That is truly blind love," Marilee said angrily. "I would rather be Maggie leaning against a cow's side for warmth than wed to such a man."

In her quiet moments of thought Marilee found marriage appealing for the single reason that life in her brother's house was so acutely uncomfortable. Abigail's wide and unpredictable mood swings kept Marilee afraid to open her mouth lest she hear furious accusations from the same lips that had smiled at her warmly the moment before.

Aside from her morning walks in the village, Marilee's one steady source of pleasure was Philip Soames. Each evening when the ship's work was finished, he came to call. Sometimes, when they walked the streets of the village together, Marilee wished that the hours would never end. Philip, having learned during the passage how she loved poetry, would quote snatches of his favorites to her as they walked. Sometimes the thready music of a spinet would spill onto the street from behind closed doors. For a few moments Marilee could imagine herself back home in England, instead of walled behind the high fence of a fort in the wilderness.

Sometimes her brother returned early enough from Martin's Hundred so that she and Philip could join Matthew and Abigail at playing cards. Philip and Matthew bantered steadily through these matches, and Abigail sparkled with beauty and vivacity, which, like her approval, came and went like shadows under a clouded sky.

While it never occurred to Marilee to burden Philip with complaints about her unhappiness, he eased it during those hours with his gentle wit and thoughtful attentions.

Sometimes, when Marilee was with Deborah and her son Willie, she had to bite her lip to keep from talking steadily about Philip Soames. Whenever his name came up, Deborah had a strange expression on her face that she either could not or would not explain. And, of course, Marilee's loyalty to Matthew sealed her lips about the joylessness of her life in his home.

Only a few days before the sailing, a morning came that brought more anguish than Marilee could carry. The moment Matthew was out of the door, Abigail turned on her in a fury about her treatment of "poor Hannah." Forced from the house by this tirade, she encountered Michael Braden in the street, and he and Timothy Reeves squared off in one of those dreadful insult matches. She fled from the street to Deborah's kitchen where she broke down without warning, lay her head in her arms on Deborah's table, and began to weep bitterly. "What will I do?" she cried. "What will I ever do when Philip Soames is gone from this place?"

Deborah stared at her openmouthed.

"What is this?" she asked. "Are you in love with Philip?"

"Oh, no," Marilee corrected her quickly. "It's just that he is so kind to me, and his good company brightens many a bitter day for me."

"A bitter day," Deborah repeated, thoughtfully. "Explain that to me."

"I simply have not adjusted yet," Marilee said, already sorry that she had broken down like that in front of anyone. "Please forgive me." She fished a dainty handkerchief from her pocket to wipe her nose.

"You are as bad as Willie," Deborah fussed, handing her an ample kerchief. "Now blow and have it done with."

Marilee blew lustily and smiled at her friend.

"Explain," Deborah ordered.

"But I hate to sound disloyal and ungrateful," Marilee protested. "After all, my brother and his wife have graciously taken me into their home."

"There is a time for gratitude and another for being honest and fair to yourself," Deborah told her. "People and teakettles are the same in that they become dangerous to themselves if they build up too much steam without spouting off."

"Hannah is driving me crazy," Marilee blurted out. "She has never been much of a worker, but since she was with me when Mother died, Father kept her on. He and I have managed her all these years by ignoring all her endless complaints and keeping a firm hold on her. All that control is gone. Between groans she is lazy and impertinent to me. It is absolutely infuriating."

Once the flood began, Marilee had no way to stop her catalogue of problems. "And that Timothy Reeves is forever tagging at my heels. If I say as much as a word to him about it, he reminds me that it is no wish of his but rather Matthew's desire. Everything I say he turns back at me. I cannot have a conversation in the street without his drawing near to listen. He made Michael Braden so angry a day ago that I feared that Mr. Braden would take a whip to him. He hates me as roundly as I hate him. But even in that, he has the advantage. He could always go away and leave me alone. I haven't that luxury.

"And furthermore," Marilee went on so hotly that little Willie, who had the terrified cat trapped in a corner, turned to stare at her, giving the animal a chance to escape, "I am deathly afraid of Abigail's changing moods. She goes from dimpling and singing to harsh words without warning. It is like living on thin ice above a swift river."

"Now, come. There must be some pattern to these moods," Deborah said mildly.

"Well, some perhaps," Marilee admitted. "She's always gay and light during breakfast. She likes the morning. And she likes guests. When Michael Braden or Philip are there, honey would not melt in her mouth. And by evening, all her mean words are spent by the time she greets Matthew with a loving smile."

"Could we say then, for the sake of argument, that Abigail is a different woman in the company of men?" The words were so delicately spoken that only as Marilee thought them over did she realize what a dreadful suggestion Deborah had made.

When Marilee didn't reply at once, Deborah went on. "About Hannah. What has encouraged her to leave off all her labors and only enjoy her illness?"

"It isn't a matter of encouragement," Marilee protested. "Abigail actually believes her, fusses over her, and strokes her painful arms or wherever that day's agony has struck. Then Abigail tells Matthew in pitying tones how tragic it is to be like Hannah, a poor, friendless old thing in great pain."

"And what does Matthew say to this?"

"What can he say when he doesn't know the truth? I hate to start his day with an argument, when he is leaving for that hard work at Martin's Hundred. The one day I did try to speak of it to him, he gave me a great lecture. He said he had been surprised to learn that I was so cruel and hardhearted to the old woman and that he had expected better of me."

At this memory Marilee's tears began afresh. Deborah sat sullenly watching her. Then she rose and went to the hearth where she poked furiously at a log that had been burning merrily without this interference.

"Now listen to me, Marilee Fordham. One would think that your head had turned to porridge on the crossing. You have listed a great number of problems. You do not have a *great* number of problems. You have *one* single problem, and it is that sister-in-law of yours. She is the one who has made your own servant useless to you by babying her. She is taking out her natural meanness on you whenever there isn't a man around to see what a shrew she really is. And, as if that was not enough, she is twisting poor Matthew's head so that he has no idea what is happening. How can he know, when you do nothing to defend yourself? As for Timothy Reeves, poor man. He worships Matthew, as does everyone who knows him well. He is resentful of you for keeping him from Matthew's side. That is the whole of that. He suffers, therefore he makes you suffer, too. Childish but natural enough."

Marilee caught her lip in her teeth and stared at Deborah. "Even if you are right, and I am not saying that you are, what can I do?"

Deborah shrugged. "Some women marry."

"So soon after my father's death?" Marilee asked, shocked at this suggestion.

Deborah laughed heartily. "Virginia is unlike England in that regard, too. It is common here for the second husband to settle the estate of the first for the freshly wedded widow. Wives here have worn their funeral gowns to their own weddings without the grace of being single overnight."

"That's absolutely shocking," Marilee said, rising.

"So is the treatment you receive in your brother's house. There is something I must say to you that I never want you to forget. There's never a time when this house is tidy or the dishes clean all at once, but there is always a bed and a place at our table for you, Marilee Fordham, and you are not to forget that."

Marilee burst into sudden tears and clung to her friend. "What a goose I am," she told Deborah. "I cry when I think I am badly treated, only to weep even harder when I am treated as royally as you do me."

"You are not a person to shed idle tears," Deborah reminded her.

Chapter
Seven

MARILEE felt better after her outburst. Maybe she just needed to have someone tell her that she wasn't being small-minded and ungrateful. And while she knew that she would never leave her brother's house unless he sent her out, she carried the memory of Deborah's generous offer as a place of comfort in her consciousness.

But those final days sped entirely too swiftly. January's sunlight had disappeared with the coming of February. Day after day dawned and darkened under a dreary, mottled sky. A perpetual chill hung in the house, even with a blazing fire. The dampness of the air made even the freshest garment feel clammy and soiled against Marilee's skin.

With the coming of Lent on February twelfth, Marilee made a solemn promise to herself that she would not lose her temper with anyone during that holy season. She

was afraid to promise not to think ill of anyone lest she break that vow, but she did
promise to try.

As uncomfortable as Marilee found it to
venture out into such weather, it was at least
more pleasant than the house where Hannah
had seized on the cold, clammy weather as
the cause of new and painful disorders. With
her hood up against the chill wind, Marilee
leaped to every possible excuse to go out. No
matter what errand she left on, she rarely
returned home without spending an hour or
so with Deborah.

Marilee tried to avoid even looking at the
Pryde of Gravesend as she moved around the
village. The frantic activity along the dock
and the beach only reminded her that the
Pryde was nearly loaded with all the tobacco
she could carry, as well as provisions for the
long journey back home.

A nearby planter, a quiet man named
Patrick Hiller, had been a tutor in England
before coming to Virginia. During that last
week he sat with his quill and ink on a bench
by the market. All day long people stood in
line waiting to dictate the letters that they
wanted sent back home by the ship. He was a
good scribe, writing endlessly in a flowing
and beautiful hand. He saw Marilee watching him and looked up at her.

"Do you have a letter you need written?"
he asked.

She shook her head and smiled, embarrassed to add that she could write her own

letters when so many about her could only make a crude X as their sign. Only then did she notice that Timothy Reeves was standing among the others waiting for the scribe. She stared at him thoughtfully. Surely Matthew would be happy to write any letter that Timothy wanted to send back. For that matter, she would be glad to do his writing for him herself. She was on the point of offering this service to him when she was struck with doubt. Timothy resented her quite enough already without her pointing out this great difference in their educations.

As was the custom, the ship's officers had planned a festive party aboard the ship the night before sailing. All the free men of the area were invited, along with their wives and families. The excitement of this coming party infected the town for days ahead of time. Even Deborah, who never seemed to fret about how she looked, wailed to Marilee that no matter how carefully she dressed, the child she was carrying would make her appear to be a "great whale in ribbons." Abigail's concern with her own costume sent Marilee to her unpacked trunks to decide what she had that was suitable.

Marilee chose her brightest dress, a clear blue gown, and an overskirt dotted with scarlet roses embroidered by hand and trimmed with a quantity of lace. She dressed and arranged her hair with care. It would never do to spoil this festive party for Philip. She hoped the brightness of the dress would conceal from Philip the shadow she felt in her heart at his departure.

If Marilee were not dressed gaily enough, certainly Abigail was. Her cherry-colored silk set off her fair beauty like a torch. The sky, which had been overcast so long, cleared that night. A pale slice of moon hung above the mast with a single star in attendance. That faint moonlight dusted Abigail's fine complexion with gold. As they made their way to the dock, Marilee saw her brother's eyes linger on his glowing wife with pride and adoration.

Oh, to be so loved, Marilee thought wistfully, stumbling a little on the stony beach.

Having never been to a ship party before, Marilee had no idea what to expect. She certainly had not dreamed that colored lanterns would swing from all the masts, sending ripples of light in all directions up and down the river. The officers, circling the deck in their dressiest uniforms, were a marvelous contrast to the rainbow of dresses worn by the planters' wives. Three crew men in blue piped and fiddled on the upper deck above a long table laden with splendidly garnished baked fowl, fragrant bowls of rich, dark stew, and oysters and sturgeon swimming in butter sauces.

Philip behaved like a proud groom, himself. He looked around at his ship with undisguised delight. At Marilee's side he smiled down at her. "What do you think of this old girl tonight?"

"The *Pryde*?" Marilee asked. "Never have I seen so many ribbons and pennants hung from a ship. She should go gaily with such a send-off."

He nodded, his face sobering. "There are those among us who dread leaving."

"Surely you must all grow accustomed to leaving places behind," Marilee said. They stood at the rail together as they had for so many comfortable hours.

Philip's answer came slowly, and his voice was gentle and sad. "It's true that we grow accustomed to leaving both places and people that we won't wish to be apart from. Sometimes I feel, as Shakespeare put it, that I have spoken 'as many farewells as there are stars in the sky.' Yet all that apprenticeship does not bring this farewell easily to my lips. I dread the coming of the morning tide. I find myself thinking of you constantly, hoping that you are finding yourself at home, peaceful and joyful in this new life."

Marilee wished he would not keep his eyes so intently on her face. For that moment she wished she had Abigail's talent for seeming to feel what she did not. Rather than speak of her sadness or tell Philip an outright lie, she summoned what she hoped was a sunny smile. "My father had a wonderful rural phrase," she told him. "He used to say that nothing of flavor grows overnight except mushrooms." She laid her hand on his arm, hoping to coax a smile to his sober face.

Instead, he gripped her hand hard. But

before he could tell her what was on his mind, Marilee felt her brother's hand on her arm. "Let an old married man give you a word of advice," he told Philip in a teasing tone. "Never court a beautiful woman lest you fall in love with her. And certainly you must never wed a beautiful woman. Let another man marry her, so that you can dance with her once in a while."

Marilee and Philip turned to see Abigail in her cherry-colored gown spinning in a dance on the captain's arm.

Then, as if the thought had just come to him, Matthew offered Marilee his arm. "But I am not without recourse. Surely you will take pity on me, Marilee."

Over Matthew's shoulder Marilee saw Philip's eyes follow them. Then he turned away to stare, as she had, into the restless lights that stirred on the river's surface.

The moon was a slender, curved thread when the four of them walked home. Matthew, full of fine food and warmed by wine, was as happy as a boy. He insisted that they walk four abreast with arms linked, past the guard and down the narrow street of the city. He sang softly, some tender song that Abigail followed with her clear, bright voice.

How young they seemed, like children playing at life. How old she and Philip seemed, trapped in the dark silences of their thoughts.

At the door Matthew invited Philip in. Instead, Philip offered him his hand. "I'll say my farewells here," he said. After bowing over Abigail's hand and wishing her joy and health, he took both of Marilee's hands in his own and held her eyes with his. " 'As many farewells as there are stars in the sky,' Marilee. Yet I find this to be one more star than my night can hold. Sleep peacefully."

His footsteps were swift and hurtful, retreating into the darkness. Matthew and Abigail having gone ahead, Marilee found herself staring out alone from that dark and silent house. An owl cried beyond the door as she pulled it shut behind her. There was a grief too bleak for tears. She knew that now.

In spite of the revelry of the night past, Matthew was up early to have breakfast before leaving for Martin's Hundred. This was not so joyous a meal as breakfasts usually were. Abigail was quieter and less high-spirited than usual. Marilee thought this normal after the late party of the night before. But even Matthew was different. She caught his eyes on her, studying her, when she glanced up. Finally, as he rose to leave, Marilee asked him, "Is something wrong, Matthew?"

His smile was sad, but he laid his arm across her shoulders and kissed the top of her head lightly. "Nothing is wrong, dear sister. You must know that I only want you to be happy."

After seeing him away Abigail disappeared into her bedroom and showed no sign of coming out.

It was early. Sukie had not even arrived with the day's pail of milk. Marilee moved around the kitchen restlessly, her mind on the ship behind the gates. She found herself wondering what time the tide would turn to take the *Pryde* out to sea. She kept seeing Philip at the rail, where they had stood so many hours together. Now he would have his spyglass in his hand, and those fine, sensitive eyes would be studying the horizon, that endless line of blue that lay between here and England.

Finally, in an effort to keep her mind from all this, she began looking for jobs to keep herself busy. She dusted the dark furniture in the great room and was sweeping the hearth when a rap sounded at the door.

After a moment's hesitation Marilee opened the door a crack and looked out.

Philip. This was not the usual Philip, relaxed and genial. This Philip stood stiff in his dress uniform. He had no smile for her as his eyes held her own in that intent way.

"May I come in?" he asked after a moment.

"Yes, yes," she said, suddenly conscious of the ribbon that held back that tumult of curls that had been unmanageable before breakfast.

He seemed not to notice that her grooming was not in order. He seemed not to notice much of anything at all. He only stalked past her in that stiff way, waited until she perched on a chair, then sat down himself, his legs crossed at the ankle as if this were an interview with an admiral, or possibly even the King.

"Philip," she said softly. "Good morning."

For a moment she thought that not even that teasing voice would melt his formality. In the end it did, and a small smile played at the corner of his mouth.

"This is the second time I have been to this house today, Marilee. In fact, it is the third time if you count my leaving you at the door after last night's party. I found I was unable to sleep and came into the fort early. I needed to talk to Matthew before he left with the others for the day."

She looked at him in astonishment as he went on hastily, "I tell you that because I do not wish you to think that I would go behind the back of my friend and partner. Now you must listen to me closely, for the time grows very short.

"Much is required of the wife of a seafaring man," he began. "She must learn to live as wife and widow in one and the same life. No warm arm shelters her in the darkness of night. No loving eye greets her in the morning when the day is dreary. The wide world is thick with perils for the one she loves, and she cannot hold him back from them. The wind will claw at his sails and the water rise against his safety. Pirates cruise

94

the seas like hawks, seeking his gold and his life as their prey."

He paused as if waiting for a moment. Then, with eyes downcast, he went on. "Knowing all this, knowing of your youth, your gentle spirit, I have come to ask you if you would like to return to England with me on the *Pryde* and become my wife. Matthew has given me his permission to ask for your hand in marriage."

These were not questions but statements. How was she supposed to handle such statements, dropped as unexpectedly as falling stars from the sky into this quiet room?

Her hesitation brought him to her side. Holding both her hands, he went on earnestly, no longer reciting carefully rehearsed words but speaking rapidly, swiftly, from his heart.

"I want you to be happy, Marilee. I want you to waken with joy to every day. I want to erase that shadow of unhappiness that has steadily darkened your eyes since I brought you here. If I could lift your unhappiness and take it with me I would do so, even if its weight sent the *Pryde* plunging to the ocean's floor. I care for you, Marilee. I care more for you than I ever thought this frozen heart could care for anyone.

"Make this any sort of marriage you want. Live with me as brother or friend or husband, as you will. Only know that I can bear any burden, except the one of knowing that the well of your wonderful laughter has run dry because you suffer."

"Philip, Philip," she whispered, laying her hands along the sides of his face. The tears that coursed down her own face were no matter. "Neither can I live with your pain. That is the kind of love we bear for each other."

Even as she spoke, Marilee felt the tiny, etched tooth in her pocket. Had he known that first night ashore that they would come to this moment together? That he would be offering not only the city of London, but also himself to hold in the palm of her hand? He had not said he loved her. She could not say she loved him as a woman ought to be able to at such a time.

In that moment she understood for the first time in her life the full power of temptation. How quickly her mind raced to the room beyond where her clothing, still mostly unpacked, could be hauled down to the sea in a matter of minutes. She thought of the peace of his friendship, the gentleness of his demands on her. She thought of English lanes green with spring beneath a sky of singing larks. London, imperial in the sunlight, broodingly mysterious at night.

Suddenly, like silent guards standing between her and this temptation, were the faces of love. Her father's face twisted above her mother's burial stone; Matthew's eyes on Abigail, dusted with moonlight; Deborah speaking of Willum with a candle behind each eye. Even Maggie the dairy maid, who warmed her head against a cow but held to the faith of her Jonathan. It would be unfair to both herself and to Philip to marry him with less love than that in her heart.

"Oh, Philip," she said, putting her arms around him and laying her head against his chest as she would have done if he were Matthew. "My dear, dear Philip. How much I care for you. I can't imagine ever loving anyone so much that I will not still have a part of my heart saved for you. I can't imagine any two people ever having what we share: perfect understanding, an instant sense of what stirs in the heart of the other.

"You have looked into my eyes as if they were windows and seen what bleak country lies there. I have done the same to you, Philip. I see you frantically searching for a way to help me, forgetting that you have a life to lead, too."

"Together," he began.

She shook her head. "Together we would be less than each of us apart. Give yourself a chance to find that real happiness. Give us both that chance. And in the meantime" — she managed a smile that was sincere enough — "I shall try to be as happy as I can to ease your heart, and you must do the same for me. We both go away with more wisdom than we had when we met. No oceans can ever separate us this way."

He stood holding her loosely for a long minute, looking down into her face. "How does one argue with young wisdom?"

"It is old wisdom," she whispered, "learned at my father's knee."

"The tide is due to turn," he said, not able to release her. "I cannot tell you good-bye."

He did not turn and go. Instead, he lifted her chin and pressed his lips softly, then harder, against hers. "To summer, Marilee."

Then, swiftly, he was gone. How empty the room felt without him. Marilee leaned against the door with closed eyes, feeling her heart thunder beneath the frail fabric of her dress.

Marilee did not hear her sister-in-law enter the room. She only heard the single word, "Fool," hissed at her from the doorway. Turning, she saw Abigail approaching as if on wheels of fury. As she crossed the room with blazing eyes, Abigail clasped her hands into fists at her side. Marilee drew back in horror. She would not have been surprised if this woman attacked her.

Abigail had not only returned to her room after breakfast, she had taken off her clothing and gone back to bed. Her fine, sheer nightdress billowed around her bare feet. That length of golden hair tumbling around her shoulders gave her the look of a handsome doll wearing a mask of hate.

And hate was what Marilee saw in her face — hate and fury.

"Fool," Abigail repeated, raising her voice to a shriek. "You selfish, pigheaded fool. It isn't enough that you have to cart yourself clear from England to be where you are *not* wanted. It isn't enough that you abuse that old woman, paw my husband as if he were yours, and ogle every man who passes your way. No. You have to lead on a fine man like Philip Soames, teasing him until he does the thing he swore he would never do. And why? Just to show that you could? Just to make yourself think you are more than a snippy little shrew?"

Marilee stared at her, unable to believe what she was saying.

"Did you think you were wanted here? How great a fool can a stupid girl be? Do you think that you will have better offers than that from Philip Soames? You haven't looked deeply enough in a mirror if you tease yourself with that."

Then, almost as if Abigail had forgotten that Marilee was even there, she began to pace the floor, wringing her hands together feverishly. "That *I* should have been such a fool. I believed everything they said about this country, about the gold and the fine pearls that could be plucked from the harbors like grapes. I believed Matthew Fordham when he promised me a gentle life, free of labor and distress. So what do I have? A servant girl who sneers at me while she makes my bread and dusts my hearth, a house no bigger than a stable, and a lout of a sister-in-law turning down an honest marriage offer to stay here and hang like a millstone around my neck.

"Fools. Fools. Fools," she was shouting as Hannah, wild-eyed, appeared at the door to listen. "I was a fool to fall for this. You are a fool to think I will let myself be saddled with you. And as for your brother" — she began to laugh hysterically — "Matthew is the greatest fool of them all . . . the fool of Virginia." She threw her arms wide and drew a breath to begin again.

Marilee felt the waves of this fury battering her, washing away her own control at the mention of Matthew's name. She crossed the room swiftly, pulled her shawl from the peg, and ran out the door into the street, blinded by her tears.

On the path beyond the stoop she stumbled on a stone and would have gone down except for firm arms catching her and holding her safe. She trembled as she looked up, unable to wipe the tears that streamed down her face.

Timothy, his face carefully without expression, stared back down at her.

Her voice came choked as she loosened herself from his hands. "Thank you, Timothy. Thank you very much. For a minute I thought I would fall."

He nodded as she stood there unsteadily, drawing the shawl around her. From inside the house came the steadily shouting voice of Abigail, still screaming even when her victim was gone.

"Would you care to walk?" Timothy asked quietly.

At her nod he offered his arm. She barely hesitated. She was too unsteady on her feet to refuse his help.

The village seemed empty of people. Only one old man stood by the market, frowning over his pipe. From her cowshed came Maggie's voice, softly singing to herself.

"The *Pryde*," she realized aloud. That was where everyone was, on the beach below the town, watching the *Pryde of Gravesend* head out to sea.

There was cheering now from the beach as Timothy nodded. Soon the people would trail back inside the fort, to their work, to their houses. Marilee looked around desperately. Where could she go? Where could she hide until she had this hateful flood of tears under control?

As if he had read her mind, Timothy leaned to her. "Perhaps you would like to walk outside the fort a little while?"

She stared at him in amazement.

"Only a little beyond the gate," he explained, "just to be clear of curious eyes. I will take the responsibility with my master."

Why did she trust him after the way they had always been together? Why should she trust anyone after the scene just past?

But she nodded. Timothy held the small gate with his arm, and she slipped through as he pulled it shut behind her.

Already there were voices in the street she had left. Already the *Pryde* would be swelling her sails into the long journey ahead.

Chapter
Eight

ONCE outside the palisades of the fort, Marilee stopped, drew a deep breath, and looked around her. The forest began here. This wasn't a dense forest with the bases of trees concealed by underbrush, but a long expanse of trees standing on smooth green. The lower branches of the trees all stopped at about the same height. She guessed it would be about as high as a grazing deer could reach.

"I guess I expected such wild tangles of bushes as I saw along the river," she told Timothy, "or the wild way everything grows on my own land up the river. This is beautiful. It's like a park."

He nodded. "Beautiful it is, and as stocked with game as the King's own preserve. The difference here is that there is no game warden to arrest a man for poaching if he takes a wild thing to feed his family. As for the brush, it is kept cleared away so that the enemy cannot creep through it to the walls of the fort without being seen."

Marilee registered this word silently. *The enemy.* She knew he meant Indians, but to her an Indian brought a mental picture of Chanco, smiling and friendly as he walked along the street.

"Whose land is this?" she asked.

His laugh sounded wonderfully friendly. "That depends very much on who you ask," he countered. "The Indians who have made their home here for countless generations claim it is still their own. The planters who were given these acres for coming to plant in Virginia say it is theirs. Have you seen the map of Virginia?"

There was laughter behind his voice as he asked this question. She nodded, trying to figure out what he found so funny in a roughly drawn map of this new country.

"Do you remember the shape of Virginia on that map?"

She nodded again. "Like a great rectangle stretching west to the ocean on the other side of America."

"Don't you think that is amusing?" he asked.

"I guess I hadn't thought about it," she admitted. "Why do you see that as so funny?"

When he dropped his voice like that, his tone turned mysterious, sending a faint shiver up her spine.

"Nobody knows what lies between this

ocean and that one," he reminded her. "They have seen the mountains that lie just west of here, where the fall line of the river is. Beyond that they have no idea how many ranges of mountains there are, or whether there are plains. Nobody knows how many natives live between here and that other ocean or how many of them will make war against the English for taking their fields and killing their animals."

Marilee turned to stare at him. He was smiling, almost as if this idea delighted him.

"I think you are with the Indians and against us," she said, feeling a little irritation that his loyalty should be so twisted.

What was there about this Timothy Reeves that he always ended up making her angry like this? He was such an attractive young man with those fine, smoky eyes and that tumble of dark, shining hair. His smile, even when he was teasing her, was wonderfully engaging, showing the whitest of even teeth. But every time they talked he ended by setting her off like this.

He laughed into her eyes, making her wonder if he had said what he did only to see her flare up like that.

"How can I be with the Indians when I have no more love of death than any man? It *is* their land we are on," he countered. "Come along," he said. "I will show you where the bread you bake begins."

She followed him, glancing back only swiftly at the fort behind them.

"Are you afraid?" he asked, pausing.

She shook her head and caught up with him. "Not as long as I am with you," she admitted. "I think I might jump every time a twig snapped if I were alone."

She heard the waterfall of the mill before she saw it. Then around a bend they saw the rude mill with its dam and spillway, trapping a clear stream that ran into the James River. The mill wheel turned idly, catching the spray and tossing it into the air, causing swift rainbows. A circle of ducks feeding on the pond rose at their coming, their wings beating a rush of air as they flew by, quacking furiously.

"Where is the miller?" she asked.

"Like every man, off working his tobacco. He gets one-sixth of all the grain he grinds, but his real income, like everyone's, comes from tobacco."

"The King hates tobacco," she told him. "He calls it a dirty, stinking weed and will not let anyone smoke it in his presence."

Timothy laughed. "He doesn't seem to hate the thousands of pounds sterling that our tobacco duty brings into his treasury."

She glanced at him quickly. There he went again, making a remark that some men at the court of King James might call treasonous. He wasn't going to get her mad this time. "I like it here," she told him.

He looked pleased.

"We can rest awhile," he suggested, pointing to the flat stones that had been piled along the bank when the pond was dredged.

They sat down, and he looked over at her. Then, for no reason that she could see, he laughed again. "What an astonishment you must be to the creatures here," he explained. "They preen their bright plumage and sing for their mates to notice. Then you come with that richly shining hair and put them all to instant shame."

This was flattery of the most forward kind, but his way of saying it had been so wonderfully clever. She laughed without looking up. "I shall believe that story when they start plunging to their death in the pond from grief."

When he stayed silent, she glanced over at him. He was staring wistfully into the pond, as if his mind had gone far from this place. Catching her glance, he sighed. "Whenever you laugh, which is seldom enough since you came, it reminds me of home. You were a laughing child from the first, you know. The villagers all spoke of it, saying that your father had been given a prince in Matthew and a jester in his merry daughter."

"A jester indeed," she said in mock insult, struggling to keep back those sudden tears that always came with thoughts of her father.

When he fell silent, Marilee leaned to look at the rich vegetation that had sprung up around the stream. There was sorrel there, browned from winter, but true sorrel that would bloom with tiny blossoms in the spring.

She began to look around with excitement. If there was sorrel, there would surely be other herbs she needed. How glorious to think of gathering them in such a place.

Timothy interrupted her thoughts with a whispered statement. "Mistress Marilee," he said softly, "we are not alone."

Instinctively she drew nearer to him as her eyes followed his. Across the pond a doe had emerged from the forest. She stood perfectly still, like a statue, her nose to the wind and her great, lustrous eyes swiftly scanning the area. Marilee could feel the warmth of Timothy's body through the shawl and her own sleeve, but she dared not move away lest she frighten the creature.

In a moment, as if she had been reassured, the doe flicked her tail rapidly a number of times and a spotted fawn bounded to her side. The mother's eyes moved restlessly all the time the fawn drank. Then she, too, dropped her head to drink. Only when they turned and disappeared back into the woods did Marilee let out her breath in a long, even sigh of delight. "Oh, Timothy," she whispered. "Thank you. Thank you."

He rose and offered her his hand. "It is better that we go back now. It wouldn't do for us to be missed," he told her.

She felt like a child being led back to school. She wanted to hang back and protest. Not only was it lovely and peaceful outside the timbered palisade, but it would be wonderful to search the woods for healing plants and see where the first violets would bloom.

Pain and humiliation and hatred were inside that timbered stockade. Even Timothy was different out here, gentler and more understanding.

"Tell me, then, about these Indians," she said as they walked. "Is all this killing and warring because of the land?"

He sighed. "The land and old wrongs," he said. "Whether a man be red or white, he shields his pride like his life. The land was taken and the Indians given false promises. Then men were killed, crops were burned, and proud men humbled in chains. They could give up the land and move on, if they didn't feel that they had to right the wrongs first."

"But wasn't there peace between our people for a long time? I thought my father talked of it with great hope."

"He probably did. When the daughter of the chief, Princess Pocahontas, was married to John Rolfe and taken to England to meet the King there, peace lasted a long time. But Pocahontas died a young woman of only twenty-two, and was buried off there in Gravesend. Since her father is now dead, too, her uncle Opechanough has his way."

"But there has been no war," she reminded him.

"Not yet. But there is talk of it all the time among the planters. Those who live outside the palisades look for signs of an uprising.

Lately many have claimed that war is close at hand."

"What do the Indians hope to gain by making war against us?" she asked.

He laughed that soft way that she had to admit was perfectly charming. "Their great dream is to kill off all the Englishmen and not let any more come in. They have never seen London, you know, or the other vast cities of England. They do not know how many Englishmen could follow this small group."

She sighed, depressed by the enormity of this problem. When they were just outside the fort, he hesitated and then stopped, looking her full in the face thoughtfully. "Sometimes it seems to me that these Indians are like the paupers of England who have had their land and their livelihood taken away. Back home such a man turns to highway robbery and stealing. The Indians, knowing this is their land and having been taught to defend it from others of their own kind, turn to war and pillage against us, even as Englishmen turn on their fellows."

Then, guiding her by the arm, he led her toward the gate of the fort that opened on the river. "We will go in this way. Anyone seeing us will think that we have only been watching the *Pryde* leave for home."

"Thank you again, Timothy," she said again as they started down the village street. She was astonished that instead of speaking to her warmly as he had during this venture outside the walls, he nodded stiffly.

"You are most welcome, Mistress Marilee," he said in a coldly formal manner. Then, before she could reply, he turned and walked away.

Only then did she realize that Michael Braden had appeared from somewhere to take his place at her side. "What was all that about?" he asked, looking after Timothy with an almost angry look on his face. Marilee was startled at his expression, realizing that he was not so handsome when he scowled like that. He also seemed a little forward in presuming that her business with Timothy, or any person, was his business, too.

She raised her eyes to his and replied without a hint of a smile. "Timothy did me a favor, and I thanked him for it."

Her manner was not lost on him. He at once smiled, took her arm, and apologized that his concern for her had sounded like prying. She nodded and walked along beside him until she realized he was leading her directly to Matthew's front door.

"No," she said swiftly, stopping in her tracks.

"What is the matter?" he asked, his eyes intent on her face. "Am I doing something wrong again?"

His air of injured innocence was assumed with that winning smile that she found nearly irresistible.

She forced a little laugh. "How ridiculous. It is just that I planned to go the other way, to Deborah's house."

His eyebrows lifted. "When Abigail sent me to see if I could find you, I looked for you there first," he told her.

She studied him a moment, her eyes thoughtful. So Abigail had sent him out to search for her. No doubt she had chosen Michael as messenger because she could not find Timothy Reeves. While Timothy had said he would take the blame for their walk outside the fort, that was not fair to him. For herself she had no intention of mentioning where she had been to Michael or Abigail or anyone.

"I didn't realize that my sister-in-law wanted to see me," she told Michael quietly. "Of course I will go home at once."

By the time Michael stepped ahead to open the door to Matthew's house, Marilee realized that she was trembling. What now? What had prompted Abigail to send for her, and what possible further humiliation did she have in mind?

Marilee didn't discourage Michael from following her in. She couldn't imagine Abigail going off into another of those rages in front of him.

As she entered the door she glanced back to see Timothy Reeves leaning against the side of the stable. His arms were crossed, revealing those firm muscles under his tanned skin. His face was changed by brooding fury as it always was when he looked at Michael Braden.

Coming in from the brilliance of the sun, Marilee thought at first that in addition to being blinded in that darkness, her eyes were also playing tricks on her. The room was filled with smoke that layered the air with a blue haze. The scent of tobacco and ale filled her head, making her a little sick. And there seemed to be a party going on. Two gentlemen with ale glasses rose at her entrance, and the third, who had been standing beside Abigail at the end of the room, stepped forward and swept her a bow.

"There you are," Abigail said brightly, as if the sight of Marilee was the dearest thing she could imagine. Abigail's nightdress had been replaced by a dress of pale green. It was entirely embroidered with bouquets of tiny white lilies tied with gold ribbons. The deep vee of the blouse was tightly fitted, making Abigail's waist appear no wider than a man's hand. The high, ruffled collar that framed her hair showed off its remarkable color. Someone — Marilee presumed it was Hannah — had woven Abigail's tresses into an elaborate style of merging gleaming coils.

The falseness of Abigail's smile, the affected brightness of her voice made cold chills go down Marilee's back. For this woman, who had screamed at her a few hours before with such hateful venom, to put on this act of lady and hostess and loving sister was more than Marilee could endure. And Hannah was no help to her mood. The old woman sat with her ankles crossed, grinning. As if her sudden health were not affront enough, Hannah had dressed the front of her gown with a fichu of fine French lace from Marilee's own wardrobe.

Abigail had no feeling for the affect she was making. She just kept on chattering, her voice rising and falling in the manner of her morning sweetness.

"You gentlemen must excuse dear Marilee," she was saying. "She is so new to the country that she would not think about Matthew's dear friends stopping in to pay their respects while they were here to see the *Pryde* leave."

So that was it, Marilee thought, relaxing a little and nodding at each of the gentlemen as Abigail spoke their names. The glasses were filled again with Michael also being served. Then questions began to be thrown at Marilee, as if this were a test that she must pass with each of these three judges.

Had her passage from England been a pleasant one?

Had she been well since arriving in Jamestown?

Did she find the city much grander than she had expected?

After answering these as well as she could without warning, Marilee fell silent, hoping that Abigail might start up her chatter so Marilee could be left in peace.

Instead, the gentleman on Marilee's right leaned toward her, smiling and exposing a large amount of pink gums in this gesture. His name was Alexander, and the green suit he was wearing had plainly either been borrowed from a generous friend or been tailored in Mr. Alexander's leaner days.

"My land is at Henrico," he told her. "The best soil for tobacco in all of Virginia lies right around there. I don't boast about my house, but the chimney is of brick, and the rooms, both of them, of good and ample size."

"Mr. Alexander was married," Abigail put in gently. "He had the great tragedy of losing his Margaret with the first frost of autumn. He and the children have been alone there since then." She paused. "Except for the service of an indentured girl. From Cardiff, isn't she?"

Mr. Alexander nodded. "And her indenture will be up before the coming winter." At this he turned his eyes full on Marilee and smiled in a way that Marilee was sure he felt was appealing.

The gentleman beyond him seized this silence for his own purpose. Leaning around Mr. Alexander's considerable bulk, he took issue with the man.

"For myself I judge the land along the south side of the river to the west to be better for the crop. This being my third year of planting, I have been able to double the production with each year." While this man, identified by Abigail as Mr. Harris, had no pitiable tale of lost wives and lonely children, he did have a single-minded eye for profit. To Marilee's amazement he even pointed out how easily her own land could be worked from the plantation where he now lived.

When the third man, the youngest of the three and the most attractive to Marilee's eye, stayed silent in what seemed an agony of shyness, Abigail, the perfect hostess, drew him out.

"How like men to gather for a social visit and talk of nothing but tobacco land," she trilled, smiling at each of them. "And I wager that Mr. Cooper here would claim his own land to be the best of the three."

Mr. Cooper, with a shy glance at Marilee, managed a nod of agreement and would possibly have gotten a word out if the other two had not leaped in again.

Through all this Michael Braden had sat lazily listening with an indulgent smile playing around his lips. When Marilee glanced his way, he closed one eye in an elaborate wink that almost sent her off into gales of laughter. He must have sensed when she had had quite enough of this marriage brokering because he rose and nodded to Abigail.

"I caught Mistress Marilee at the point of visiting with Mrs. Yarrow. I am sure that each of you will excuse her if she keeps her appointment with this dear friend."

Although Michael's speech caught Marilee off guard, she was quick to seize this opportunity to escape. She was instantly on her feet, ignoring the frown that changed Abigail's face for that startled moment. Then, regaining her grace at once, Abigail rose.

"Of course, my dear," she said. "We would not think of further interrupting your day. And we do appreciate the time you have given us. Don't we, gentlemen?"

After a general flurry of farewells Marilee made her retreat on Michael Braden's arm.

Marilee, giddy with relief, had quite forgotten that Timothy Reeves would be somewhere about, waiting for her. Her only thought was gratitude that Michael had rescued her from that dreadful situation. Once outside the door, she seized his arm as she would have if he had been Matthew. As she smiled up at him the laughter she had fought so hard inside the house came spilling out.

"My life, Michael," she cried. "You saved my life. How can I thank you?"

"It is always a gentleman's pleasure," he told her, "to pluck a rose from a bed of thorns."

She raised her eyes to see Timothy watching her. What had happened to their easy truce of the morning? How could he change the warm, friendly smokiness of those eyes to cold steel drawn against her? She tightened her hand on Michael's arm as they turned down the street toward Deborah's house. But she was totally aware of Timothy's eyes on her.

Chapter Nine

SINCE Deborah often paused in her housework to watch the street from the window, she usually saw Marilee coming before she reached the door. It was strange that afternoon to have to rap a second time before a reply came. Then, instead of Deborah appearing at the door, Marilee heard her friend's muffled voice calling, "Who is it?"

When Marilee identified herself, Deborah called again, "Let yourself in, but watch out for Willie."

Sure enough, as Marilee opened the door, the child struck her knees as he ran for the street behind her. Catching him firmly by the waist, Marilee thrust him back into the room before pulling the door shut behind herself.

Deborah still hadn't risen but stayed in the low chair by the hearth. The smile she gave Marilee was weak at best, in spite of its warmth.

"Forgive me for not getting up," she said. "I'm just tired and dizzy enough that I've spent the entire day here. I hoped that it would be you when I called out."

A glance around the room confirmed the truth of Deborah's claim of spending the day in her chair. At best, Deborah was an indifferent housekeeper, but this state of disorder was past what Marilee had ever seen. The kettle was off the trivet, having run dry, and the wood basket was empty except for a single withered log. Willie's playthings littered the room, and the basin of water from Willum's morning shave stood half-full, with a curdle of soap gathered around its rim.

Deborah had made some effort to care for her child. She had clearly managed to stir up a pot of porridge to feed Willie. Frustrated in his attempt to escape past Marilee, the child raced back to the bench, seized his bowl of porridge and clamped it on the cat's head. After one protesting yowl the cat flew across the room, leaving a trail of cold porridge in his wake. When he finally shed this peculiar hat, he leaped on the counter top and sat there dripping.

Although Deborah's face looked thinner than usual and large smudges of darkness circled her eyes, her cheeks flamed with color. "Leave all that mess there," she protested when Marilee began to roll back her cuffs to clean up after Willie and the cat. When Marilee only smiled and reached for the cleaning cloth, Deborah tried to insist, bracing herself to rise. "No, no, just be comfortable. Willum will clean up when he comes."

"Nonsense," Marilee told her, taking a soapy cloth to the trail of spilled porridge. "I'm glad to be able to help for a change instead of just stopping your work." As she scrubbed, Marilee teased her friend. "Not used to such partying as last night, are we?"

Deborah smiled wanly. "Not used to it at all. I woke up so tired that I would have asked Willum to stay home but for the work he has promised."

With the porridge cleared away Marilee lifted the wood basket from beside the hearth to refill it. "We'll make a crisper fire, put the kettle on, and then I'll be comfortable."

"I'll not have my dearest friend be a scullery in my house," Deborah wailed.

"Nor will I have my dearest friend in a sorry situation without lending her a hand," Marilee told her.

With the fire crackling and a hot mug of tea in her hands Deborah relaxed. With a slice of buttered bread inside her she actually looked healthier. By the time Marilee had minced some venison and onion and set it to simmer over the fire for the family's evening meal, she began to feel nervous about how late it was getting.

"Surely you don't think your brother's wife misses you," Deborah teased when Marilee began to get ready to leave.

Marilee paused and frowned thoughtfully. She had been too busy getting Deborah's house under control even to think of the dreadful day just past, and her fortunate escape from Abigail and the planters.

"I think, with Michael Braden's help, that I left the house rudely," she admitted. "Abigail and Hannah, dressed in my finery, were entertaining three planters who are supposed to be friends of Matthew's."

"Ah." Deborah nodded. "In for the sailing of the *Pryde*, no doubt."

"And for the seeking of a wife," Marilee added. "Those men were like pigs at a trough. They were all lined up with their hooves dug in, ready to grunt to me about their riches and have me choose whose tobacco land I wanted to pool my own fields with."

"And help you spend that five hundred pounds that comes annually from your mother's estate, no doubt," Deborah added, beginning to laugh. "But you saw no groom to your taste?"

Marilee groaned. "What a glorious choice, a tub of green butter with a house full of young Willies, no doubt. A man whose very eyes have the sign of money set in them, and then a poor dolt so shy that he would have swallowed his tongue if Abigail had not done his talking for him."

"Stop it, stop it," Deborah wailed. "Laughter is my favorite kind of music, but I cannot draw breath enough to laugh like that." Tears streamed down her face, and her cheeks flamed from the effort of her breathing. "At least Michael saved you from having to turn down a wedding proposal then and there."

Then, seeing Marilee's stricken face, she asked, "He did, didn't he?"

Marilee let herself down on the bench with a sigh.

She hadn't really forgotten Philip's proposal of that early morning. But Abigail's violent attack on her, that wonderful walk beyond the walls of the fort, and this last fiasco had driven poor Philip's words from her mind.

Matthew.

Philip had told her that he had been to the house twice that morning, the first time to ask Matthew's permission to make his suit. Until that moment she had forgotten how strangely Matthew had spoken when he left to go to his work at Martin's Hundred.

What had he said to her with his hand warm on her shoulder?

"You must know that I only want you to be happy."

Without explaining her sudden change of mood, Marilee dropped a kiss on her friend's head, patted her hand, and wished her better health in the coming hours. Even as she did, she realized that Willie, anticipating her opening of the door, had gathered his small, sturdy body into a firing ram to shoot himself past her when the opportunity came. She waited until she had her hand on the latch to turn and growl so fiercely at the child that he stopped in astonishment long enough for her to escape into the street. From beyond the door she heard the faint sound of Deborah's laughter.

After walking swiftly through the village to her brother's house with Timothy behind her, Marilee was amazed to lift the latch to a quiet house. She passed through to the kitchen where Sukie was turning a brace of ducks on the spit.

"Is the mistress about?" Marilee asked her.

Sukie shook her head and nodded toward the front of the house. "Not her or the old one, either," she said quietly. "The minute the gentleman callers left, the two of them tucked themselves into bed like so many chicks going to roost with the sun still high in the sky."

"The mistress said nothing about being ill?"

"She said nothing at all," the girl replied.

When Marilee had finished laying the table for the evening meal, she curled on a bench by the window with a book. When she heard Matthew's horse whinny beyond the door, she hurried to the door, hoping to warn him that his wife was sleeping. She was not quick enough, only managing to catch him at the door.

"Marilee," he cried as she swung the door wide. How handsome and happy he looked standing there, his face widening in a delighted, loving smile at the sight of her. She was to remember the open joy of that welcome with a dull grief during the hours to follow.

Before she could explain, he was inside the house, looking around in a puzzled way. "Abbie?" he asked. "Where is my Abbie?"

"She has been resting since I came in," Marilee told him.

Frowning at her in a most confusing way, he did not reply but brushed past her to disappear into the room he shared with his wife. After a long time had passed without his coming out again, Sukie came to the door, her apron twisted in her hands.

"The birds, mistress," she said. "They're done."

"Set them away from the fire then," Marilee said. "Surely the master will be ready to eat soon."

The minutes stretched to half an hour with only the steady sound of soft voices behind the door. When Matthew finally came out, his glance at Marilee was dark and forbidding. Striding past her, he went directly to the kitchen where Marilee could hear him speaking to Sukie.

"Be free to go, Sukie," he told the girl in a tone of unaccustomed curtness. "The women will tend to the kitchen when we are through with our meal."

Sukie, with a frightened look, scuttled past Marilee out the door. She was no more than gone when Matthew called to his wife.

If Abigail had designed this entrance to

bring tears to an observer's eyes, she could not have done better. The golden hair was loose again, a tumbled fall of light around her shoulders. She was wearing a loose wrapper of pale blue that exposed the creamy beauty of her throat. She had assumed a look of virginal shyness as she paused in the doorway with her eyes clinging to her husband as if she were afraid.

"Come, my love," Matthew said gently. "Come here and sit by me."

Marilee heard the door in the back room open slightly and realized with anger that Hannah had set it ajar so that it would be easier for her to hear what went on in this tense room.

Matthew, who had helped Abigail into the carved chair, could not settle down anywhere himself. Instead he paced back and forth in a restless, harried manner.

Marilee watched him soberly, frantically trying to figure out what had hardened his face into this mask of pain and anger. When he finally spoke, his voice was low and thoughtful with remembering.

"When our father told me that he had few months left on this earth, he had but one request of me. 'Take Marilee,' he said. 'Shelter her and love her and keep her safe.'" Matthew paused and looked at Marilee steadily. "Can you imagine with what joy I took that stewardship? I had not seen you since you were a child, a lovely girl, full of jest and laughter, a strong child, devout and loving. Never a moment did I doubt that you would bring that joy into our home that you brought our father. How can I now face the truth of what you are?"

Marilee dropped her eyes. Sidelong, she could see Abigail, her face set in wounded sweetness, her hands folded in her lap with eyes downcast.

Marilee could hear the effort Matthew was making to keep the anger from his voice. This effort was wasted, and his voice rose almost to a shout as he recited the catalogue of Marilee's sins.

"From the day you came into this house you showed your true colors by your heartless treatment of that poor old woman who came dependent on your goodwill —"

"But, Matthew," Marilee tried to interrupt.

"*Be silent*," he said in a tone that turned her heart to stone.

"You showed my poor wife how little you enjoyed her company by constantly going forth in the streets like an idle woman seeking entertainment. Instead of warm laughter and your famous gaiety, you showed us only a face withdrawn as if in hate or fear. All this was forgiven by my wife with the excuse that our father spoiled you by letting you continue as a willful child at an age when you should bear the responsibilities of a woman. But today, Marilee, you have strained me past forbearance."

Today, Marilee echoed to herself. Had he then thought that it was she who lured Timothy outside the fort? How had he known? Had Timothy himself told a great lie to his master?

"I come from my work to find my beloved wife lying in pain and tears. In one day, in one single day, you have managed to reduce a healthy, happy women to this."

"Matthew," Marilee wailed, unable to take more of this assault in silence.

"Listen to me! For hours on end through the middle of this day you disappeared totally from view. Since the streets were crowded with strangers here to watch the sailing of the *Pryde*, naturally my poor wife was frantic, concerned that you had fallen into evil hands. By the time a loyal friend located you Abigail was pressed to entertain friends with only poor, sick Hannah as companion. Then when you did come, you sat briefly, spoke tersely, and excused yourself with unforgivable rudeness.

"Is it any wonder that my wife, who is herself tender of spirit and thoughtful of others, took to her bed, made ill by pain and embarrassment? And to think that this morning I left lighthearted, thinking that my dear friend and agent and my equally dear sister might be joined in holy wedlock as husband and wife? Were you then as rude to Philip as you were to the other gentlemen? Do I see in you, sister, a woman who bewitches a fine man like Philip until he would offer you a city for the palm of your hand, only to throw him aside once your use for him was through? Life has not been kind to Philip Soames. God forgive me that I exposed him to your heartlessness."

He stood staring at her as if puzzling the means to manage such a creature.

"You would not hear my side of all this?" she asked quietly.

"This is not a war in which we take sides and raise arms against each other," he said. "I have lived here in this house with you all these weeks and have been steadily informed of what went on."

"Informed," Marilee echoed. "What information have you taken from me?"

As brilliant as Abigail had been in poisoning Matthew's mind, she had yet one more strategy to play. She reached out and caught the hem of his coat. Her voice was small and pitiful as she appealed to her husband.

"Please, Matthew," she begged softly. "If the girl claims to have any charge to bring against me, her side of this as she calls it, let me endure all the pain of it at once."

"You hear her?" Matthew asked. "This is the woman you have so grievously wronged. I would have you ask her forgiveness and pray that your ways be mended in the future."

Marilee looked at him a long time, feeling the green of nausea behind her throat. Matthew was a mountain of angry waiting.

Strong. Her father had told her to be strong. If she could be strong enough not to lie at this moment, she could claim that strength he had believed in.

Within her heart she railed at the unfairness of this demand. She had been charged without recourse to protest. She had been judged without opportunity for appeal. Worst of all, her sentence was to admit and recant what she had never been guilty of.

"I ask your forgiveness," she said carefully, her eyes full on Abigail's, "for any fault you truly found in me. I solemnly pledge to be fair in all my dealings from now on."

Matthew seemed to go weak with relief at her words. He patted her clumsily on the shoulder and turned to lift his wife so that she stood within his arm.

"All is over then," he said. "Come, let us eat together."

Whether it was the dryness of the duck, the lump of pain in her throat, or Hannah's triumphant look from across the table, Marilee wasn't sure. She only knew that the food could not be chewed, and once chewed, could not be swallowed.

Fortunately Matthew, giddy with his relief that Abigail was not ill and that he had handled this domestic problem with such success, became exuberant, refilled his ale mug over and over and seemed not to notice that Marilee's meal lay uneaten on her plate.

That was the darkest night Marilee could ever remember. Not even the coming of dawn would promise light.

Chapter
Ten

MARILEE was wakened by such a frantic banging on the front door that the shutters of the window by her bed shook in response. Startled, she sat straight up in bed, her heart thumping wildly. Every peril she had ever heard of flashed through her mind as she tossed her braid back over her shoulder and tensed to hear what was happening. She doubted if it was past two or three in the morning. Dawn couldn't be coming because it was so dead-dark that no glimmer of light showed beyond her window.

Hannah was no help. Her snoring choked to a stop for a moment. Then she groaned and flopped over in her bed like a great whale leaping from the surface of the water. Once landed again, she pulled her goose-down pillow around her ears like a hat and began sawing away again as if she had never been disturbed.

By the time Marilee figured out that the sound had been a fist beating against the wooden door, the noise stopped. The muffled rumble of men's voices in conversation came from the room beyond, rising and falling as if something urgent was going on. Marilee had no sooner identified one of the voices as Matthew's than he was at her door, rapping softly and calling her name.

"Come quickly," he added in a hoarse whisper. "You are needed." She trembled as she fished her dress from the shelf in the darkness and struggled into it. Naturally she was all thumbs, struggling with the buttons and unable to find her second shoe, which she was sure she had placed neatly by its mate on the stool. She caught the end of her long braid and wound it around her head like a crown, fastening it any which way with all the pins she could locate in the dark. In spite of every attempt to control herself she was trembling as she let herself out to where Matthew was waiting.

The man standing behind the candle loomed like a giant in that wavering light. Willum Yarrow. Marilee only recognized him because she had been briefly introduced to him the night before at the party aboard the *Pryde*. There on the ship in the confusing light of all those lanterns, she had not realized that he stood half a head taller than even her brother, who was among the tallest of men she knew.

Willum was not only tall but broad, a heavy, barrel-chested man whose head rested on a thick neck. Even his face seemed heavy, with curled brows that nearly concealed his eyes and a broad, solid chin that suggested stubborn strength.

"Mistress," he cried, stepping forward as she entered. "Mistress Marilee, thank God you are here. Thank God." His voice was hoarse with fear and relief.

"Your friend Deborah has been taken ill," Matthew explained. "William came for you, hoping you might be able to help."

Marilee's heart sank, remembering the dizziness and nausea that had kept Deborah in her chair all day. Then she was suffering from something more than the aftermath of her night of rich food and strong drink. "She's not better, then?" Marilee asked. "Tell me how she is."

"Her mind," Willum began. His voice broke, forcing him to pause, clear his throat, and draw a deep breath before he could go on. "Her mind has flown. She sings and laughs and has no idea where she is or who I am. All this while she flames with fever."

Marilee paused, studying him, trying to think what she had in her store of potions that would help a person who was delirious with fever. Apparently Willum thought she was hesitating about coming with him because he began to plead with her pitifully.

"No, no," she assured him. "Of course I will come. I really hated to leave her alone there today with only the child, the way she felt. I was only trying to think what I have here that might help to break her fever."

"Then she was already ill when you were with her earlier today?" Matthew asked quietly.

Marilee, her mind still off sorting through her supply of herbs and teas, frowned distractedly and nodded. "Aye, she was very weak and so dizzy that she was afraid to stand and try to walk. I left thinking she was feeling a little better."

"An angel, this girl is," Willum told Matthew. "It's not enough that your sister's visits have brought Debbie real delight all these weeks; today she came as lifesaver. Debbie couldn't say enough of what she had done, drawn the water and rebuilt the fire and cleaned up after a great mess that Willie made. And she didn't leave until my supper was simmering and Debbie herself comfortable." He paused, remembering. "Then, in the night, she wakened like this, her mind gone." He turned toward the door. "We must go," he said urgently. "She's alone there in that shape with only the child."

"Run back to her," Marilee decided aloud. "I will get my herbs and come along within minutes. I am sure that Matthew won't mind seeing me to your house safely."

"Of course, of course," Matthew assured them both. He spoke as if her words had roused him from deep thought.

Hannah stirred and sat up in complaint as Marilee set the candle on the stand beside her trunks. "How is a body to sleep?" she whined. "What kind of a business is it to be setting the room to light in the middle of the night?"

"Close your eyes and go back to sleep," Marilee advised her. "I'll take the light away in only a minute."

"There's no rest for such as an old woman as I. Who would believe that I cannot even have a night of sleep without —" Hannah railed on in a tone of insulted complaint. Then, seeing Matthew in the doorway, she fell suddenly silent, her eyes widening with fright.

Outside, the night was cold but clear under a sky cluttered with winking stars. The watchman halted them, then nodded them on as he recognized Matthew. Their hurrying footsteps echoed through the empty street in a bleak and lonely way. Awakened by that sound, a dog began to bark from a stable they passed. As something swift and silent darted past Marilee's head, she drew her shawl tighter around her hair, shivering. Even the breath of a bat passing that close made her blood cold.

"You have spent a great deal of time with Deborah then?" Matthew asked thoughtfully after a few moments.

"We are good friends," she told him.

"So it was to visit your sick friend and help her that you excused yourself from the guests today?" he asked.

Temptation. How easy it would be to let him believe that she had known Deborah was sick when she left with Michael Braden. That would certainly justify what had been referred to as her unforgivable rudeness. Abigail's game was one of twisted truth and half-lies. How easy it would be to play that same game herself on Matthew. And certainly his angry attack on her had given her cause, if such cause were ever just.

She did not completely resist that temptation. "She was expecting me," she told him.

He walked in silence for a moment. "Deborah is fortunate to have you for a friend," he said.

"I am fortunate to have a friend," she replied, not realizing until the words were out that he might take them for a rebuke.

After an awkward silence he mentioned Willie. "That is not an easy child to handle, I understand," he commented.

They were nearing the door of the Yarrow house as he said this, and Marilee laughed softly. "That is carefully said," she told him.

At the door Matthew paused a moment as if in indecision. "When do you think we can expect you home?" he asked.

Home. Even if he had no idea how she had dreaded entering his house every day that she had lived there, how could he think after the evening past that the place was home to her?

Marilee avoided his eyes. "From what Willum says, Deborah is delirious with fever. Even when the fever is brought down, she will be weak and need to take many liquids. I

can't even guess how long it will take before
I can leave her in comfort."

He seemed to have something more he
wanted to say, but Willum was at the door,
his great, fleshy face twisted with worry.

"There you are," he said with relief. "She
is no better. She may even be getting worse."

"I will be in touch," Matthew said in a
hurried way. "God bless your wife, William."

"God bless your sister," Willum replied,
taking Marilee's basket and seeing her inside.

Deborah, her eyes wide and glittering, was
propped up in her bed. Her hair was in a
great, rough tangle, and spots of brilliant
color stained her cheeks. She was waving her
bare arms around and laughing in a strange,
loud way.

Although she did not recognize Marilee she
hailed her with a warm and hearty greeting.

She cried, "What have we here? A lady
with a basket." Then, leaning forward and
running her tongue along her parched lips,
she began to whisper. "Violets. You have
brought me violets and primroses and daisies
for my hair. We'll dance." She began to laugh
again, wildly, and tried to struggle to her
feet.

Marilee shook her head and laid her hand
along Deborah's throat, just beneath her ear.
She concealed her terror from Willum's
watchful eye. Deborah flamed with fever. The
touch of her flesh was like a poker from a
raging fire.

"But first we get you cooled off," Marilee told her. Her friend was bound in a comforter like a great worm in a cocoon.

"I feared she might catch a chill," Willum said in a worried tone.

Marilee nodded. Willum was echoing what most people thought about fevers. Marilee's own mother had taught her that fever held close to a body only feeds itself into more fever. "If a chill comes we will warm her," Marilee assured him. "Would you do me the great favor of dampening a cloth in that cool water?"

Deborah's fever was slow to break. Dawn began to stripe between the shutters, finding Marilee still working with her friend. Deborah went from feverish heat to chilling, begging for the comforter one moment and thrusting it away the next. She pushed away the herb tea that Marilee prepared until Willum thought to stir a generous spoon of honey in it to mask the flavor. Through all those hours that Marilee bathed Deborah and wrapped her close and kept her from jumping from the bed to dance, Deborah sang and laughed and thought herself a girl in London again.

The room was flooded with morning light before Marilee was sure that she had won this round at least. Deborah began to yawn, then fight a heaviness of her eyelids. When at last she slept, the roosters had crowed morning and the business of the day had begun beyond the window.

Willum, gaunt from the strain of the long night, set mugs of sassafras tea on the table and asked Marilee to sit with him. "I wish there was bread to offer you," he said wistfully. "Or even a bite of meat to restore your strength after such labor." Then he smiled, a twisted grin that gave him the look of a giant, mischievous boy. "In fact, I wish there was gold to offer you and fine linen and your heart's desire. You are all that my Debbie has said of you, and more. You've a debtor in Willum Yarrow should you live to be a hundred."

Little Willie was only stirring when Matthew rapped at the door. Startled awake, the child looked around the room, saw his mother sleeping, and was out of his bed plunging toward her in a flash. Marilee, as quick as a cat, darted out and caught him just as Willum opened the door to Matthew.

"Willie," Marilee whispered to the wriggling child. "Willie, listen."

The child stared at her, his eyes wide and his mouth hanging open. "Can you hear your mother sleep?" Marilee asked him.

The child rolled his eyes toward Deborah doubtfully. "Come," Marilee urged, still whispering. "Come and listen with me."

Lifting the boy on her hip, Marilee knelt by his sleeping mother.

With his round mouth puckered into an O, Willum strained to hear his mother's even breathing. Then, with delight, he turned to

Marilee and tried to put the sound into whispered words.

"Ah ha," he said. "I hear Mama sleep, ah ha."

Marilee nodded and smiled at him. "Let's surprise her and have breakfast all gone before she wakes up."

When he grinned, his nose tightened into a cunning little wad. " 'Sprise." He nodded.

Only then did he notice the three men, his father at the door and Matthew and Timothy outside on the stoop. He looked at them sternly and laid a finger on his lips.

"Hush up, now," he told them sternly. " 'Sprise Mama."

"But surely you are exhausted," Willum told Marilee. "Surely you need to go with your brother and be rested."

"What about yourself?" she asked him. "Surely your work will go hard today after such a night. Harder by far than I will have with Willie here to help me."

When Willum looked from Marilee to her brother, Matthew shrugged. "She makes a good argument," he said. "But are you sure you don't need rest, Marilee?"

She shook her head. "How could I rest at home not knowing how Deborah was getting along? If you think it would be all right with your wife, I would prefer to stay and care for Deborah and my friend Willie today. I could come home when Willum is through with his day's work."

Not until the words were out of her mouth

and she saw the change come over Timothy Reeves's face did she realize what her spending the days at the Yarrows would mean to Matthew's servant. After all these weeks he would be free to work at his master's side. His smile was like a lantern in the doorway.

"What Willie and I need is bread," she told her brother. "Deborah was too ill to bake, and Willie and I need to eat if we are to make surprises all day."

"Bread," Willie repeated, nodding importantly. "Bread for 'sprises."

Later, Timothy brought a loaf of Sukie's good bread to Deborah's door. Marilee looked at him there on the sunlit stoop. What a healthy, wonderful-looking young man he was, with that fine, strong face and those unusual eyes. He seemed about to explode with happiness as he looked down at her.

"I hope you are going to get to work with Matthew today at Martin's Hundred," she told him.

His smile was brilliant with delight. "Indeed I am, Mistress," he told her. "Indeed I am."

The memory of his joy stayed with her as she fed the child. He seemed to enjoy his " 'sprise" breakfast. He ate slice after slice of buttered bread spread with honey until his eyes were glazed and he leaned back groaning.

" 'Sprise." He grinned at her, pulling his blanket up against his cheek and rubbing it between his fingers.

Marilee grinned back at him, hoping that

he wouldn't add an extra surprise by getting sick from that great quantity of food he had stuffed into his tiny body.

Deborah drifted in and out of sleep all that day. When she first wakened with her mind intact, she was astonished to find Marilee there. She protested at once and would have leaped out of bed and tried to work if Marilee had not practically held her there by force. She gave up when she realized how well her household was running. Little Willie played happily with his toys beside her bed while fresh bread dough perfumed the air from where it sat rising by the hearth.

"I might as well give up and play the grand lady," she admitted ruefully. "And, indeed, I have little strength to do anything else."

She stared off thoughtfully awhile. "Dear Willum," she told Marilee gently. "I must have been a sick one for him to go for help. He's a proud man who does not find it easy to ask for favors."

"He's a dear man," Marilee told her, "and I am proud that he came to me when you needed help."

There was no way that Marilee could ever tell Deborah what a lifesaver her sickness had been to Marilee. She could not imagine spending that day and the days that followed cooped up in the house with Abigail's ferocity and Hannah's gloating.

As it was, she enjoyed playing housewife and make-believe-mother to Willie, as Deborah gained strength. Maggie the milkmaid, hearing that Deborah was ill, brought a bowl of soft cheese that she flavored with the onions that grew in the woods beyond the fort. Willum shot a wild turkey in the woods. Simmered all day over a low fire, the bird made a rich stew that brought healthy color back into Deborah's cheeks.

Marilee went home each evening when Willum returned from his work. Those hours were the only ones that Marilee dreaded. The men who had come to call on her on the day of the sailing of the *Pryde* proved to be only the beginning of a great tide of suitors. Every night one or more young men stopped in to pay their respects to their friend Matthew Fordham and tell his young sister about their good land and great prospects. Without fail, each man had a plan to get her out alone with the hope of selling himself to her in the role of husband. Although they all invited her to walk in the village or enjoy the night air, she turned them all down.

After the first few days of this she remarked to Matthew that he had an astounding number of "good friends" who cared enough for him to seek his house every evening.

He laughed, knowing that her words were spoken with irony.

"You must forgive them, Marilee. This is a country of single young men," he reminded her. "And many men would have you as their wife. It is certainly not my company or that of my lovely wife that they come for."

She remembered Abigail's harsh words the day of Philip's proposal, and Matthew's equally stern judgment on her refusal of his friend as husband.

"Must I marry at this young age?" she asked without looking toward Abigail for fear she would see a change of expression there.

"When your heart cries out for marriage it will be soon enough," he told her. "Don't you agree, Abigail?"

But Abigail had begun another quiet conversation with Hannah and seemed not to hear the question. Therefore she did not have to reply.

Although Marilee turned down all other invitations to walk out with these gentlemen, she made an exception for Michael Braden.

The third time she left the house with him, Matthew raised his eyebrows at her. "Is there something between you and Michael that I should know about?" he asked.

She shook her head. "Only that Michael alone has the good taste not to try to push me toward the altar every time we say hello."

Abigail had been listening that time. She found Marilee's remark amusing. "I am sure that Michael Braden's only possible interest in you is to show kindness to his friend Matthew," she said with a sly sneer.

Matthew, not being given to sarcasm himself, was insensitive to other people's use of it. He shook his head. "I rather think that

Michael hangs back from pressing his suit to her because of his own experience. He knows how tender a heart is after the loss of a loved one. I think he would hesitate to suggest anything as joyous as a marriage to Marilee so soon after losing her father."

It took an entire week for Deborah's strength to return enough for her to assume her own housekeeping duties. Although Marilee would have preferred to see her friend return to her old schedule gradually, Deborah would hear none of that.

"You have spoiled my husband too much already," she said, laughing. "I will never be such a cook as you are. The less of that good food he gets, the better he will be able to keep on swallowing mine."

During that week the winter weather retreated halfway, bringing springlike days with a full sun, even though the nights stayed chilly. While Marilee no longer spent the entire day at Deborah's, she did pay a daily visit to check on her friend. In addition, the change in weather gave her a new excuse to be outside of the house. She spent happy hours stripping away the old growth, breaking up the earth, and getting her garden under way.

On the Tuesday before Easter, a ship, *Early Lark,* out of Plymouth, arrived from England. The news that it was in Norfolk passed quickly up the river. High excitement stirred along the beach for two whole days as everyone vied to be the first to sight its sail coming up the James. The arrival of the ship plunged Marilee back into memories of her own passage, her first sight of land, the wonderful feeling of earth beneath her feet, and, of course, her dear Philip.

The crowd gathered on the beach as they had when the *Pryde* hung at anchor there. Since Marilee didn't know anyone who was arriving and didn't have any goods on board as many people did, she watched the ship unload just for the fun of having something new to see.

The ship had been in less than an hour when Matthew arrived from his work. He came immediately down to the beach and joined her and Timothy. They had stood there only briefly before one of the ship's officers approached Matthew and greeted him warmly. After being introduced to Marilee the young man smiled and took a packet from inside his coat.

"I see I shall do all my duties at once." He smiled. "I am carrying a letter for each of you."

Matthew turned his in his hand and smiled. "Ah, that is from Philip. I would recognize that handwriting anywhere."

"How can that be?" she asked, taking the sealed message with a rapidly thumping heart. "Philip can't be in England yet."

The young officer at Matthew's side smiled and nodded. "We passed the *Pryde* on the open sea," he explained. "They took mail from us back to England and we did the same for them here."

Marilee tucked the letter in her pocket, thinking she would read it later in privacy. After a few moments she realized that she was far more interested in hearing from Philip than in anything that could happen there on the beach. Excusing herself to Matthew, she went back to his house to sit on a cool stone by her garden and read the letter slowly.

Philip's handwriting was just as it should be. The letters were gracefully and perfectly formed. When she read his phrases, she could hear his voice speaking them.

He spoke of the loneliness at the ship's rail without her, adding that he often stood with his eyes closed there and talked to her, pretending that she was by his side.

He wished her joy, and if that was too great a demand, then pleasure of each day in peace and contentment. She sat a long time with the pages folded in her hand, feeling the peace and contentment he spoke of. She had been right when she told him that no other love could ever displace what she felt for him. Theirs was a love that was altogether caring, and such a gentle caring even soothed her heart in this far place.

She wondered if he were standing before her at that moment, if she would turn down his offer of marriage again.

She rose and put the letter away. "It is

foolish even to ask yourself that question," she told herself firmly.

That night Matthew asked what news Philip had to tell. She handed him the letter to read. He seemed to enjoy the letter, since he smiled and nodded once in a while as his eyes moved down the page. Only later did she realize that he had not even offered to share his letter with her.

Chapter Eleven

MARILEE's letter from Philip Soames gave her the first sense of warm belonging that she had enjoyed for a long time. Even as the tiny ivory tooth had given her the city of London to hold in her hand, that letter reminded her that a whole world of love and understanding and caring still existed for her in one human heart. She knew that Deborah and Willum loved her. There were brief moments when she thought that Michael Braden loved her, although she guiltily wondered if he were not playing the role of the handsomest man in Virginia, proving that he could also be the most attentive and flattering.

Philip's love was different. He neither needed nor asked anything from her. Philip only held her in his heart, wishing the simplest of all things for her, the thing she had never guessed would be so far from her life — happiness.

It was not realistic to think that Philip's caring could have any effect on the causes of her misery. Yet, just having his words tucked into her pocket along with that etched tooth gave her a feeling of strength.

The unbelievable thing was that Philip's love and caring did manage, during that Easter week, to change her world into something she could bear.

The first astonishment came on the morning after the arrival of the ship that brought both her and Matthew their letters from Philip. Marilee was still slicing bread for breakfast when Hannah came out of her room and slid with a groan into the bench by the table.

From where she stood Marilee could see her brother. Matthew looked up and studied Hannah with a thoughtful frown.

"Is this going to be another day that your health is too poor for you to do your work?" he asked quietly.

Although the question itself was polite enough, something in the tone of his voice changed the very air in the room.

Hannah looked up and stared back at him as if amazed. Her mouth grew slack while she considered the question. Before she could answer, Abigail stopped the stirring of the spoon with which she had added sugar to her milk. Her round mouth dropped open in an almost stupid way.

Matthew continued to look at the maid calmly while he waited for her reply. Hannah flushed a deep ruddy color and cast an appealing glance at Abigail.

Abigail did not turn to her, nor let the woman catch her eye. Finding herself without a supporter, Hannah answered him in that whining voice of pain that she could produce as dependably as she could a sudden flow of tears.

"The pain comes and goes," Hannah told him with only a little hesitation in her voice. "The worst is when one ache leaves only to have another descend on me." As if to illustrate how dire her condition was, she cleared her throat and began to cough in a deep, hacking way, covering her eyes as well as her mouth as if to shield those who were watching from seeing how great her agony was.

"Since that is true," Matthew said quietly, "I have decided that we need to think again of the solution that my sister suggested for your problem before Philip left on the *Pryde*."

Hannah stared at him as if she did not understand. Whether she understood or not, she was clearly upset by his words. She gripped the edge of the table with such force that her fingers whitened around the nails.

"Solution?" Abigail asked, her tone challenging.

"Solution," Matthew repeated quietly. "Philip's letter reminded me that Marilee had offered to pay Hannah's return passage to England on the *Pryde*, as well as the expense of a coach to her sister's house."

"But I don't want to go," Hannah wailed.

Matthew's eyes were steady on her face. "Neither does my sister want to continue to pay the salary of a servant who is unable to work for any reason, whether it be a series of complaints or a simple desire to live beyond her station. It is in the tradition of the Fordham family to give generously where there is need. The family has an equally firm policy about not being robbed."

"Matthew," Abigail said in a hushed tone tone of shock, "I can't believe what you are saying."

Hannah, encouraged by this expression of sympathy, began to sob quietly into her handkerchief.

"You need to believe it, my dear," he said gently. "I have learned from Philip that Hannah's is a longer story than we have been told. Since she was never my own nurse, and not known as a pleasant person to be around, I avoided her at home. It seems that from her earliest days of employment with the family, soon after Marilee's birth, she has seized on the pretext of one illness after another to avoid the work that she was fairly paid for. Upon the occasion of my mother's death my father and Marilee made the compassionate decision to keep her on. Part of this was based on her advancing age. More considerable was their fear that no one else would put up with her ridiculous games."

"I'm a poor old woman, broken in health," Hannah wailed. "I don't want to go back to

England. I know that my health will be better. I am sure that I will feel strong when spring comes."

"Spring and summer are the unhealthiest times of the year in Virginia," Matthew told her. "If Marilee does not want to pay the cost of Hannah's return to England on the *Early Lark,* I shall do so myself. I have made the firm decision to take the burden of all this complaint and cost from this household. It is unfair for my sister to assume the work as well as the support of an ungrateful woman."

"Matthew," Abigail protested with a hint of warning in her voice, "this is unlike you. I enjoy Hannah's company and have sympathy with her plight. While she may not have been able to assume full duties yet, she has been helpful to me in many ways. I want her to stay."

"My dear Abigail," he said gently, "you must remember that Hannah is Marilee's servant, not yours. It is unfair for Marilee to assume the payment of her salary from her own private fortune when the woman does nothing but arrange your hair and provide you with company. Marilee and I can do with this woman as we desire. She returns to England."

"But, Matthew," Abigail argued, "you could pay her salary yourself."

Matthew had risen. "I could, but I do not choose to," he told her. "Neither Marilee nor I enjoy having Hannah in this house. She leaves for England with the sailing of the *Early Lark.*" With that, he turned and walked out the door.

Both women turned as one on Marilee. Hannah was weeping, and Abigail was shouting in fury. Marilee dropped her eyes and tried to control her trembling.

She heard the door open and looked up. Matthew had returned. He stood in the doorway, looking from his wife to the maid. Their voices fell silent in a breath. He held his wife's eyes until she flushed and dropped her gaze. Had he ever seen Abigail in one of these screaming fits before? Marilee wondered.

"I came back to tell you to pack your things," he told Hannah, his words quietly distinct in that silence.

Then, turning to Marilee, he asked, "Would you like to walk through the village with me on my way out? I am sure that your friend Deborah would appreciate a visit from you this lovely sunny morning."

Marilee did not hesitate but followed him out the door without a backward look. He said nothing of what had occurred in the kitchen, and neither did she. Marilee walked silently beside his horse until they reached Deborah's door. "My letter from Philip was very informative," he told her. "I would certainly not blame you if you decided to stay with your friend and her son until I return."

She nodded, unable to find words.

He glanced at Timothy. "In fact, if you do intend to stay with your friend, I shall have no concern for your safety or your happiness. I would also feel free to have Timothy come along to give me a hand today. I am conscious that I have been careless in the running of my own household. We will be through at Martin's Hundred in only a few days. His help will speed my getting back to my proper responsibility."

Marilee nodded. "That is a good plan," she managed to say just as Deborah, having seen her through the window, threw open the door.

Willie, who had decided during his mother's illness that Marilee was his private friend, launched himself across the room to seize her around the knees. She caught his arms and hugged him close.

"I have just been invited to spend the day with you," Marilee said.

Deborah angled her head to stare at Marilee like a skittish horse. "By Willie here?" she asked.

Marilee shook her head.

"By Matthew."

Deborah laughed. "Never question where the gold falls from. It all spends the same. I was going to make some special bread for Willum and the child to have on Easter Sunday. We can bake it together."

The thought of Easter baking flooded Marilee with homesickness. The kitchen of her father's house had been famous for holiday sweets. In autumn there was spicy gingerbread baked in the shape of men.

Christmas brought plum puddings that one stirred, always to the right, getting a wish for every time the spoon circled the bowl. Marilee's favorite sweet of the year was the great platter of hot cross buns that appeared at Easter.

"Oh, what I wouldn't give to be able to buy sugar and white flour to surprise Matthew with buns like we had at home."

" 'Sprise," Willie whispered from the floor. "More breakfast 'sprise."

Deborah laughed. "I will never get that boy to separate breakfast and surprise in his mind. But, listen, let me share my flour and sugar with you. I have a good supply."

"It wouldn't be the same," Marilee protested. "I would feel greedy taking from that expensive store of yours."

"If that is really how you feel," Deborah said, "Mrs. Harmer has such things to sell from her kitchen at double what they should cost."

"I feel reckless," Marilee told her, pulling her shawl from the chair to go back out.

Deborah frowned. "Didn't I see Timothy leave with Matthew?" she asked pointedly.

"You go about the village all the time by yourself," Marilee told her. "I don't know why I can't be free to come and go if you can."

"Because you don't look like me. Besides, there is a ship in port. You know about sailors. Come, use my sugar and flour. I promise to let you repay me."

It was such a glorious day altogether that later Marilee could hardly believe how miserably it ended. She and Deborah decided that little Willie was in danger of wearing his button nose out while the dough was rising. The smell of the cinnamon and allspice grew stronger as the fine dough rose in bulk. By the time the rolls were actually in the hot oven and baking, Marilee herself was tempted to snatch one from the pan half-baked and eat it.

Maggie, the milkmaid, passing by the house, rapped at the door and asked what fine smell filled the air.

"It's the smell of Easter," Deborah told her, showing the pans of shining buns.

"The smell is enough to pull a man off a horse," Maggie said. Then, eyeing Marilee, she shrugged. "You're an unlikely-looking cook, but the proof is in the eating, I suppose."

Deborah studied the finished product with a frown. "I have never made buns so light or with such wonderful flavor. You may have to make them with me every year after Willum sinks a tooth into these."

Marilee finished packing her share into a basket and covered it with a fresh towel. "Let's just hope that none of those eager suitors come tonight to sit and drink Matthew's wine and ale and act like friends. They are a remarkable lot for eating and drinking, and it would be sad for Matthew not to have his fill of these, since he loves them so much."

"Matthew is a generous man," Deborah

admitted. "But I have a feeling that his open-handedness might stop right there at that basket. Remember, he has a wife who neither cleans nor bakes. He is not apt to take such a treat as this lightly, nor to share it with fools."

For a moment Marilee looked at the buns thoughtfully. Was it possible that Abigail would take offense at Marilee's baking Easter buns for her husband? That was ridiculous. She had no other gift for her brother except this skill and the love it took to spend all those hours at this task.

Matthew rapped at the Yarrow door when he rode in from Martin's Hundred. He laughed to see little Willie shake hands in sober fare-well with Marilee, then hold his dirty little face up for a good-bye kiss.

Matthew was in an expansive mood. He chattered happily all the way home. "What a good day it was to be out in the sun working," he told Marilee. He smiled over at Timothy. "And we made a good day of it, Timothy and I. The two of us can outwork any team in these parts and have no modesty about it," he told Marilee. "Now I can figure that this Friday will be the last day I need to be there. Then my friends can set their furniture in and begin their life in style."

"But this will be Good Friday," Marilee protested.

He nodded. "I'll start early, to be sure and get back for the evening service. I need to be here working with my own land next week if my crop is to prosper. What do I smell?"

Marilee hid her smile and shrugged. "The wind off the river? The breeze from the stable?"

"No," he said, shaking his head. "It is something wonderful that smells like home." His voice drifted off as he tried to identify the elusive fragrance he had caught.

He was still shaking his head in a puzzled way when they reached the house and Timothy disappeared into the stable with the horse.

Although Abigail met her husband at the door as usual, her smile was stiff and forced. Matthew managed to be like always, bright and affectionate, full of the day's talk. Again, how like their father he was, Marilee thought. If there was unpleasantness to be done, her father had always faced it squarely. Once it was past and done, he never looked back in rancor.

Abigail clearly was not the same.

The moment the door was shut behind them, the fragrance of the spiced buns filled the room like perfume. "It's you," Matthew cried, as excited as a child. "What do you have in that basket that smells of home and happy times?"

Marilee exploded in laughter and laid back the cover on the basket she had borrowed from Deborah. A fresh wave of fragrance rose at the gesture. Matthew stared at the basket of buns in disbelief. "Hot cross buns," he said. "As I live and breathe, hot cross buns. Where in the world did you get them?"

"We made them, Deborah and I," Marilee told him. "I owe her for the sugar and flour, but I wanted them as an Easter gift to you and Abigail."

"Abbie, look," Matthew cried. "Better yet, smell. When did you see such as these before?"

"I can never remember seeing such buns as those," Abigail said in a distant tone.

Matthew lifted one and examined it from all sides and breathed its wonderful scent before taking a great greedy bite of it. He finished that bun and another while dinner was being served up. He offered one to Sukie. She accepted it with wide-eyed delight but asked permission to take it home so that she could share it with her family.

"I would offer you more," he told her, laughing, "but I intend to eat one for every year I have gone without them. That's ten buns, Sukie."

She giggled and wished him a hearty stomach for the task.

He was like a child about the buns, so much so that Marilee decided recklessly that she didn't care that Abigail only picked at one and didn't even finish it. Hannah did not appear at the dinner table at all.

Sukie was still clearing the table with Abigail helping when the rap came at the door. Marilee suppressed a groan. Please, not another planter come to smile and talk about tobacco and whether or not his chimney was made of brick.

To her delight Matthew opened the door to Michael Braden.

He greeted both her and Abigail with gentle gravity and congratulated Matthew on having more flowers in his house than most men had in their gardens.

There he went again, being so flowery that his words meant less than nothing. The longer she knew Michael, the more confused her feelings toward him were. As her life at Matthew's had become increasingly uncomfortable, she had found herself thinking about marriage in spite of her protests. But when she thought about marriage, she thought only of Michael Braden.

How confusing love was. Sometimes she wasn't sure that she would know it if it came flying out of the blue and knocked her down. Never for a single moment in all of the time that she had known Michael had she been as comfortable in his presence as she had been with Philip from the moment she met him. As a matter of fact, unless Timothy was in one of those scowling moods or was teasing her in an impudent way, she was even more comfortable around her brother's indentured servant than she was with Michael.

But then there was the matter of his beauty. She had never known a man who was so delightful to look at. No matter what clothes he wore — and he did have a handsome collection of clothes — the colors and fittings were perfect on him. She knew this was not a particularly good way to feel, but she always felt a surge of pride when she walked along the street with Michael, seeing the eyes of other women following him, knowing the handsomest man in Virginia walked at her side.

Then there was the way Michael made her feel about herself. Ten minutes with Michael and she felt like the most beautiful, witty, charming person in all the world. If her hair was neatly in place, he compared her with a woman of fashion like the ones who promenaded in the fine parks in London. If the wind had caught those unruly curls, twisting them loose into ringlets around her face, he talked of how the classical artists of Greece and Rome made just such spiral curls fly carelessly around the faces of goddesses.

"But that's not me," she told herself swiftly when he was puffing her up with such vanity.

Temptation. If one were married to a man like Michael, perhaps one would feel so beautiful all the time that it would come true and she would be comfortable with it.

But in any case, he was there, greeting Matthew and looking around in a puzzled way.

"What do I smell?"

Matthew roared with laughter. "Abbie, listen to this," he called to his wife. "Michael walks in here and asks —"

"Wait, I'm coming," Abigail called from

the kitchen where she had taken some dishes after Sukie. The moment she spoke, her words were followed by a cry, a crash, and the unmistakable sound of something dripping.

"Oh, Matthew," Abigail wailed, as if she had been hurt.

Matthew was on his feet and to the kitchen door in swift strides. Marilee could only see his back, but she heard Abigail's wail of distress. "It was an accident," Abigail kept saying. "I turned too fast and caught the handle of the pitcher in my sleeve."

Somehow Marilee knew what had happened even before she rose to join Matthew at the door. The tray of hot cross buns was on the kitchen table where Sukie had placed it. The jug of wine that Abigail had accidentally caught with her sleeve had emptied into the tray, soaking the buns into a scarlet, sodden mass.

"Of course it was an accident," Matthew said quietly. "Now let it be cleaned up." When he turned back to Michael and Marilee, his face seemed to be made of stone.

"What you smelled, Michael," he said in a flat, level tone, "were the finest hot cross buns ever to have been made in the New World. They might even be the only hot cross buns ever made in the New World. But now they are slop for pigs, having been carelessly drowned in red wine."

Michael looked at Matthew and then at Marilee with a stunned face.

"Perhaps I came at a bad time," he said.

Matthew had regained his presence. "There is no good time to spoil fine food," he said, "but what is done is done. Come and sit."

"I brought a special gift for my lovely friend here," Michael said, smiling at Marilee. "I left it outside in case there was some problem with having it here."

"A problem with a gift?" Matthew asked.

"It's not just any gift," Michael admitted. "It's a living gift, for Marilee's Easter."

"A living gift for Easter," Matthew said, frowning with puzzlement. "Well, let us see," he urged. "For heaven's sake, stop the suspense and let us see."

Michael let himself out, only to reappear within seconds with a midsize basket. He set it on the floor and raised his eyes to Marilee's. "For the joy of Easter," he said warmly.

Before anyone could lift the kerchief that covered the basket, a puppy nosed it aside. He stared up at Marilee and pushed the kerchief clear off the basket. He was a leggy little creature with short, wiry golden hair and large dark eyes. When he tried to leap from the basket, he landed on the floor in a great tangle of legs and feet.

"He's only two months old," Michael explained, "but he comes from the finest of Irish wolfhound stock. He'll make a dog twice the size of his mistress, big enough to bring down a wolf or a deer and certainly to protect her life from anyone of evil intent."

All of that didn't matter to Marilee at that

moment. What mattered was the way the puppy looked at her, the way he flew into her arms and twisted around not to lose sight of her face, the way his rough tongue scraped across her cheek.

Tears came at the warmth of him in her arms, at his delicious babyness, at his wriggling life.

"Oh, Michael," she said. "I love him. I love him. I can't ever thank you enough."

Michael's eyes met hers, filled with joy. At that moment she knew. She could be happy as Michael Braden's wife. She might not be comfortable with him, but he understood her need for affection, her love of living creatures.

She felt Matthew rise. She knew that he had joined Abigail at the door. Not until she heard the low insistence of his voice did she realize that she had been party to another breach between them.

"Not in my house," Abigail was saying in a low, intense voice. "Not a single night. Not in my house."

Chapter Twelve

ABIGAIL got her way.

Even though Michael had to be as conscious of this heated exchange as Marilee was, he acted as if he had heard nothing. Instead, with that instant smooth social skill of his, he turned and smiled at Marilee.

"The night is clear and lovely," he told her. "Would you like to take your new little friend for a walk through the village? The poor little creature is still nameless. You might even want to think about what you want to call him."

Marilee was quick to get her shawl and join Michael at the door. A tense silence in the house warned her that Abigail only waited to have Matthew alone before resuming her tirade.

It was cool outside. The air in the street was fragrant with rich food smells from meals being cooked and served behind closed

164

doors. As they passed Maggie's stable, Marilee heard the girl's voice lifted in soft wisps of song, broken now and then by humming as if she entertained herself happily as she worked.

At first Michael carried the dog in the basket. Almost at once, the animal's curiosity proved to be too intense to make that work. He kept sticking his head up this way and that, threatening to unbalance himself and tumble out onto the street. Finally Marilee lifted him out and fitted him into the crook of her arm, leaving Michael the empty basket to carry.

How warm he was against her. Even though the texture of his hair was wiry, his skin felt soft to her touch. He nestled himself into Marilee's arms as if he had been designed for them. Through the fabric of her sleeve the beating of the tiny animal's heart was like a muffled, rapid drum beat.

"I love him, Michael," Marilee told Michael again, overwhelmed by tenderness for the little creature.

Michael laughed softly, looking over at the pup. "He seemed to figure that out fast enough." Then he reached for Marilee's free hand and folded it lightly in his own as they walked along.

How peaceful and lovely it was to walk quietly in the darkness like that. From beyond the high fence of the fort Marilee could hear the sound of the river lapping at the beach.

"What a pleasant night for a walk, Michael," Marilee told him.

Michael sighed. "I wonder if you have any idea how pleasant I always find your company?" he asked. "A lovely night helps, but it is really you, Marilee, who makes the difference between pastime and pleasure for me."

"I know how much I have enjoyed your company," she replied. "Your friendship has meant a great deal to me."

Michael nodded. "It is good to have you say that, Marilee. I never want this warm friendship between us to come to an ending."

She glanced over at him. What a strange remark. Why should their friendship ever end? Unless, of course, it changed to some new and deeper relationship. Startled by this thought, she could only murmur that she knew of no reason that it ever should.

She felt herself waiting, waiting for Michael to declare himself, waiting for him to move his definition past friend to beloved.

When, instead, he continued to walk with her in silence, his hand warm on hers, she sighed.

She was beginning to think that there was a mystery in every life but her own. Matthew had suggested some mystery about Philip's leaving the university to go to sea.

More than once Matthew had made veiled references to how great an understanding Michael had about death.

How simple her own life had been. How

simple it promised to remain. If Michael learned to love her he would put the question to her and she would fly into marriage with him without looking back. Well, maybe she would look back a little. She could see herself married to Michael. She could not imagine in marriage with Michael that deep devotion and heartbreaking caring that she still had been seeking when she refused Philip Soames's proposal. Was she so quickly giving up her wonderful idealism about love? Or was she only recognizing that such a love was a child's romantic dream that she must stop seeking if she was ever to become a married woman?

"I am not at all sure that I like that dog after all," Michael said suddenly.

She turned to him in amazement. "What do you mean? Of course you like him. How could anyone resist him?" Even as the words left her lips she remembered the scene back at the house. "Except Abigail," she added to herself.

When he laughed, flashing that wonderful smile that only made his handsome face more appealing, she realized that he was teasing her. He tightened his hand on hers. "Look at how he has affected you," he pointed out. "You had barely tucked him under your arm before you slipped off into some sort of dream and stopped giving me any attention at all."

"I'm sorry," she said. "That was really rude of me. But at least it was a happy dream."

167

"I am sure that your little Irish friend was in that dream," he said. "Just so I was included."

She hadn't expected to look up and meet his eyes like that. The intensity of his expression made her flush. "You most certainly were," she assured him, feeling his hand tighten on hers.

The night had deepened. Marilee felt that Michael was as reluctant as she was to return to Matthew's house. Even though their steps slowed, they still finally wound their way back to where they had begun. Michael paused outside the door. He hesitated a moment before he asked his question. "Perhaps it would be better for me to take the dog home with me tonight?"

She said nothing for a moment. The last thing she wanted to do was give up the warm comfort of the little creature there against her arm. "We could ask Matthew," she suggested, and was delighted at his nod of agreement.

Matthew rose from his chair as they entered. He looked more like her father than Marilee had ever seen him look. Perhaps this came from the lines of concern that were newly visible on his forehead. Abigail was nowhere to be seen.

"There you two are," he said, smiling warmly at them both. "I hope the evening air agreed with your new friend here."

"He seems to have found it very relaxing." Marilee laughed, showing him the puppy limp in sleep across her arm. "Michael suggested that perhaps he should take the puppy back to his home tonight. What do you think, Matthew?"

Matthew shook his head. "That won't be necessary, but it was thoughtful of you to ask, Michael. While you were gone I made sleeping arrangements for your new friend. Have you given him a name?"

"Brian Boru," Marilee said swiftly. "His name is Brian Boru."

The two men exchanged a startled glance and then both laughed at once. "How in the world did you come upon a strange name like that?" Matthew asked.

"He's Irish," Marilee reminded him, "and certainly he will grow to be a king in size. Brian Boru was the Irish king who turned away the Norse invaders before England was even a nation."

Michael whistled softly and shook his head. "Your sister is a remarkable woman, Matthew."

"I am learning more about that all the time," Matthew agreed. "But she is also the child of a remarkable scholar who studied history all his life. We both are. Brian Boru is a fitting name, if a little unwieldy."

Marilee wakened the puppy and gave him a bowl of fresh water to lap up. Watching him drink, she wondered how she should feed him. As young as he seemed, she hesitated to offer him meat. She meant to ask Michael about his food, but the men had fallen into a hushed conversation in the next room. She sighed. Without hearing all their words, she was conscious that they were discussing the threat of an Indian attack again, a subject that men in Virginia never seemed to tire of. Well, she was tired of it even if they weren't. In all the time she had been here, the talk had gone on while peace reigned as usual. She joined them, her puppy in her arms, deliberately distracting them from this unhappy subject.

After drinking a glass of ale Michael told them both good night. When he had disappeared down the street, Matthew lifted the puppy from Marilee's arms.

He said nothing about Abigail's angry remarks. "Your room will be crowded until the *Early Lark* leaves with Hannah," he explained. "Timothy has agreed to keep your puppy in the loft with him until we can make more permanent arrangements."

This was a compromise then, Marilee thought. She had only seen the single window of the loft above the stable where Timothy Reeves slept and took his meals. As Matthew let himself out to deliver the puppy to the loft, Marilee felt suddenly bleak and lonely. She was even a little envious of Timothy, who would have that soft, loving warmth at his side through the long night to come.

The house had been so quiet except for their conversation that Marilee had thought that both of the women had already gone to sleep for the night. Even as she crept into bed she realized her error in this. Almost immediately from behind the wall Abigail's voice rose, almost shouting at Matthew.

Marilee shuddered under her coverlet and tried to close her ears as well as her eyes for sleep. Possibly she would not have gone to sleep right away, anyway, but Abigail's angry tones could not be shut away. Matthew did not shout, but the tone of his rumbling answers was not one that she had ever heard from her brother before.

Silence only came after she heard a door being slammed in anger. She lay wakeful a long time, trying to sort out the days ahead. Matthew had only said that Philip's letter had been "most informative." Clearly Philip had managed to give Matthew a better history of Hannah than he had heard from Abigail. The truth about Marilee's own "idleness in the streets" had been pretty well cleared up during the days of Deborah's illness. And Abigail herself, in that scene after breakfast and her fury over the dog, had surely done much to disillusion her husband.

While this was good for Marilee, in the sense that at least Matthew could not be so easily led to misjudge her, it promised little but trouble to come.

That first night, when she and Matthew had talked about the coolness between Philip and Michael Braden, Matthew had said, "We must forgive much in each other if we are to survive." She had no doubt of Matthew's ability to forgive much in Abigail. She did not have the same faith in Abigail's being able to do the same.

When a happy, sharp, high yip was the first sound that Marilee heard on wakening, it took her a moment to realize where it was coming from. The moment she remembered, she whispered the dog's name to herself and hopped out of bed as excited as a child. She felt a rush of joy like Christmas morning, knowing that she would have that companion all day long. Dressing was easy enough, but as always when she was in a hurry to make herself presentable, her hair flew every which way in a tumble of curls.

"Fly then," she told her ringlets, blowing them from her eyes as she let herself out of the room.

The house was empty. Except for Hannah's steady snoring, it was also silent. Abigail's door was still shut, and there was no one in the kitchen. When the yip came again, Marilee heard Matthew laughing and realized the sound came from outside.

She opened the door and stood watching the three of them for a long minute before they noticed her. Timothy, his lustrous curls gleaming in the morning sun, was kneeling just outside the stable. He was gripping a leather strap with both hands. The puppy was making a fierce effort to tug it away from him. Brian had braced his legs against the earth and was shaking his head wildly as he tried with his baby strength to get the leather from Timothy's hand.

As Marilee watched, Timothy looked up into Matthew's face, and they laughed together. Something warm and wonderful flooded Marilee's heart. How much love and friendship these two men shared. Remembering the bitter arguments that had kept her from sleep the night before, Marilee felt a surge of great love for Timothy Reeves. Indeed, at that moment she loved him with all her heart. No matter how false and unpleasant Matthew's wife determined to be, at least Matthew had this, the love and loyalty of a fine, strong man like Timothy.

She often thought of her earliest conversations with Timothy. He had told her almost at once that his indenture was nearly through. Surely his becoming a free man wouldn't change anything as powerful as this friendship. They would be equals instead of master and servant.

Timothy, seeing her, rose to his feet with a smile.

"You do have a sturdy little fighter here," he told her. "And a snuggler, I might add."

"You were so good to keep him," Marilee said. "I do thank you for that." The puppy, having lost interest in the strap when Timothy released it, bounced to Marilee and pawed at her ankles to be picked up.

With his wriggling warmth against her neck, she turned to Matthew. "Have you had breakfast?"

"Neither Timothy nor I have eaten," Matthew replied. Then he frowned. "Maybe you

could find something for us all to eat and
bring it out here." As she nodded and turned
he called after her. "If you could pack a little
extra while you do that, I will take it with
me. I plan to stay the night at Martin's
Hundred."

At Timothy's stricken look and her own
amazed glance, he added quickly, "To get an
early start on my last day there."

When she set down the puppy, he lunged
after her eagerly. Timothy laughed, scooped
him up by his round belly, and held him aloft
and wriggling while Marilee made her escape.

She piled buttered bread and slices of meat
spread with mustard on one of Abigail's pewter trays. She slid the rest of the meat in
between slices of bread for Matthew to take
with him. She felt a moment's guilt about
carrying the last shred of meat from the
kitchen, but Abigail preferred jam and honey,
anyway, and a working man needed solid
food.

The three of them sat on the smooth stones
by Marilee's garden and ate with wonderful
appetite. The puppy watched her eat with
such whining excitement that she finally fed
him most of her own food in tiny bites that
he chewed with loud enthusiasm.

Marilee hoped that she was imagining how
unlike himself Matthew appeared. He looked
as if he had not slept. When she noticed that
Timothy kept glancing at him with worried
concern, she knew her fear was founded on
fact.

Matthew, watching her eyes, smiled at her as if to reassure her. "I have been admiring your little garden," he said. "Every day I see more spikes of green. What will you do with all these herbs and spices?"

Marilee looked over at them and laughed, remembering her mother's words when her father had teased her about her great bounty. "Cook and heal and give away, just as Mother always did," she explained. "What I am excited about is to find out what useful things grow wild in the woods here."

Matthew nodded. "Timothy and I will take you exploring when I am home next week. I know it has been hard for you to be so cooped up. Believe me, no one wanted it to be that way." His smile was tender on her face. "Maybe I have been too cautious with your safety, but all this growing talk of an Indian uprising made me a coward for you."

"Do these planters ever talk of anything else, or have they some reason for these dire predictions?" Marilee asked.

"The Indians have planted no corn," he told her. "They do not plant corn if they think a war might drive them from their crop."

This thought might have depressed Marilee a great deal if Timothy had not risen and brought Brian a bowl of fresh water. The puppy drank with such fervor that his foot slipped and he ducked his head in the water, coming up blinking and bewildered.

Matthew laughed and rose. "I could watch

that little creature all day," he admitted with a sigh. "But watching isn't working." He studied Marilee a moment. "What do you plan to do all day, Marilee? I don't want you to feel that you have to stay around here if there is a more comfortable place you could be."

Marilee tried to conceal her surprise at his blunt words. "I will probably go introduce my new friend to my old ones," she said. "Perhaps Timothy —" She was going to suggest that Timothy might go with him to hasten the work, but Matthew didn't even let her finish the sentence.

"No," he said firmly. "Timothy will stay here in the fort with you today. I don't want him that far with all the talk that is in the air."

She dropped her eyes to keep from seeing that hard change come in Timothy's face. This had been such a happy hour, with the three of them and the puppy comfortable and loving together. As Timothy turned away to ready Matthew's horse, Matthew took her hands and lifted her to her feet. He looked at her tenderly for a long moment.

"How strong you have been, my Marilee," he said gently. "As strong as our father claimed for you. God knows I grieve for the pain I visited on you. God bless Philip Soames for his love and loyalty that risked our friendship for your comfort."

She didn't want to cry. More than that, she couldn't stand for Matthew to call her strong in one breath and see her weep in the next. She buried her head against his chest and clung there until the clop of the horse's hooves told her that Timothy had come out of the stable with the horse.

"I love you, Matthew," she whispered against his chest.

"And I you, Marilee," he replied, his hand warm and firm against her back.

Unable to make herself go back into the house to stay, Marilee returned the pewter tray to the kitchen and went out to work in her garden. Timothy, working in and out of the stable, saw how difficult it was for Marilee to make the puppy stay out of the freshly planted earth. He disappeared into the stable and was gone a long time. She heard the sound of a hammer on metal and Timothy whistling softly to himself as he worked. When he returned, he was smiling broadly. From a worn set of reins he had fashioned a leather leash for the pup that was exactly the right size for little Brian's neck.

He put a circlet around the puppy's neck and pulled the leash through a loop. "This will work as a choke collar," he explained. "He will train easily, as smart as he is."

"Train?" Marilee asked, looking up at him.

"He must be trained to obey your commands, both with your voice and with a leash like this," Timothy explained. "Remember how your father's old dog Bruce stopped at a gesture of his hand? He was taught that as a puppy, along with other things."

"I hope I can do that," Marilee said doubtfully.

He smiled down at her, his fine, smoky eyes laughing. "Given how small and light you are and what a great strong beast he will grow into, you had better learn that job."

Even after Sukie came with the milk, there was still no sound from inside the house. When Marilee heard Abigail's voice raised in anger from inside, she remembered the breakfast she had fixed with a stab of guilt. All the meat was gone and most of the bread. She rose, wiped off her hands, and took the dog's leash.

"Would you give me the first lesson in training Brian now?" she asked Timothy, trying to keep her voice from mirroring the trembling that had begun when she heard the sound of Abigail's fury.

He smiled, his mouth tightening in that private way, as if he were hiding his amusement from all eyes but her own.

"The village street would be the best place to start," he suggested. "He'll need to behave there all his life."

Only when they were walking the animal along the street, being stopped constantly for the puppy to be admired, did Marilee even think about Michael Braden.

It was awfully ungrateful of her, but she really hoped that Michael wouldn't be out this morning. She could imagine him turning pale with anger to see her and Timothy together with this dog that had been his gift. But the puppy was swift to understand what was expected of him. Almost at once Brian began to walk briskly along beside Timothy, instead of stopping every few feet to chew on his leash.

The sun was high before the puppy tired and dropped in his tracks, having to be dragged along. Marilee picked him up and thanked Timothy warmly.

He nodded. "It was a good morning's work," he told her "The little fellow did well to last so long." He paused. "Can I take you somewhere now?"

She was so grateful, she couldn't protest his coming along to Deborah's with her.

They were almost at the door when she looked up and saw him grinning broadly.

"Did I miss something?" Marilee asked him.

He shook his head and grinned at her. "No, but I fear I will. I was thinking of that young Master Yarrow, who is such a terror. It will be a sight to see the two of these creatures play together."

Marilee was smiling at the thought as Deborah opened the door. Her friend cried aloud with delight at the sight of the puppy.

"I forgot about the cat," Marilee said as she stepped inside the door. The cat had leaped to the sill at the sight of Brian. She stood there stiff-legged, her back arched in prickles, hissing in warning.

Deborah laughed. "No dog is going to bother a cat who has survived Willie," she pointed out. "Come in, sit down a while. Let the cat work this out her own way."

"Thank you," Marilee said, "but I have really come to spend the day."

"If you meant that as a warning you are wasting your time," Deborah told her. "That's the best news Willie and I could ever have." Deborah knelt with a groan and held Willie's hand to show him how to pat the sleeping puppy gently.

"And maybe the night?" Marilee asked. "Matthew and Abigail had a great row, and he is spending the night at Martin's Hundred."

Deborah's glance was swift and searching.

"Matthew is sending Hannah home on the *Early Lark*," Marilee added.

"The day had to come," Deborah said, being careful not to meet Marilee's eyes.

"He got a letter from Philip," Marilee explained.

Deborah looked at her thoughtfully. "Trust Philip to reach a man from across the seas and scold him for his blindness."

"It was a brave act," Marilee said. "He risked Matthew's friendship if my brother did not believe what he said."

"Philip is not a man to stand off because of risk," Deborah reminded her. "Nor is Matthew a man to turn away from the truth if he has it plainly before him. As for staying, you are as welcome as morning."

Then Deborah nodded. "In fairness I'll give you warning. Willie snores."

Marilee laughed and pressed her friend's hand gratefully. "I cannot believe that he can hold a candle to what Hannah can do to the quiet night air."

Chapter Thirteen

WILLIE did not really snore, he snuffled. Marilee, drifting in and out of sleep in a strange bed, was conscious of a different rhythm in Deborah and Willum's house. Little Willie and the dog curled together as if they were both puppies, each one stirring and settling again when the other moved. Marilee smiled at the memory of Willie and the pup in the day just past. Willie, finding the name Brian too hard to say, promptly nicknamed the dog "Briny."

Deborah laughed. "Briny? That means salty."

"So he will be the salt of the earth," Marilee said. "Willie knows what he is saying."

Drifting in and out of sleep, Marilee watched the moon pass beyond the window and out of view.

She hoped she had made the right decision in staying the night at the Yarrow house.

Timothy had come to the door at twilight asking if she wanted to return home.

"I really don't," she admitted, hesitating at making such an obvious break but unable to face the prospect of a night alone with Abigail and Hannah.

"Send a message by Timothy," Deborah prompted her. "There is no law that says a friend cannot visit the night."

Timothy waited silently, his face unreadable.

"Please just tell your mistress that I am staying the night with my friend, Mrs. Yarrow," she told him.

In that half-light his smoky eyes seemed as dark as Philip's. He hesitated a moment, studying her.

"You will be all right?" he asked.

She nodded, touched not so much by his words as by the tone in which they were spoken.

"I don't think Matthew expected me to go back there," she added.

He bent his head, kicking at a clod of earth at his feet. "Probably not," he agreed. "Probably not." Then he nodded and said, "Rest well."

"You rest well, too," she told him.

She stood, watching him walk away in his distinctive light-footed tread. Somehow he had done it again. He had tugged at her heartstrings in a painful way. It was ridiculous. Most of the time he was rude to her or glared at her fiercely. He was a huge, strong man and the son of a yeoman in her father's village. Yet, sometimes, like this evening, like the day beyond the wall of the fort, he seemed wonderfully like an understanding gentleman. More even than with Philip, she sometimes had the sense that she didn't even need to speak to have him understand what was in her heart.

In spite of what Michael had said, Timothy Reeves was not a dolt. He was not stupid or insensitive. And since he was not blinded by love for Abigail as Matthew was, he must have seen the woman's falseness long before now. That would explain why Abigail hated him so much that she had said to Marilee more than once that Timothy Reeves would get put down in time. Marilee sighed. Her own experience had taught her not to envy any person who had Abigail Fordham for an enemy.

Only when Timothy was wholly gone from her sight did she close Deborah's door and rejoin her host and hostess.

Marilee wakened to the common sounds of breakfast being made. Off in the kitchen Willum and Deborah were talking, a low, friendly hum. Willie still slept, but the puppy's eyes were watchful on her as she dressed. When he caught her eye, he drummed the coverlet with his ungainly tail.

"Come now," she whispered, pursing her lips and whistling softly to lure him from the bed without wakening the child.

She caught him and was easing the door

open when she heard the extraordinary sounds begin. She heard the horse first, a horse being galloped through the fort, its rider shouting something Marilee could not understand. Later she remembered a moment of stunned silence. Maybe it had only been in her own heart. Within seconds the tumult began.

It was as if the world had exploded in sound. More voices answered until shouting came from everywhere. Doors were banged explosively, and she heard a woman scream, and then another. The village dogs began to bark, and the sound of running feet drummed along the street outside. Before Willum even got to his feet, someone passed the house running, hesitating only long enough to hammer on the wooden door with his fist, shouting at the top of his voice. The same cry came from everywhere.

"Indian attack," the voices shouted. "All up and to the battlements. Indian attack."

In a single motion Willum crossed the room, pulled a gun from the rack, and threw the door wide open. An acrid scent of gunpowder and smoke poured into the room with the crisp morning air. The puppy, tight in Marilee's arms, seemed to be the only silent creature inside the fort. Horses whinnied in panic, and the braying of a donkey failed to drown out the frantic barking of the village dogs.

Willie, startled awake by the wild confusion of noise, began to scream. As clumsy as she was with her coming child, Deborah hurried to him swiftly. Even as she folded her child in her arms, her eyes followed Willum. Her voice was weak with fear.

"Willum," she called after him as he let himself out to join the running men in the street. "God bless. God bless."

Marilee followed Willum into the street, only to be pressed back against the rough wall of the house by the traffic in the street. Men bearing guns and swords spilled past her toward the gate that opened onto the river. Above her on the walls of the fort, soldiers in scarlet shouted at each other as they loaded the cannon, their plumed helmets shining in the sun of Good Friday morning. In a matter of minutes the fortress wall was bristling with armed men.

"What is it? What is happening?" Marilee called helplessly.

"Have you no eyes then?" a voice asked. "Look to the sky."

The sky.

As far as she could see, pillars of smoke rose against the blue sky. The world looked to have been set afire. Here and there a vast pillar of flame licked scarlet above the height of the fort.

"Arms," Deborah cried behind her. "Arms."

Somehow Deborah had settled little Willie into a glazed coil of terror, cringing in the kitchen corner.

"Here," Marilee said, thrusting the puppy

into Willie's arms, "you take care of Briny for me."

Marilee stared stupidly at the gun Deborah pressed into her hands. "Load it," Deborah said sternly, "while there is still time."

Marilee watched Deborah's swift skill at this unfamiliar task, tamping the cone of powder down, getting the shot fitted into the barrel.

"Deborah," Marilee wailed, "what does this mean? What is happening?"

Deborah shook her head. It would have done no good for her to speak. The steady explosion of guns and the roar of the cannon would have drowned out her words. And through it all sounded the high, hysterical screaming of unseen children.

When that morning came back to haunt Marilee, either in memory or in long, painful nightmares, that battle seemed to have gone on for hours. In truth, it was over almost as swiftly as it had begun. Everything went at such a frantic pace. Within minutes all the horses were gone from the fort, being ridden madly out the gate to accost the enemy. All the men were gone except those soldiers crouching on the walls, manning the cannon and the towers. The cannon shattered the air with waves of thunder, and gunfire came from all directions. Then the voice of the cannon stopped, and the gunfire rattled into silence.

But beyond the walls the fires still raged,

darkening the sun with the masses of smoke that seemed to be rising for miles, for the length of Virginia, smoke swaying like a shroud along the river, smoke bringing tears to Marilee's eyes and tightening her throat into painful coughing.

Only when the firing ceased did Marilee remember Abigail, Matthew's wife. Without a backward glance, Marilee fought her way into the crowded street, pushing her way toward her brother's house.

Although the door was still closed with the latch string tight, Marilee could hear Abigail wailing inside the house.

"Help," she was crying. "Oh, please, God, help."

Marilee found the two women huddled together in Abigail's room: Hannah, wide-eyed and weeping, and Abigail frantic with fear.

"Save me, save me," Abigail moaned, reaching for Marilee with clawing hands.

Even as Marilee hesitated in the door, uncertain what to do, a voice called urgently from the door. "We seek the sister of Matthew Fordham. If you have medicines, come."

"Medicines," Marilee repeated dumbly, turning.

The milkmaid Maggie, her voice turned hoarse by smoke or screaming, repeated her words impatiently. "Where are they?" she went on. "We need your help. They are bringing back the wounded, woman," Maggie went on angrily. "Where are your medicines?"

Wounded. Maggie followed as Marilee

rushed back to the tiny room where her trunks were stored. Thank goodness she had unpacked her medicines, even though most of her things still waited the coming of Hannah's strength. She found a large basket in Abigail's kitchen and filled it and another with supplies before Maggie, fretful with haste, hurried her out onto the street.

"What about Martin's Hundred?" Marilee asked as she followed Maggie's swift passage through the crowd. "Has anyone had news of Martin's Hundred?" There was no answer.

Marilee had seen death in the village back home in England. A blacksmith had lost his hold and smashed his leg into pulp. Men caught their own scythes during harvest and cut themselves wickedly. Marilee had seen burns and broken bones and men kicked by horses when she had gone out with her mother on the business of healing. She had never seen such carnage as this.

"What about Martin's Hundred?" she asked as she brewed the strong solution of herbs that was designed to prevent infection.

There was no answer.

But the wounded kept on coming. They limped through the gate, supported on the shoulders of friends. They were carried like moaning logs by white-faced companions. All these men were strangers to Marilee. Not once did she see any of the people she was accustomed to greeting in the streets of Jamestown. Along with the wounded came weeping women and children wide-eyed with horror. Strangers, all of them strangers, finding refuge inside the fort with the fighting already past. But beyond the walls the fires still burned sullenly, pillars of destruction.

"What about Martin's Hundred?" she asked as she bound a groaning planter's leg with strips of clean fabric, praying that his bones had been wrénched back into their proper position.

While no one spoke of Martin's Hundred, everyone had something to tell about the attack. This word came out in such a confused jumble that Marilee found it hard to sort it into any kind of sense.

When she did begin to understand, Timothy Reeves's words came back to her. This morning had brought the kind of attack that Timothy had warned of that day that she walked with him beyond the wall. Opechanough's warriors had tried to wipe out all the Englishmen on their land in one great attack. At the last possible moment the governor had been warned. He had reacted swiftly, sending all the couriers he could summon to ride to the plantations and give warning. Because of the lateness of the hour, only the plantations within five miles of Jamestown had been reached. There had been no time to alert the others.

"Tell me about Martin's Hundred," Marilee begged, without stopping her hands from their gruesome task.

She got no answer from those around her

until she felt a sudden hand on her arm. She looked up to see Willum Yarrow at her side. She didn't recognize him at first. His face was black with smoke, and his eyes almost swelled shut. His hand on her arm was tight, as if he meant to pass on to her his own great strength by this laying on of his hand.

"It went badly at the outlying plantations," he told her, his voice heavy with foreboding, "but the news comes slowly at such a time. Pray, sister of Matthew Fordham. Pray."

Chapter Fourteen

THE alarm had first sounded at eight that morning. By noon there was not an inch inside the fort of Jamestown that was not filled with either refugees from the outlying plantations or wounded struck down in battle. The survivors had arrived on foot, on horseback, and by boat down the river. There was not food enough to provide for the living. There were not hands enough to care for the wounded. There was not room enough to store the dead until graves could be dug.

All the women with any skill at tending the sick were pressed into service. The ship's doctor from the *Early Lark* had been rowed in to direct and help with the growing tide of patients. All day Marilee worked at Maggie's side. By late afternoon she fought a growing dizziness, having to brace herself when she rose from kneeling by a suffering man. She had not stopped for food and would not have stopped for drink if Deborah had not twice shouldered her way to her friend's side. Deborah watched sternly while Marilee forced down a second steaming mug of hot sassafras tea generously sweetened with wild honey.

"I suppose there is still no word from Martin's Hundred," Marilee asked her, no longer even hopeful of an answer.

Deborah could not meet her eyes. Instead she caught her lip between her teeth and dropped her eyes.

"There is word then," Marilee said, feeling a leap of hope in spite of herself. "What of Matthew? Is there any word at all of Matthew?"

"Word has been coming in from Martin's Hundred," Deborah told her. "So far I have heard no man who knew anything about Matthew Fordham. They say that those men who were working on the outlying plantations bore the brunt of the attack, men working in their fields, men building new structures, making brick."

"Matthew was helping build a house," Marilee reminded her, feeling her heart tighten painfully in her chest.

Deborah's tone turned very stern. "Remember that there is still no firm word. You are not to give up hope until his name is spoken." This was an order, not advice, Marilee decided.

Although the pillars of smoke no longer rose at day's end, a dense pall concealed the sky. The setting sun stained this blanket of smoke with deep tones of red and lavender. The exhausted population seemed to have worn out with the day. The village grew quieter with sunset. The last of the men who had pursued the escaping Indians had returned to the fort. Many had been wounded in skirmishes with the retreating enemy. Others simply wore shock and exhaustion on their faces. Only an occasional wail of grief or the sobbing of a child broke the quiet of the streets.

Deborah had been right to tell Marilee to wait to hear Matthew's name. With only twelve hundred Englishmen in Virginia, these men knew each other's names. The names of the dead were spoken quietly. Worse even than the names that were recited were the numbers. Of these twelve hundred citizens in the tidewater settlement who had begun that Good Friday, almost a third had not survived to see another sunrise.

The wounded men had been placed as close together as logs, on rough pallets hastily formed to keep them from bare floors. Marilee's basket was emptied of any herb that could help any man heal. With her heart as empty as her basket she leaned back against the post of Maggie's stable to rest. She was standing there with her eyes closed and her arms crossed over the handle of her basket when she heard Matthew's name whispered for the first time. Waves of chill shuddered down her body, and a sudden, hot pressure of tears swelled behind her eyes, but she felt no surprise.

Marilee was still trying to control the anguish that racked her tired body when she realized that Maggie was talking to her. Rousing, Marilee looked over at this milkmaid who had been such a tower of strength that whole day.

Marilee sensed that Maggie had not overheard those fateful whispered words, because the girl was smiling crookedly as if she had a joke to share. "Here we are," she said. "The two of us as worn as old shoes. Yet in truth, we might as well have been pouring water through sieves all day, you and I."

Marilee frowned. Maggie was certainly right about how tired they both were. But how could Maggie see such a day as wasted when they had worked side by side, cleaning wounds and binding them, setting broken bones with wooden splints? "What do you mean by that?" she asked.

"How little you know of life in this place," Maggie scoffed. "It is a lesson of war that you need not kill a man. To wound him is enough. Infection and disease will put him into a grave soon enough."

"I won't believe that," Marilee told her. "I can't bear to."

Maggie shrugged and turned away. "Wait until the morning," she said. "The fever will have begun by then."

Marilee studied the girl. Who would know what to expect better than Maggie? After all, Maggie had lived with the fever and lost her beloved husband to it, yet the girl's air was so flippant. She talked of death as other men would talk of a wager. Was this how a person became when all hope was gone, so callous that she could even jest about death?

"You are still expecting to hear good news of your brother," Maggie said quietly. She was not asking a question. It was as if she were making a sad statement about Marilee's foolishness.

The word *no* came instantly to Marilee's mind, but she caught herself before she spoke that lie. It would be easy enough to tell Maggie that she had heard Matthew's name whispered among the dead and accepted her loss. She would have been telling only half of the truth. The reason she had not been surprised was that she had felt her own hope dying with the fading day. She was exhausted past tears, past active thinking. Her realization that Matthew was lost to her had come, not to her mind by whispered words, but into her consciousness, seeping in slowly like foul water polluting a clean well.

And there was the evidence of time. If Matthew were still alive he would have managed to come to Jamestown long before now, if only to ease Abigail's mind and her own. If he had been wounded he would have been brought here for safety long before now. Matthew was dead. To fight away an anguish that threatened to weigh her to the ground,

Marilee straightened up and looked around for something more she could do.

She drew a fresh pail of cool water and carried it into the chapel. The benches that usually served as pews for worship had been stacked against the wall to make room for the wounded. The room was dim and airless with only a few candles flickering here and there.

Dully, she walked between the rows of wounded men, pausing now and then to kneel and wipe a flushed face or pour a freshening trickle of water over a moaning man's wrist. Sometimes one of these strangers caught at her hand in thanks. Once in a while a soft groan came from parched lips. She wasn't seeing the faces of the men, really. She kept seeing Matthew as she had seen him that first day from the rail of the *Pryde*, walking toward her briskly with that wonderful smile of welcome on his face. Then he had grown hazy, his outline uncertain in her view, as if he, like their father, was fading into death before her very eyes.

Her eyes swam with tears as she moistened the cold cloth to wipe the forehead of the man who lay at her feet. His wound had been dressed with white fabric that covered half his face, leaving only one eye exposed. One of his legs was bandaged, too, showing that whatever enemy he had encountered had struck him a double blow. She had lifted the moist cloth when a hard, firm hand seized her wrist, forcing the cloth away from his face.

"Don't touch me," the man said, his voice harsh with hatred. She stared down at him, the wet cloth dripping cold water down her arm, soaking into her sleeve, chilling her so that she trembled. Only then did she really see him. She stared at those dark, matted curls, that wing of a brow above a single smoky eye, and realized who had seized her wrist so roughly. Timothy Reeves.

She breathed his name gratefully. "Timothy, you live."

"Not by any fault of my own," he said harshly. "The fault is yours, all the fault." Still holding her, he tried to rise on his elbows, an effort that brought a swift rising of sweat to his forehead.

"He is dead, do you understand? Matthew Fordham is dead because of you. If I had been there at his side where my duty lay I could have stood off an army of the enemy to save his life. But, no. I was here to guard a worthless girl, and they cut him down. God forgive me that I live and he lies butchered."

He released her and fell back, turning his face away from her.

"Don't do this," Marilee wailed softly. "Don't reject your life because Matthew lost his. Rejoice that you live even as he would rejoice if he knew. He loved you, Timothy, and believed in you."

"I want no part of any life that is bought with my master's death," he said furiously.

"Listen to me, Timothy," she begged. "Remember what Matthew stood for. He believed in men and their chances for fuller lives. And look at you. You will be a free man right away. The better and fuller you use your life, the better you serve the Matthew we both loved."

"Let your mouth be silent," he said angrily, turning to glare at her with that single haunting eye. "I want no part of life. I want no part of you or your fine words. I want Matthew alive again, as he still would be except that I was left to guard you. How can either of us live with the guilty knowledge that the world lost a great man because I was guarding a fool?

"Leave me to die in peace, Marilee. With your vain pride and your giddy beauty you are not fit to be called by the name of Fordham. To think that I was forced to let the master die for nothing but the last worthless remnant of a long and noble line."

It was not the cruel unfairness of his words that drove Marilee to step back from him. It was the flaming, furious hatred in his voice and in that single eye pinned on her.

Then he began shouting so wildly that others around craned to stare at both of them. "Go," he shouted. "Go and let me die in peace."

Marilee lurched from the church unsteadily, unable to see the ground for her tears. When someone took her arm to steady her, she tried to shake herself free. "Leave me be," she said. "Just leave me be."

"How can I do that?" Michael Braden asked softly. "How can I let one so dear to my friend Matthew stagger about like a poisoned horse? Come home, Marilee. You are needed."

"Needed!" she cried, turning to him. "I might better walk out of those gates into the arms of the enemy than face life here. Matthew is dead, don't you understand? Matthew is dead, and my own life with him."

He hesitated a long minute, looking at her soberly. "You were sister to Matthew," he reminded her. "Matthew also left a wife."

When she dropped her eyes, he waited for her to look up again. The sternness in his voice was not reflected in his eyes, which watched her in that intent, tender way. She felt herself weaken under that glance and shook her head. "Oh, please, Michael, don't be kind to me," she begged. "I can bear all things but kindness right now."

"Then I will be firm," he told her. "The woman your brother loved past reason has collapsed, unable to bear the weight of her grief. She is helpless."

"She is surrounded by help," Marilee reminded him angrily. "What about Sukie? And what about Hannah?"

"Marilee, Marilee," he said softly. "Sukie never got here this morning. Her plantation was too far to be warned. She never made it, nor did her husband, nor did their children."

"Children," Marilee whispered, remembering the day that Matthew had given her the single Easter bun that she wrapped to share with her family.

He nodded. "Sukie had three fine young sons who stayed with a friend on a neighboring plantation while she worked here for Matthew and Abigail. Now all are dead."

He had taken her gently by the arm again and was guiding her along the street.

When he spoke again, his tone was one of sober thought. "I guess you have to ask yourself what Matthew would have wanted you to do," he said quietly.

His words brought Matthew as fully alive in Marilee's mind as he had been when they had shared a sunlit breakfast with Timothy and Briny the morning before. Then he had stood holding both her hands and looking into her eyes. What pride had been in his voice as he told her, "As strong as our father claimed for you. Bless Philip Soames."

She stumbled a little in the path, and Michael leaned out to brace her with an arm at her waist.

"Bless Philip Soames."

Until that moment she had not realized how much she owed to Philip Soames, how much she would owe him all her life. Without Philip's letter and Matthew's careful reading of it, Matthew would have died thinking her an enemy instead of a loving friend. He would have gone down to the weapons of the enemy disliking her, thinking ill of her, misjudging her.

But they had made peace. "I love you, Marilee," had been Matthew's last words to her.

"Matthew would want his wife cared for," she admitted to Michael, falling back into step with him.

The hearth fire in Matthew's house had long gone out if it had ever been laid that day. With Michael's help Marilee set it to flame again. In spite of her past troubles with her sister-in-law, Marilee felt her heart go out to Abigail. Her sister-in-law did not weep. Her eyes did not even show the red of weeping past. She only lay against her pillows, staring off into a corner as if her mind had been swept from her. Hannah, for once on her feet and moving, rustled around the pale blonde figure, moving a coverlet, clucking and muttering to herself.

When Marilee brought Abigail a warm cup of soup and the last of the bread buttered and spread with jelly, Hannah stepped back without meeting her mistress's eyes.

Michael hesitated at the door. "I hate to leave the three of you here alone," he said. "That worthless Reeves seems to have taken his leave of here."

Marilee marveled that her words in defense of Timothy came so swiftly after the way he had talked to her. "He is wounded," she told him.

Then, remembering where she had been when this day began, she thought of the puppy Briny. "Oh, Michael, I haven't once thought of that puppy since the first alarm was sounded. I handed him to little Willie Yarrow. I guess he has been there this whole day. Surely Deborah will care for him until I am free to get him."

"I will stop and ask that favor of her for you," Michael said. "After such a day you need a long, sweet sleep."

Marilee looked at him, neat as always in trim breeches with well-fitting stockings on his shapely legs. His pale hair caught the light, and the line of his face looking down at her tempted her to lift her hand and caress his face.

"How good you are to me, Michael," she whispered, overcome by sudden emotion. "What a warm friend Matthew had in you."

"It is no strain to be kind to people one cares so much about," he told her.

The coming of morning brought rush after rush of fresh grief. As Marilee fanned the fire up for breakfast she realized that no tanned and smiling Matthew would come through that door to join her, not today, not any day ever. She carried a tray to Abigail. Her sister-in-law did not acknowledge her presence and only toyed with the precious food. Back in the kitchen Marilee found herself half-listening for Sukie's arrival, only to stand in horror when she remembered Michael's words.

Not until the governor sent his soldier to the house did Marilee hear a word from Abigail's lips. When Maggie entered with the man, Abigail seemed to summon her mind from a distant place. Supported by Hannah and clad in a loose, flowing dark blue robe, Abigail summoned a sad smile for him and asked what he wished.

"I have been sent to ask the help of Mistress Marilee Fordham," he said. "She is needed to nurse the wounded."

"She is a mere girl with no skill," Abigail told him. "She is needed here in my household."

"Begging pardon," he said. "She was noted for her skill by all the village this day just past." He glanced at Hannah, hovering behind Abigail. "Few houses have the good fortune of even one servant."

"But I am a sick old woman," Hannah began.

"She will return to England on the sailing of the *Early Lark*," Marilee put in quietly. "But in the meantime, you are quite right. She can care for Mrs. Fordham while I come with you."

Abigail opened her mouth to protest but fell silent as the man turned to walk toward the door. Marilee followed him, taking all the herbs that were left in her dwindling supply.

When she stepped from the door, Marilee found the soldier gone but Maggie waiting.

The two women walked in silence until they reached the entrance to Maggie's stable. "I will join you later," Maggie told Marilee as she stopped there. She smiled wryly. "They knew you only as the beauty with the shining curls who labored with the milkmaid."

Maggie had been right about the fever coming with the night. As Marilee moved from pallet to pallet, changing dressings on wounds darkening with infection and holding cups of ale to parched and swollen lips, the stench of illness made her own stomach heave.

At noon Deborah, with Willie at her side, came to insist that Marilee stop and eat and drink against the long day and night ahead. There in that friendly house, with her puppy glued adoringly to her knee, Marilee felt like a real person again for the first time since the attack began.

"We listened for you to come until well into the night," Deborah told her. "When did you stop?"

"It was dark," Marilee said. "Michael came looking for me and took me home."

"You don't have to go there, you know," Deborah said hotly. "You're welcome here, as you know."

Marilee sighed and quoted her brother's words. "There are few enough of us here, as Matthew told me. He said that for that reason we must put up with much in each other."

"Matthew was too good a man to live," Deborah said. Then, realizing what words had passed her lips, she fell to weeping and had to be comforted.

Only late in the day did Marilee's work bring her into the chapel again. When she heard Timothy's voice from the door, her heart sank. His temperature had risen until he was delirious. He was talking brightly and laughing once in a while at some jest that passed his fevered mind. Stubbornly she worked her way to his side and looked down at him.

That great, smoky eye fixed on her, and his hand rose to touch her arm.

"There she is," he said brightly. With that bandage across his face she could see only half his smile, but it was joyous, sending her heart lurching.

"Come, little Marilee, and I will show you where the gray cat has hidden her kittens. Blind they are as bats of the night but warm to your touch."

Marilee fought back tears as she lifted away the bandage on his face and dressed the long wound that ran from under his left eye almost to his jawline. But the wound was clean and looked to be healing. She breathed a sigh of relief to see that whatever blade had sliced his cheek had not injured his left eye. Her mind raced. If this wound was doing well, where was his fever coming from?

He was still babbling about the kittens in her father's stable as she unwound the cloths that bandaged his leg. Her heart sank. The deep wound on his calf was rank with infection and the flesh reddened past his knee.

Simply cleaning the wound and laying moist cloths on his flesh gave him some comfort. He stopped babbling halfway through a sentence. His dark lashes fluttered, and he drifted into sleep. She stood watching him sleep, her heart pulled every which way with pity and pain . . . and something else she couldn't define.

Then the man who lay next to him groaned and muttered a prayer between clenched teeth, and she moved on.

Chapter Fifteen

On that second morning after the attack, Marilee did not wait for the governor's messenger to come for her. While Hannah and Abigail still slept, she rose, dressed, and had a solitary breakfast in Abigail's untidy kitchen. She let herself out of the house into a crisp March day whose air was musical with songbirds. She paused a moment on the front step. The sky was a deep, rich blue, and the pale glint of first green was showing on the twigs of the trees outside the palisades. As she stood watching, a bird with scarlet wings darted to the topmost limb of a nearby tree and burst into a torrent of song.

How could a world so filled with grief and suffering be so beautiful to the eye and ear?

To her astonishment she was no more than three steps from the door before Michael Braden fell in beside her.

"You startled me," she confessed, smiling

up at him. How fresh he looked in the morning light. She found herself a little intimidated by the perfection of his appearance. How could he, or anyone, stay so perfectly groomed in such difficult times? She blushed to think how little time she had spent on her own appearance, tossing on the dress she had worn the day before, adding only a fresh apron. She could only claim being distracted by concern over Timothy and her hope that the fever that had ravaged his mind when she saw him last had abated.

"I was waiting for you," he said. "I wanted to suggest that you not go into the village today."

She stared at him. "But why?"

That wonderful smile lit his face, and he shook his head as if to chide her. "What other woman would even ask?" he countered. "As Matthew's friend I need to remind you of who and what you are, Marilee."

He must have realized her confusion. He laughed softly and took her hand very gently in his own. "My very dear Marilee," he said tenderly. "You are not a common servant but an English gentlewoman. You are not an aging and bitter crone but a young and lovely girl. What should such an innocent creature as you have to do with death and dying? As sad as it is to see men injured and dying, few of those wounded planters are even of your station. None of them are your responsibility. Let others do this menial and disturbing work. Those who are ill would be better served if you kept yourself decently at home and offered your innocent prayers in their behalf."

"Safe?" she asked tartly. "How could I possibly think myself safe if I didn't do all I could to help, whether the wounded are servants or masters."

"Listen to me," he pleaded, holding both her hands to bring her to a stop. "You are not safe there with all that illness and death. Disease and fever follows injury. You must not punish yourself by seeing what terrible things are being done."

"Terrible things?" she asked, struck with a sinking dread. "What terrible things?"

"You must know that the ship's surgeon is there," he reminded her, dropping his voice a little. "After all, you worked by his side the past two days. And you must also know what a surgeon is obliged to do to save a man who has poisoned blood. He has only one course, and it is not a pretty one."

Marilee felt her breath leave her lungs as she grasped the meaning of his words. Amputation. At the very thought she heard again in her mind Timothy's delirious voice and remembered the dreadful condition of the wound on his leg. "No," she cried, "it is too soon. He must not give up so soon." At the thought she pulled herself free of Michael's grasp and would have walked away if he hadn't caught her arm.

"Think, Marilee," he pleaded. "Think of

those who love you and keep yourself from this horror. You are Matthew's sister —"

"And my mother's daughter," she told him. "There is a time for a surgeon when cutting is needed, but there is also a time for healing so that no cuts need be made."

"What a stubborn creature you are," he said, following her, his tone indulgent. "If you were mine . . ."

His words struck her heart. If she were his wife would he truly try to keep her from such acts of mercy? She couldn't believe that, remembering her father's pride in his wife's loving care of the poorest peasants in the village at home.

Yet his words struck a deep and warming chord. If she were his, as wife and lover, how much easier these hard days would be. In her mind she saw how Willum and Deborah stood close together, bound in love and mutual support. How Willum's eyes sought his wife's across a room that he might send her a comforting smile. "I have no one," she thought bleakly. "I am alone in this far place."

Although she was stiffening herself to win this argument with Michael one way or another, she was relieved when one of the governor's men hailed Michael with a request that he accompany him on the governor's business. Although Michael excused himself with his usual gallantry, Marilee sensed that he was not as pleased at this interruption as she was.

Maggie, on her stool, was finishing the milking when Marilee reached the stable.

"I think I heard bad news this morning," Marilee told her. "Is it true that the ship's surgeon has begun amputating so soon?"

Maggie tugged fiercely at the cow without looking up. "It is a quicker death than blood poisoning," she pointed out.

"But what about leeches?" Marilee insisted. "Leeches should be tried first."

Maggie stopped her milking to stare up at Marilee. "Even a foolish child knows that," she scoffed, "but who has leeches?"

"Has anyone looked for them?" Marilee asked. "In England I know many streams where they can always be found."

Maggie turned back to her cow. "You are not in England," she said in a final tone.

"But there are streams out there," Marilee insisted. "I saw one —"

Maggie stared at her with narrowed eyes. "I thought you had been kept within the fort."

Marilee dropped her eyes. "There are streams out there, and in them there will be leeches," she said stubbornly.

Marilee walked straight from the stable to the chapel to see how Timothy was faring. By standing inside the door she could see him. He lay quietly with his eyes closed, as if he were sleeping or had lost consciousness. Her heart leaped to see that his leg was still there under the crude bandage. At least the surgeon had not reached Timothy with his crippling, and often killing, cure. But that did not mean that the threat of it was gone. The threat would not be gone until someone provided leeches to battle the infection. Making her way out swiftly, she went to where the ship's doctor, Jones, was bending over a patient.

Kneeling by his side, she spoke swiftly. "I think I know where there are leeches."

He turned and stared at her, openmouthed. She saw a momentary flicker of high interest in his eyes. Then she saw him sweep his eyes over her. Angrily she realized that she could almost read the man's mind. She was young. She was a woman. She was a busybody. He laughed in a rude, short way.

"We all know where there are leeches," he told her bluntly. "But the governor has ordered all planters and their families to secure themselves inside the fort. Are you suggesting that someone defy the governor's order and go out searching for leeches in these wild woods where the enemy lies waiting?"

"But many men who could be saved will die," she protested.

He said, turning away, "Go and tend to your embroidery and leave us to a man's work."

Laughter followed his words. A bearded patient nearby rose on his elbow and grinned at her, revealing a lecherous mouth half-emptied of teeth. "Come over here, dolly," he coaxed in a mincing tone. "Perry here will be happy to see you."

Marilee rose, her cheeks flaming, and walked away with all the dignity she could muster. Once back in the street, she looked around the village thoughtfully. The feeling of aloneness that had struck her earlier returned in double measure. Who could she ask to go with her into the woods to search for leeches? Who did she know well enough to ask, and who cared enough about the suffering men to take the chance?

Not Michael Braden. Certainly not Michael Braden, who so completely misunderstood her that he thought she would shrink from helping the wounded for her own safety's sake. Worse than that, if Michael thought she might go he would even try to prevent her. That would be easy enough to do with Governor Wyatt's order in force.

Who else did she know? Deborah? Willum? Maggie?

Deborah was out of the question, of course. Not only did she have Willie to think of but her unborn child would slow her too much on rough ground, even if they took a squadron of soldiers along to protect them.

That left Willum.

Deborah's house was fragrant with the aroma of a simmering fish stew. After a most affectionate greeting at the door from both Willie and Briny, Marilee found Deborah in the kitchen. Every surface was covered with pans of more bread than Marilee had ever seen set to rise. Marilee stared at the neat rows in disbelief. "You're a baker now?" she asked.

"Trying to do my part," Deborah explained. "Though how they expect us to feed all the people crammed inside this place, I'll never guess."

"Is Willum around?" Marilee asked.

To Marilee's amazement her friend turned away and began stirring the fish pot briskly. "He was ordered out on the governor's business along with some other men," she said, her voice charged by sudden emotion.

Marilee stared at her friend's back.

"What business is that?" Marilee asked. Surely the governor had not already organized the war marches against the Indians that she had heard talked of the day before.

Instead of answering Marilee's question Deborah began to chatter very rapidly as if to bury Marilee's question in a torrent of words.

"What did you want Willum for?" she asked. "Whatever it is I know he'll be glad to help once he's back here. He's very fond of you, as you very well know —"

"Deborah," Marilee interrupted firmly. "What business did the governor call Willum out to do?"

Deborah's shoulders slumped, and the spoon slowed in its passage. "Burying," she said in a small, pained voice.

Burying, Marilee's mind repeated. The

thought of that friendly giant of a man bent over a shovel digging graves for his friends was more than Marilee could endure.

"I'll be going along," Marilee told her. "I was just wondering."

She felt Deborah's eyes follow her as she opened the door to leave. The puppy plunged for the door with the same wild speed that Willie used to. This time it was the child who caught the escaping animal. "No, Briny, no," he shouted, catching the wriggling creature in his arms.

Had they all been changed, even the children, by the events just past?

Back at the stable, Marilee found Maggie straining her morning milk. She watched for a moment silently before Maggie looked up.

"What is it now?" Maggie asked impatiently. "Do you come to tell me more of what good medicines are to be found in England? Will you ever have an end to your dreaming?"

"I wish you weren't so cross," Marilee told her.

Maggie stared at her and broke into a wide grin. "You learned more healing than you did manners from your mother, didn't you?"

Marilee ducked her head. "I'm sorry if that was rude," she said. "I seemed to be frustrated at every turn, and it doesn't help my temper. I simply have to find someone who will go looking for leeches with me, so that more of those men can be saved. I can do nothing for Matthew now, but maybe I could save Timothy Reeves."

"I thought the two of you behaved like cats and dogs," Maggie said. "I always see poor Timothy scowling behind you as you go by with your nose in the air."

Maggie did have an unfortunate way of putting things. Marilee felt herself flush at the picture that came into her mind at the girl's words. "Matthew loved him, and he loved Matthew," Marilee reminded her.

Maggie wiped her hands and set the milk aside.

"Now let us talk like sensible women," she said. "You tell me what kind of a fool would walk beyond the walls of this fort into the woods and defy the governor's orders? You heard him, him in his fancy-colored silks with his wig freshly curled. And it's not as if it's only him and his orders. When Indians take up war, they do not stop until a peace is made. What kind of a person would go prowling around in the woods in such a time?"

Marilee studied the girl a moment before answering. "A person who had nothing to lose but his life," she said quietly.

Marilee had not meant the words to hurt as much as they clearly did. Maggie's face crumpled into pain, even as she stood there. She sighed and turned away so that the dampness in her eyes would be hidden from Marilee.

"I wish you had never come here from England, Marilee Fordham," she said angrily. "And if you had to come, then I wish you had never exchanged the first word with me. How do you dare to lay a tongue on me like that?" Then she turned back to Marilee furiously. "But what of yourself? How can you claim to have nothing to lose? The gossips say that besides your hundred acres of land, five hundred pounds a year comes to you. You are young." She eyed Marilee and shrugged. "Even not bad-looking if a person happens to like your kind of looks."

"You have a roof over your head and food enough," Marilee reminded her. "You even have work you love and memories. Yet we are alike in being alone."

For a long moment Marilee thought she had lost her gamble. Maggie turned without a word and disappeared into her shed. Marilee even thought Maggie might have forgotten that she was there, when she heard Maggie humming softly to herself as she put feed into the troughs for her two creatures.

Then, when Marilee was close to giving up and going away, Maggie came out carrying two jugs with firm handles like pitchers.

"We face the small problem of getting outside the gates without being stopped and hauled back," she told Marilee.

Marilee recovered quickly from her surprise and answered her question in a matter-of-fact way. "There is a gate away from the place where people commonly walk," Marilee said, remembering how she and Timothy had slipped out there without being seen.

"Go along and I will follow you," Maggie told her.

Marilee was grateful that no straggling families with pitiful bundles of possessions were crossing the open area just outside the walls of the fort as she and Maggie made their escape.

"Once we are in the woods, anyone seeing us will think we are on our way to seek refuge in the fort," she told Maggie.

Maggie nodded. "If they considered us to be anything but crazy, they would think just that."

It was easy for Marilee to retrace the path that she and Timothy had taken to visit the mill. She had been so interested in the growing things they passed that she even remembered one sweet gum tree and knew to veer left after passing it. She had remembered the tree as a note to herself to come back when the resin was running. Her mother had taught her that few things were as healing for skin disorders as that fragrant gum. When they passed the clump of white elm surrounded by the stumps of hickory trees, she could hear the water tumbling over the spillway.

They knelt alongside the pond, searching the water for the telltale vertical movement of leeches. When they had explored every one of its banks without finding a sign of a leech, Marilee sat up with a frown.

"These leeches of England," Maggie said thoughtfully. "Did you find them in salt water or fresh?"

"Mostly we got them from the ponds and streams around the village," Marilee told her. "Like all of England, we are not far from the sea, but the water was fresh."

Maggie grunted and rose. "That is the problem then. When the tide comes up, this river is salt and spills into the pond."

"But the stream that feeds in above must be sweet," Marilee told her.

Maggie's eyes on her were a challenge. "Are you game to go farther upstream?" she asked.

Marilee shrugged. "We are too near success to stop now."

Upstream the woods grew more dense. Marilee only realized how far they had gone when the last sound of noise from the fort disappeared. Birds and squirrels set up a great clamor at their approach, only to fall silent when they actually neared the nesting places.

"My husband Jonathan had something to say about men who had nothing to lose," Maggie said suddenly.

Marilee looked questioningly at her. Maggie's face was pale, and her forehead was wet in spite of the chill.

"He said that the most dangerous man in the world is the one with nothing to lose."

Marilee nodded.

"In our case," Maggie went on wryly, "we are dangerous only to ourselves." With that, she grinned at Marilee and nodded her head. "That pool ahead, blocked by the fallen tree, is where we will find our leeches."

The birds and squirrels grew accustomed to their presence and began their tumult of sound again. Within an hour they had found enough leeches that the first of the jugs was filled with them. They were straining the water from a good supply in the second jug when a jay screamed in the tree beyond, setting up a general alarm. Maggie seized Marilee's arm and whispered, "Don't move."

Marilee tightened her muscles to keep from leaping to her feet. A squirrel ran halfway down a tree and began to scream furiously at something behind them.

Then the laughter came.

"Look at them, a tumble of maidens flirting with death. What do you see there that is worth having your scalp carried away?"

Maggie leaped to her feet, furious. The man behind them stood unsteadily and stared at them with wild eyes.

"Be still, you fool," Maggie said angrily. "Do you want to bring every enemy in these woods to our side?"

"Ha," the man said, "Live or die, it is the same. Stand or sleep, it is the same. Life is nothing, death is everything."

Marilee was also on her feet. "You are the scribe," she said in wonder. "I saw you writing letters for the ship that left."

"Ships come and go," he said, shrugging. "It is all the same."

"He has taken leave of his senses," Maggie whispered. "Poor creature, God only knows what horror drove his mind away."

Marilee realized that she had never heard Maggie's voice so gentle.

Maggie handed her pitcher to Marilee and clambered up beside the man. "When did you eat last?" she asked him.

"Eat?" he repeated dumbly. Then his eyes widened as if he saw phantoms. "Eat. We were at breakfast when they came. My wife. My child." He covered his face with his hands and began to weep pitifully.

Maggie motioned with her head for Marilee to follow, and took the scribe's arm. "Come," she said softly, "I know where there is fresh milk with oaten bread and soft cheese."

He came like a child, stumbling as he walked and sobbing softly now and then. At the wall of the fort they hesitated. "You use your gate," Maggie told Marilee. "I will meet you by the chapel, and we will find that dumb Welsh surgeon."

"Welsh?" Marilee asked, startled by her words. Maggie, leading her companion firmly by the arm, looked back over her shoulder.

"Why would a man call himself Jones if

he had a name an Englishman could pronounce?" she asked.

Marilee reached the chapel before Maggie did. She waited only a moment before slipping inside and taking her jugs to Timothy's side. She gave a prayer of thanks to see that the leg was still there, even though Timothy himself lay unconscious.

"What are you doing?" the man on the pallet beside Timothy asked as Marilee stripped off Timothy's dressing, wiped the wound clean, and bound it again with some of the leeches under the bandages.

"Just trying to help," she replied, giving him what she hoped was a blinding smile.

The surgeon Jones looked up impatiently as Maggie and Marilee approached. "You again," he said to Marilee with annoyance. "What silliness is in your head now?"

"We have leeches," Maggie spoke up.

He frowned at her. "Leeches? Where did you find leeches in such a place?"

Marilee swallowed her grin at Maggie's swift reply. She didn't lie. You had to give it to Maggie that she didn't even lie. Like Socrates, she made the day with a question.

"Sire," she said almost humbly, "have you looked at the water in the horse troughs here?"

"Horse troughs," he asked, peering into the jugs. "Upon my word, what a quantity of healthy leeches you have there. It's a good work you did here, you women," he said, nodding. "A good, lifesaving work."

Chapter Sixteen

MICHAEL alone was suspicious of the story that ran through the village like wildfire. He was not only suspicious about the story that the Fordham girl and the milkmaid had found lifesaving leeches in the horse trough but also of these miserable creatures being as valuable as everyone claimed. He was not only suspicious but even a little haughty about Marilee's name being on every gossip's tongue.

"These are disgusting things to have linked with the name of a fair young girl," he told her. "Horse troughs? Leeches?"

When Marilee only held her eyes on him without comment, he backed off a little. "This is not to say that the end result was not good. The surgeon claims many lives were saved and more than a dozen limbs. But, Marilee, it is mysterious to me that you should want to be so involved in what at best is a filthy business."

"Death is not the prettiest business in this world," she reminded him. "And I am sick of death and dying."

Only at that moment did it occur to her to wonder what damage had come to Michael and his holdings from the Indian attack. "Tell me, Michael," she asked, "did you come off scot-free in the attack, so that you can now treat the saving of life so lightly?"

He paled in that way he had when Timothy had angered him. "Marilee, I cannot believe you are asking me that when you know I lost my dearest friend in Matthew."

"That was a loss that many of us shared," she reminded him. "But what of your own plantation? Did you lose servants? Were your own crops burned?"

"I have the good fortune that my plantation is located near enough to Jamestown that my people were warned in time by the governor's couriers." His tone had turned distant and cool.

When she only nodded, he went on defensively. "That has been not only my good fortune but your sister-in-law's, too."

Marilee looked up at him, puzzled. "How can that be?"

He shrugged in a distinctly pettish manner. "You must know that the foreman who was running Matthew's place in the absence of that village boy, Timothy Reeves, was killed. And that Reeves charged off at the first warning and got himself injured there near Martin's Hundred. He has not been on his feet to serve his mistress since."

"He went in search of Matthew," she reminded him, "hoping to be able to save him."

His smile was as charming as usual, but somehow it seemed less than genuine. "Your loyalty to that village boy is very worthy of you," he said coldly. "But, if your sister-in-law was to have a crop this season, someone had to be put in charge of running that plantation. Because my people were spared, I was able to provide her with a foreman."

"Until Timothy Reeves is well enough to assume his duties?" she asked.

"Abigail will make her own decision on that. But at least Matthew's land is being tended."

That village boy.

Michael's phrase about Timothy rankled in Marilee's mind. Why did he always have to refer to Timothy Reeves as something less than a man? Michael had even sounded as if he disapproved of Timothy's effort to reach Matthew in time to save him. It was easy enough for a man who had lost nothing to criticize a servant who had lost everything. For the hundredth time she was glad to know that Timothy's indenture would soon come to an end, taking his welfare out of Abigail's control.

Not that Timothy was any longer her friend.

The morning after she and Maggie

brought the leeches back from the woods, Maggie had warned Marilee not to go into the chapel. "Nobody is fonder of that curly-haired Reeves man than I am, but he is a caged bull and dangerous," she explained. "He carries on like a madman about your prying into his business. He blames you for saving a life that is worth nothing to him."

"He grieves for Matthew," Marilee explained.

"Timothy and I have been friends from the first, even as he and my Jonathan were. But now he is behaving like an ungrateful wretch who should be on his knees to you," Maggie corrected her.

Remembering Maggie's free tongue, Marilee felt a moment of panic. "You wouldn't dare say such a thing to him, would you?"

Maggie grinned and thumped her with an elbow. "What? And lose both of my great friends?"

Marilee said nothing, but it began to look as if Maggie had acquired a third great friend. The scribe, whom Maggie had brought home babbling from the fields, seemed better and stronger with every day. Although he did nothing but sit for long hours outside the stable staring sadly at nothing, he no longer burst into peals of wild laughter nor looked glazed and ill. Marilee had to admit that not all the change was for the better. He no longer looked the neat scholar he once had. While it was natural for a man who slept in the hay with the cows to have some problems with his grooming, the scribe seemed unconscious of the flakes of straw that clung to his coat and hair. As if in contrast, Maggie herself looked better than Marilee had ever seen her. Her pale face was sometimes rosy with a happy glow, and her thatch of hair, while not arranged in anything that could be called fashion, was neater and drawn back with a ribbon.

Within a fortnight many changes came about. March had given way to April, turning the thoughts of the planters away from the tragedy and toward the growing season ahead. The governor had declared an all-out effort to drive the Indians from that whole stretch of land that lay between the York and the James rivers. To achieve this he organized parties of men that went on long marches, patrolling the area and driving out, by force if necessary, the Indians still left. The fort gradually emptied to its old, uncrowded state as the planters took what was left of their families and went home.

With spring came an influx of ships into the James River. By mid-April ten ships hung at anchor there. While some of them had brought immigrants and goods to the Virginians, many of them were tavern ships, carrying only a cargo of strong liquor that was for sale to all comers. Willum fretted about the safety of his family as well as Marilee's, cautioning her not to go about the streets alone for any reason. He was not sure

that even Briny, as fast as the dog was growing, was protection enough for her.

Meanwhile, in the harbor, the *Early Lark*
readied to return to England.

Marilee needed to send two things on that
ship: Hannah . . . and a letter to Philip
Soames. Marilee found herself dreading both
these tasks almost equally.

"How do I tell Philip that he has lost his
dearest friend?" Marilee sighed to Deborah.

"He has heard that by now," Deborah said.
"The sea is a great back fence with sailors
gossiping across the waves."

"But I must write him," Marilee said. "I
may not have another such chance to contact
him for many months."

"With fair winds he may be back the first
of August. Tell him whatever you think will
make him comfortable until he gets here to
see how things are for himself."

Marilee stared at her. She couldn't tell
Philip what he wanted to hear because it
would be a lie. She was not happy. She was
not at home in Virginia. She was, if anything,
more restless and lonely than she had been
when he left. She could not even tell him she
had a wedding planned because Michael,
distracted by his obligation to help and comfort his friend Matthew's widow, had not
spent enough time with her even to ask for
her hand, if he meant to do it at all.

"I know two good things to tell him, anyway," Marilee said, rising. "I shall tell him
that Timothy Reeves is now up and able to

walk about with the aid of a cane. And that Hannah is going back to England on the *Early Lark*."

The Irish wolfhound Briny had grown at an astonishing rate. He had doubled his size since his arrival at the Yarrow house. In spite of his great bulk he was still a puppy at heart, trying to get onto her lap whenever Marilee sat down and racing for the door to go with her when she left. Willie, catching the dog by the neck, held him with both arms, tumbling them both on the floor where they lay, Willie giggling wildly and Briny thumping his tail like a drummer.

"You are so good to me," Marilee told Deborah. "I drink your tea, cry on your shoulder, and dump my great animal into your keeping. How shall I ever repay you?"

Deborah laughed. "If there were debt, Briny himself has paid it in joy for Willie."

Marilee found herself humming a little melody as she walked toward her brother's house. Although she spent little time in the house except in sleeping, she and Abigail had managed a cold truce in the days after the attack. And there was Deborah to give her life pleasure. How dear a friend Deborah was. And truly, how wonderfully Willie had changed for the better with the playful companionship of Briny. She was so deep in thought that she did not see Timothy until she was almost upon him. He was leaning against a stable post, as he had in the old days when Matthew had left him to guard her.

How tall he seemed. Perhaps he only appeared taller because he had lost so much weight during his long illness. One leg was a little bent as he braced its weight with a black oak cane in his hand. He looked more the gentleman than ever, with his face lean enough to show his fine, high cheekbones. The scar down his cheek had healed pale, as light as the glowing whites of those smoky eyes.

She hesitated, not knowing what to do or say. He had not spoken to her since the day she had found him in such a delirium from fever. He solved her problems for her. When she stopped, he turned his face and looked the other way as if he had not even seen her coming.

"Never mind," she whispered fiercely to herself through her tears. "Matthew would be glad that Timothy still lives." Almost without meaning to, she had made this single standard her rule in all she did. If she could do all things as Matthew would have wanted them done, she could not really go wrong.

As usual, Michael Braden was in the house visiting Abigail. Marilee heard a ripple of laughter that stilled as she opened the door. Michael rose with instant gallantry. Abigail looked her up and down without comment. Hannah sat grinning in the third chair.

After greeting them Marilee excused herself, explaining that she had a letter to finish before the sailing of the *Early Lark*. Michael took that occasion to leave, too, bidding them all a pleasant evening.

As Marilee took down her writing board, she realized that something was changed in the room. Every stitch of Hannah's clothing was back out of the trunks and stacked on the shelves. She looked at this display in amazement before going back into the other room.

She purposefully kept her voice calm as she put the question to her maid. "Hannah, what does this mean? Why are your things all spread out again when you are to leave for England?"

Hannah's eyes flew to Abigail's face. Abigail met Marilee's glance in a haughty, taunting way. "Hannah isn't going to England. She is staying here with me."

Marilee stared at her. "I am sorry, Abigail," she said slowly. "It was Matthew's decision as well as my own that Hannah must return to England on this ship —"

Abigail did not even let her finish that sentence. "Your brother is dead," she said bluntly. "I am mistress here now, and Hannah stays with me."

"She is then, at this moment, no longer in my employ," Marilee said, turning away to hide her pain at hearing Matthew's death announced like that — coldly, brutally — by his own wife's lips.

"I realize that," Abigail said softly. "The amount of her salary is a small price for your board and room in my house, but I shall accept it for a time at least. You may pay it to either her or me as you wish. It is all the same."

Inside the door of that small room Marilee stood very straight, straining for control. Her new rule for behavior was not a good one. She didn't have the slightest idea how Matthew would have dealt with this problem. She was pretty sure he wouldn't have done what she wanted to do, which was take every single rag of that old woman's clothes and throw them out of the window.

She wrote and tore up three letters for Philip before she finished one that did not shout her bitterness from between the lines. Since it had been arranged that Philip would be her agent in London as well as Matthew's, she did have to tell him that no more salary was to be drawn for Hannah, but that same amount should be issued to Abigail Fordham, widow of Matthew, for her own room and board. To this directive she added no comment.

The planters who survived the attack proved to have short memories. They grumbled when they were called to take their place in the marches against the Indians, complaining that they could not spare the time from their tobacco planting. They even complained when the governor agreed to take their servants as replacements, protesting that a man did not buy a servant's time to have it used away from his plantation. The first wave of marchers went out, and then the second, with the grumbling growing worse with each march. The skirmishes with the Indians took some toll on the men. The deadly snakes of the wetland made more than one woman into a widow during those marches.

Willum came privately to Marilee when his name was called for the next march. "As little as I like leaving my wife and child, I need to do it now and have it behind me," he told Marilee. "I want to be back to care for my Debbie when our child comes."

Marilee nodded in agreement. "If you have doubt of leaving Deborah and Willie there alone, I will be happy to go every day and help out Deborah. I would even stay the nights, if having me there would make you more comfortable."

His wide face broke in a delighted grin as he seized her hands. "Bless you, Marilee. I had sworn to Deborah that I would not ask you to help, but you have offered it, which is quite a different thing. If I knew you were there with her and the child during the day, what peace it would bring me." But then he added, "As to staying the night, that won't be necessary. Willie wears himself out and sleeps from sundown until morning. Deborah is the same. As for worrying, for all his youth, that dog of yours is a fine guard. You should hear him when something moves around the house at night. But you must be sure to tell Debbie that I did not ask. We had a long talk about that, believe me."

"I believe you," Marilee said, laughing softly. She could imagine what a scene that "long talk" had been between these two strong-willed people. "You knew I would want to come."

He nodded. "I had hopes," he admitted. "I had my own high hopes." He turned to leave but hesitated, then came back, his forehead creased with concern. "You have heard that Mistress Fordham has put in the name of Timothy Reeves for this march?"

"That is impossible," Marilee cried. "That man is still recovering from his wounds. His leg must heal at least another month before he is fit for long days of marching."

Willum nodded. "I thought the same," he told her. "I took the liberty of putting a word into the captain's ear that such a man would make danger for all the men in the group." He winked broadly at that. "He may well be rejected so that he won't hold back the healthy men."

On the very day that the men set out on the march, Marilee left early for Deborah's house, carrying only a little needlework and a book she thought Willie might enjoy looking at. Abigail, still in a loose nightdress, looked up as she passed the kitchen.

"Whether you eat here or not you will be charged for the room and your food," Abigail told her.

Marilee nodded. "I expected that to be the case," she told Abigail. Then, in one of those rare lapses of good sense, she added the fuel of embarrassment to the fire of Abigail's hatred. "I have notified Philip Soames of your arrangement," she told her sister-in-law. "He will pay you from my personal income."

Abigail's eyes widened with astonishment. "You told Philip!" she cried furiously.

"He handles my affairs," Marilee explained, letting herself out of the door.

She heard Abigail's screams of rage begin inside the house as she walked away. She glanced back with only one regret. If she spent her days with Deborah she would not have time to tend her garden, which had been planted with such love and hope. But if Deborah stayed well until Willum's return, even that price was not too high.

Deborah was awash with tears when she returned from watching the men march away. "They don't always come back, you know," she told Marilee. "Even without the Indians, there are snakes and accidents and illness from bad water."

Marilee held her friend to comfort her. At the knock on the door Willie ran to see who was there. Timothy Reeves stood glowering on the stoop.

"Why are you not amazed to see me here when the men have marched away?" he asked Marilee, his voice rough with anger.

"Should I be?" she asked.

"I was in the list to march out," he told her. "Then at the last minute another man was sent in my place."

"With no reason given?" she asked.

He looked away. "I was said to be unfit on account of my leg."

"Why blame me?" she asked. "Is the commander blind that he can't see by himself that you are lame and not yet healed?"

Before he could reply, Deborah put in her own words. "Don't be foolish, Timothy," she said. "Would you have marched and been a handicap to all the other men as well as yourself? Give yourself time to heal."

During this exchange Marilee studied her brother's servant. His thinness broke her heart. His well-shaped arms, once so firm and muscular, were lean as stakes. She had a horrifying thought. Was it possible that Abigail was not feeding her servants properly? There was a law that masters must provide food for their servants, but it required so little that a young man like Timothy might well shrink to skin and bones with no more to eat than that. Her father had always claimed that only a fool starved his servants, since it was the same as taking money from his own pocket when men were too weak to work.

Distracted by Timothy's poor appearance, Marilee only heard the last of his conversation with Deborah.

"As for taking care of myself, Mrs. Yarrow," he said bitterly, "if you think the work that Mistress Fordham gives me *here* is less difficult than the march, then you don't know my mistress very well."

He turned and walked away, sparing the

injured leg as he moved. Marilee turned to
Deborah, white with shock.

"She wouldn't dare," Marilee cried. "Not
even she would dare to put an injured man
into work beyond his strength."

"Remember, he works now for Michael
Braden's foreman," Deborah said. Then she
echoed Timothy's own words, only a little
changed. "You do know his mistress pretty
well."

Marilee turned away with a grief past
tears. Over and over she was failing Matthew
and her own standard for herself.

Chapter Seventeen

WHEN Marilee had first seen Michael Braden from the rail of the *Pryde of Gravesend*, she had thought him the handsomest man she had ever seen in her life. During those endless months that followed the attack, while the women of Jamestown waited for the return of their marching men, she decided he must also be the most thoughtful man in Virginia.

It was late and dark when Marilee returned from Deborah's house that first evening after Willum's departure. Having insisted on seeing the child into bed for the night and Deborah settled down before returning to her sister-in-law's house, Marilee was dead tired. She let herself into the house without even a glance around and fell immediately into bed.

She awakened refreshed that next morning, grateful that she had important work to tire her body and keep her mind busy.

She knew better than to try to find breakfast at Abigail's house. With Sukie gone and only Hannah to bake the bread and dust the rooms and keep the hearth fire fed, there was neither bread fit to eat, a clean surface anywhere, nor a fire to bring a pot to boil.

As always, the first minute she stepped out the door, she turned to examine her garden. She stopped and stared at it aghast, barely able to hold back a cry. Her neat rows of green had been all stirred together like a mess of weeds. The hoof marks of horses had dug deeply into the soft earth. Those plants that had not been sliced in two had been pulled out by the roots and were gone.

Before she even recovered from that shock, Michael Braden stepped to her side and stood looking down at the garden with her.

"I grieved to see that all your good work had gone to nothing," he told her sympathetically.

She turned with childish tears in her eyes. "What happened, Michael? How could such a destructive thing ever happen?"

He shrugged. "You know those planters. The only green thing they recognize is a tobacco plant. One of them must have tied his horse here while he paid his respects to Abigail."

She stared at him. " 'Paid his respects,' " she quoted. "You couldn't mean what I think by that. No man could possibly be here to court Matthew's widow before there is grass on his grave."

He took her arm gently and smiled down at her. "Why do I always forget how tender your spirit is, Marilee? I understand, and you understand, but most Virginians don't share our sensibilities. They do not even think of Matthew and how recently he was a living man among them. They see only Abigail. They see her as a woman of great beauty, unencumbered with children, the owner of fine, cultivated land and no husband."

"That is sick," she said, beginning to walk along so swiftly that he had to quicken his pace to stay beside her.

"If you think it sounds sick you should be there when they come," he told her.

"You see them?" she asked, unable to believe all this. "Do you mean that you sit there and watch those dreadful men brag and boast and make those ridiculous eyes?"

The pressure of his hand tightened on her arm as he laughed. "Marilee, you put things in such a way that I see them happen again before my eyes." Then, more soberly, "Of course I go and sit with them. What else am I to do as Matthew's friend? Would you have me leave Abigail to deal with them with only that old woman at her side? And, in fact, Marilee, they are not dreadful men. They are simple men for the most part, who forget that a wife is more than a housekeeper and a source of new land. Haven't you ever wanted anything enough to make compromises for it?"

"Not that sort of compromise," she told him. "And I really don't understand why you don't just tell them to go away until a decent time for grieving is past," she said angrily. "Order them out of the house and add that they had better tie their horses in some sensible place if they don't wish to find the beast butchered on the spot."

"There is a limit even to the rights of a friend," he reminded her. "I go and do what I can to comfort and distract her. And, of course, to discourage these eager suitors."

Marilee sighed. "You have more stomach for fools than I have."

"I wager that I know more fools than you do," he replied, smiling at her in that tender way that twisted her heart.

She smiled back at him. "Remember, I met a number of them myself when I first came."

He fell silent for a moment before sighing deeply. "Oh, Marilee, when will we ever have such time together as I desire?"

She only shook her head. When, indeed, would anyone have time for simple things like courtship and laughter? ordinary people that is, she told herself silently. Abigail seemed to have no problem finding time to laugh and be courted.

"I did have an idea that I wanted to suggest to you," he went on. "That Briny, as you call him, must be growing like a horse himself. A great animal like that must be taught to obey or he will be dangerous. Perhaps I would help you learn to control him. Maybe we could walk out together with him sometime during the day?"

It was on her tongue to tell him that Timothy had given her a fair start in training the animal, but she held her words back. "You will be surprised at how well he behaves," she told him. "Some of the time, anyway."

They were nearing Deborah's door. He smiled at this last and then frowned. "Surely there is some hour of the day when you can leave your friend. Does she rest, she and the child? Tell me the hour and we will take Briny along the beach and teach him the ways of a gentleman."

Marilee looked at him, astounded at his thoughtfulness and concern. "Michael, you are too generous. Isn't it enough that you spend all those tedious hours in Abigail's behalf without making time for my concerns, too?"

His eyes rested on her face, a small smile playing on his lips. Then, to her astonishment, she saw his eyes move from her own eyes to her lips and hesitated a moment as if he were imagining the feel of her mouth against his own. She felt her face flush with color from the intimacy in that glance. She would have pulled away, but his hand was on her arm, holding her.

"Marilee," he said intensely, "don't you

understand? Don't you know how much *more* I feel for you than friendly concern? I am trying to find a time that I can be with you. You are like the wind to me. I feel you near, only to have you gone in a breath. How can you have whole days for your friend Deborah and not even scattered moments for anyone else who loves you?"

His words had made her breath come short. She did not have to look up into that wonderful face to know how intently he was watching her.

"A little after the noon hour," she told him breathlessly. "Each day right after lunch both Deborah and Willie sleep." She paused. "But only for about an hour."

His tone was exultant. "Only an hour? When did we last have an hour together? That is more than I dared to dream." He frowned. "I know the time must vary from day to day. Therefore I won't knock for fear of waking them. Come out with your puppy and I will be watching for you."

She nodded, suddenly unable to speak, and let herself into Deborah's house.

Deborah, sharp-eyed as always, watched her all morning curiously. "Is there something afoot that I don't know about?" she finally asked.

"Not really," Marilee began, then laughed. "Yes, there is, really. Michael Braden is coming by during your rest to teach me to handle Briny."

When Deborah said nothing, Marilee looked at her. "You have no comment?"

Deborah shook her head. "Only surprise," she said. "The gossip is that Michael Braden pays daily court to Matthew Fordham's widow. It seems amazing that he has time to court the two of you at once."

"I didn't say that he was courting me," Marilee told her. "And as for his courting Abigail, *that* is ridiculous." The longer Marilee thought of this, the angrier she got. "Michael was one of Matthew's dearest friends. I know he goes there every day. He told me himself. He goes to represent Matthew when those stupid planters press their questions on Abigail."

"Michael is a planter," Deborah pointed out. "He only seems to be different from the others because he leaves the actual work of planting to his servants. He also leaves the management of his land to a foreman so that he can wander around the fort like an idle gentleman."

"Are you criticizing him?" Marilee challenged her.

Deborah shook her head. "Every shoemaker to his own last," she said, turning away.

As much as Marilee looked forward to that early-afternoon hour, she had no idea how glorious it would be. The air inside the fort was warmed by cooking fires and the flames of the forges. Because the high walls of the stockade kept any cooling breeze from entering, the place was miserably hot.

Outside the gates a sweet wind stirred up the river with the tide. Instead of smelling like smoke, it brought the fresh salt tang of the sea along with it. It caught at her hair and billowed her full skirts, making her feel young again, gay and free.

Briny was in ecstasy. When Marilee showed Michael how neatly Briny padded at her side when she ordered him to, he was delighted.

"I knew the moment I saw that animal that he would be a winner."

"He's wonderful," Marilee agreed. "And so loving with Willie."

"Just so he keeps his teeth for your enemies," Michael said. "Here, hand me the leash."

He drilled the animal in sitting quite still as he walked away. Briny performed beautifully until he got tired. Then he flopped to the sand to stare sullenly at Michael from between his ears.

"Perhaps that's enough for today," Michael agreed, loosening the leash so the puppy could roll over in the sand. A small boat came up the tide from Norfolk bearing fishermen with a fresh catch from the sea. Michael hailed the man who poled his craft ashore.

Having ordered fine sturgeons to be delivered both to the Yarrow house and to Abigail Fordham's, he paid the man for his catch.

"That was generous," Marilee told him.

"But you need not do that. We are fine, as I am sure Abigail is."

"I find great pleasure in doing things for you," he told her.

The hour passed all too swiftly. As they walked back inside the gates Marilee saw a figure in the shadow of the stable, watching her. She waved, thinking it was Maggie. She was startled to see the scribe step from the shadows and wave genially at her. She was sure that Maggie had told her that the man, being cured, had returned to his plantation beyond the fort.

Michael laughed at her astonished expression. "Are you surprised that your friend the milkmaid has a gentleman caller?"

"Yes," Marilee replied. "I was told that her great joy with her husband kept her from being interested in other men."

"That's not the way it is supposed to work at all," Michael told her. "It is said that if a person is happily married, then a new marriage is looked for quickly, seeking a return to that joy."

She wondered if he was trying to warn her about Abigail and her suitors.

Although the month passed slowly, Marilee found herself enjoying even the most tedious of household tasks because of Deborah's easygoing companionship. Willie, over those weeks, completely won her heart. Since the puppy Briny had as much lively energy as the child, the two of them played happily together by the hour. Apparently what had seemed like an inexhaustible supply of mischief had really been an active little boy's boredom.

During her days at the Yarrow house Marilee realized for the first time how closely knit the little community was. This startled her because she could not remember a single woman friend coming to call on Abigail. Yet, as the days passed and the stream of visitors continued to call to see how Deborah was getting along, Marilee met every woman of the village that she had not already known.

These guests never came empty-handed. Sometimes they brought a fresh loaf of bread or a basket of dried fruit or wild plum jelly. Some of these women became favorites with Marilee at once, so that she smiled as broadly as Deborah to find them at the door. Others she enjoyed briefly when they dropped in, without feeling that they would ever be close friends. Two of these local women, sisters named Em and Vi, Marilee would have been perfectly happy never to see again in her life. She told Deborah that the first time they came.

"Those are women of genuine ill will," Marilee announced.

"How can you say that?" Deborah asked in amazement when Marilee blurted this out after they left. "Why, Em and Vi were as sweet as honey to you."

"They spread honey to catch flies," Marilee told her. "Did you really listen to them talk?"

Deborah stared at her and then shook her head. "I guess I have heard them talk enough that I no longer listen. But maybe I do know what you refer to. They are gossips. In fact, they can carry more tales than any two women I ever knew. But that's just their way. How else is public news to get around?"

"I have no objection to hearing public news," Marilee told her. "What they spread is not news at all but rumor. I would not tell either of those women the day of the week for fear they give out Tuesday on Wednesday and say I confided it to them."

Deborah laughed. "They do make everything sound very secret and confidential, don't they? That's just their style."

"Then it's their style I don't like, not them," Marilee grumbled. The women had truly irritated her. Every story they told was introduced by some confidential phrase, such as, "You must never tell anyone who told you this."

After that first time Marilee managed to have an errand outside of the house every time the two sisters came to the door.

But most of the time the days went pleasantly, brightened by Marilee's hour on the beach with Michael Braden. Strangely, only when Marilee returned from her daily walks with him did Deborah ever become withdrawn and quiet.

"I am going to stop telling you how well Briny does with his training if you aren't interested," Marilee told her friend.

"I am interested enough in the dog," Deborah told her. "It is the man who comes with him who makes me cross. I hear so much gossip about him and Abigail that I wish you wouldn't walk out with him. But, in truth I have never been much of an admirer of his."

Philip Soames's anger at her admiration of Michael Braden came back swiftly. But that would be jealousy, she told herself. Michael was too handsome for another man to admire.

"What has Michael Braden ever done to you?" Marilee asked.

"To me, nothing," Deborah replied. "To others, much."

"To whom, then, has he done wrong?" Marilee challenged her.

"Not wrong, perhaps," Deborah said, retreating a little. "But he is a man of peculiar habits that sometimes bring harm to others."

"What peculiar habits?" Marilee asked.

"He is a gambler, for one thing," Deborah said hotly. "Surely you can't have missed the fact that he would give you odds on the leap of a frog if there was nothing else to name a bet on."

Marilee laughed. "Oh, that. I did notice that the first day we met, and we have laughed about it. He even confessed that he won Briny for me on a wager."

"That doesn't strike you as a dangerous habit?" Deborah asked.

Marilee frowned. "Not really, Deborah,

250

not the way he explained it to me. He pointed out that any man who left the safety of England to risk his life and fortune in this wild country had to be a gambler at heart. Such harmless entertainment as betting on a leaping frog seems a small thing to dislike a man for."

"What if that bet were based on how fast a horse could run, and then the winner took the horse that meant the difference between success and survival to a family?"

"Now you are into some particular story," Marilee said. "And before you tell it, I have a single question. Did the man who lost this horse make the bet of his own free will?"

Deborah looked at her a long moment before dropping her eyes. "He did," she said quietly. "And since he did, and that seems to make it right to you, there is no point in my telling the story."

"But I am interested in the story," Marilee protested.

Deborah shrugged. "There is more grief than entertainment in it. I would remind you, though, that luck in gambling is a whimsical thing. It comes and goes. One day's winner is the loser on the next."

When Deborah turned away and indicated that the conversation was over, Marilee tried not to feel hurt. This crossness wasn't like her friend. But, after all, Deborah's child was very near term. She was awkward and miserable from carrying that great weight. She was also fighting against her worries over Willum. It was long past time that the men should be returning from their march, and yet no word came. "Under such circumstances I would be short-tempered, too," Marilee told herself.

Deborah was not alone in her concerns that summer. When Marilee passed through the village, she saw knots of men and women talking in worried tones. Although she did not purposely listen, she couldn't fail to hear what was weighing on their minds. They spoke of how long the men had been absent on the long march. They talked of Indian ambushes and the diseases that could strike men so far from help.

"And what of their crops?" one woman reminded them. "With no one to reset the tobacco there will be no crop and no money even for taxes."

"Taxes," her companion echoed. "Who cares if taxes get paid? It is food that I worry about. What will we eat? With the half-grown corn being burned in the field we will all starve for winter bread."

One afternoon, as she and Michael rested after exercising Brian Boru along the beach, she asked him about those field fires that hazed the distant sky day after day.

"Why do you worry?" he asked her. "You will draw your money the same whether the corn is harvested or not."

"I'm not worried about myself," she told him. "I worry about people who have no resources but this land. How will they eat with the governor ordering all those fields burned?"

"He is taking a chance on having a starving winter," Michael admitted. "But cornfields make perfect cover for the enemy to creep near a plantation. Men have better odds against starvation than they do against hatchets and arrows."

"Odds," he had said. Indeed, Virginia was a world for gamblers if even the governor studied the odds of life against death.

But hunger was on her mind. Leaving early and returning late as she did, she had not exchanged any more words with Timothy Reeves. Yet once in a while she caught a glimpse of him in passing. He was too thin by a great deal for a man of his height. He no longer limped but put his weight firmly on both feet again. But he did not walk the same nor look the same as he had before Matthew was killed. His gait was that of a beaten, miserable man. His face looked as if it had forgotten how to smile.

She comforted herself that now that summer had come he must be within weeks of being a free man at last.

Sometimes when she sat with Michael during that precious hour they spent on the beach, she wondered at herself. When she was with him, she felt light of heart and lovely and cherished. Only then was she able to forget the heavy concerns of both the colony and her own life. It was almost as if her time with him was spent under an enchantment. Was love a magic that could sweep away all the troubles of life, filling one with joy and warmth? If so, then she must love Michael, in spite of the fact that she never felt wholly comfortable with him.

Chapter
Eighteen

WHEN a rap come on Deborah's door that late June morning, Marilee opened it to find the sisters, Em and Vi, grinning at her from the stoop. Inwardly she groaned as she forced a cordial smile and threw the door open to welcome them. As always Briny had risen and walked to the door with her, quietly alert against danger that might threaten his mistress.

The two women took chairs side by side, their bright eyes searching everywhere.

"That is certainly a fine dog that Michael Braden won from that planter up at Henrico, isn't it?" Em asked.

Deborah, knowing Marilee's dislike for these women, spoke up quickly. "However Michael came by the dog, Briny is a wonderful animal and a good friend and companion. It was thoughtful and generous of Michael to give Briny to his friend Matthew's sister for her protection."

In the moment of silence that followed Marilee rose and picked up her basket. "If you ladies will excuse me . . ." she began.

"Not again," the two women said, laughing and speaking almost in unison. Then Vi leaned forward to take the offensive. "My sister and I have often discussed your habit of getting up and rushing off on errands every time we put our feet inside dear Deborah's door. I hope we have done nothing to offend you, dear child, that you feel the need to avoid us like this."

Startled, Marilee groped for some civil response, only to have Deborah beat her to it. "Offense?" Deborah asked with a merry laugh. "What an idea! I certainly hope that none of my other friends have been offended by Marilee's attempt to take the best possible care of Willie and me. You are certainly not alone in having only brief visits with my young friend." She smiled warmly at Marilee. "Marilee takes the occasion of any visitor in the house to do her errands. That way she avoids leaving me and Willie alone, except when we are napping, of course."

Marilee saw the sisters exchange a wise, knowing glance at Deborah's words and wanted to lash out at them. No doubt they had given other people reports (in absolute confidence, of course) about Marilee's walks along the beach with the dog and Michael Braden, while her friend and Willie slept.

After a flurry of apologies for their having misunderstood her, Marilee finally escaped. Outside the door, she whistled silently. So her escapes had not gone unnoticed. Then she smiled to herself. How clever of Deborah to put such a good light on her rudeness. Deborah's words were true, of course, but Marilee herself would never have been able to give that excuse without blushing at the added truth that indeed she tried her best to avoid those two women.

At her stable Maggie had finished her milking and, with sleeves rolled back, was stirring a great pot of cheese over a slow fire. Marilee watched her a little sadly for a moment. She really missed the warm friendship she had established with Maggie during the days following the Indian attack. Once the nursing of the wounded was past, Maggie had gone back to her old, unfriendly ways, greeting Marilee almost crossly, as if they had not worked together side by side in easy friendship.

When Marilee realized that the scribe had disappeared from the stable, she had been curious about his fate. She had casually asked Maggie what had become of the man.

"He lived or he died," Maggie had told her, shrugging. "Once fed and among friends, he was no longer any business of mine." Then she shrugged again as if it hadn't mattered to her that even that much had been done for him.

Marilee looked at her thoughtfully. Behind

that rough manner, more mysteries lay hidden than the daring that had taken Maggie into the woods with her. There was also that gentleness that came forth in the girl's singing and in that one incident of concern that she had shown for the maddened scribe.

"You are early for the milk," Maggie told her without looking up.

"Guests came, and I left," Marilee said.

Maggie's eyes sought her own. "This early in the day? Men seeking wives again?"

Marilee laughed and shook her head. "Not that, thank goodness. These were friends of Deborah's." Marilee went on. "A pair of women who chatter of everyone's business but their own."

"Maybe they have none of their own," Maggie commented. "If you can wait five minutes I will send along some extra cheese that I have for the young mother."

"You are very good to Deborah," Marilee said. This would not be the first treat she had carried from Maggie's stable to her friend.

"Some give time, some give cheese," Maggie grunted. "And others give words better left unsaid."

To Marilee's astonishment Maggie seemed to want to talk.

"Do you remember the man we found wandering crazed in the wood?" Maggie asked.

At Marilee's nod Maggie smiled. "He has

his health again," she reported. "His house is back up and some crops put in."

"That's wonderful," Marilee said. "He is fortunate to have recovered at all."

Maggie nodded. "It would be a waste for a fine, bright mind like his to have been destroyed," she agreed.

Marilee agreed, saying nothing of her surprise. She could not remember Maggie ever saying a good thing about any man before, except that Timothy was her friend. Perhaps Maggie was softening in spite of herself.

When the cheese was ready, Marilee accepted it with Deborah's thanks. Maggie held her eyes a minute, wiping her hands on her apron as she frowned.

"He sends his greeting to you," she whispered. As soon as she spoke the words she turned away swiftly to hide the rise of sudden color in her cheeks.

Marilee smiled to herself as she went on her way. Maybe she was being a romantic dreamer, but she wondered if more than the return of his wits had come to the scribe while he was in Maggie's keeping. Could they be in love? The thought sent her humming along the street on her errands.

Marilee took pains to be gone long enough to give the sisters ample time to finish their visit and leave. By the time she returned to Deborah's house, her basket was full. Instead of setting down her basket to rap on the door, she clung to it with one arm and lifted the latch to go in.

Em and Vi were still there in the same chairs. Em was leaning forward talking, her eyes glittering with excitement. "I wouldn't want you to say where you heard this," she was saying, "but the betting was all wrong on this one. More men put money on that one getting married again in three weeks than they did on three months."

Deborah raised stricken eyes to Marilee, and the voice snapped into silence. The silence, in fact, was too heavy for even Deborah to bear. "Em and Vi," she said quickly, "have only stayed so long that I not be left alone."

Marilee, still standing inside the door, nodded stiffly. "That was generous of them," she said. "My sincere thanks." It was all she could do to walk past them into the kitchen with her market basket without betraying her shock.

Three months.

The subject of that gossip was clear. Em was telling of the marriage of one woman widowed from the Indian attack. Marilee had not made note of the day, but it had indeed been three months since the Indian attack.

Em's glittering eyes disgusted her. But more disgusting by far was the readiness of some widow of that day to change her name and forget. Only when she heard Deborah return from the door did she turn to her friend.

"Then the betting men of the colony had even laid odds on the remarriage of the widows?" she asked without trying to hide the sarcasm in her voice.

"As you said yourself, those are women of ill will," Deborah reminded her after a moment. "I paid the price of my quick excuse to them. I never got so tired of a pair of women in my life. I even imagined myself in pain because I wanted them gone so much."

"In pain?" Marilee asked.

Deborah smiled. "The pain was imagined, but they did wear me down with their chatter. I think I will rest in bed awhile if you can spare me."

"Who were they talking about when I came in?" Marilee asked.

"Widows from the Indian attack," Deborah said, walking away without looking back. She had grown so heavy with her child that she waddled uncertainly across the rushes on the floor.

"Any particular widow?" Marilee insisted.

Deborah turned, her eyes streaming. "I am in pain," she admitted. "Oh, Marilee, it was your brother's widow."

Marilee stared at her is disbelief. Abigail. As she looked at Deborah she saw her friend's face twist with pain and watched her bend a little. Too much was happening too fast. In one moment she must absorb the fact that Abigail was marrying. In the same breath she must find some comfort for Deborah.

"Is it the real pain, the final pain?" Marilee asked.

Deborah, unable to walk farther, gripped the wall and the back of a chair as she nodded. "Yes."

"I am no midwife," Marilee whispered. "Nor am I a doctor."

"There is neither midwife nor doctor here," Deborah whispered. "Willum took care of Willie. Willum meant to be here."

"Who would know what to do?" Marilee asked desperately. There had been midwives in the village at home, wise women who had brought more lives into the world than they remembered.

"Maggie," Marilee said suddenly. "Would Maggie know what to do?"

Deborah's eyes widened. She tried a weak smile. "If I were a cow she would," she said, nodding. Marilee saw the pain strike her again. "Yes, yes," Deborah panted. "Get Maggie and hurry."

It was a matter of a minute to bring Maggie running. When the two of them had Deborah safely into her own bed, Maggie chased Marilee out with Willie.

"Keep the kettle hot and the child comfortable," she ordered Marilee. "If I need anything from you I'll call."

With Willie fed, his eyes never leaving his mother's closed door, Marilee sat with him and sang to him until his eyes grew heavy.

She did not once think of Michael Braden waiting for her until she lay the sleeping child on his bed. The moment she opened the door, Michael stepped forward to approach her. At that same moment Marilee heard a cry from Deborah's room.

Willie, startled from sleep, ran from his room and seized Marilee around the knees, wailing, "Mamma, Mamma," in a heart-broken tone. She clasped him against her and spoke to Michael.

"I cannot see you today," she told him. "I'm sorry if I kept you waiting."

With barely a glance at the weeping child he reached for her hand. "But I must talk to you at once, Marilee. This is urgent."

"Not now." She shook her head. "I am really sorry, Michael."

"But I must." His voice was almost a wail.

As if in answer, a cry came from behind the door. Maggie appeared there and called to Marilee, "Bring cool cloths and a basin, quickly."

"No, Michael, no," Marilee said, shutting the door and starting off for the kitchen with the child still hanging to her knees.

The day was destined to last forever. Unable to get Willie to go back to his bed, Marilee sat with him, singing to him, until he drifted off to sleep on her lap. Briny, his wise eyes full of questions, leaned his head on her knee and stared up at her dolefully.

The brightness faded beyond the shuttered window, and twilight settled on the village. Marilee heard the horses returning the men from their plantations and dogs welcoming their masters' return.

Maggie, her face slack with fatigue, let herself out of Deborah's room. "She is finally asleep," she told Marilee. "I will take a chance and go tend to my beasts. If we are lucky she will sleep until my return."

"And if we aren't lucky?" Marilee asked, frightened by the thought.

Maggie crooked a smile at her. "Then we will find how fast you can run from here to the stable."

Maggie must have passed the word of Deborah's condition along the street. After what seemed forever to Marilee, Maggie returned with help — an older woman with a kindly face who had often come to sit with Deborah.

The two women took turns through the night waiting on Deborah. Marilee caught snatches of sleep on the bed beside Willie, who would not let her leave his side.

The child was born at last a little after dawn. Marilee leaped awake to hear the faint, mewling cry from the next room. She slid from Willie's grasp and was waiting in the outer room when Maggie came out carrying the baby.

How ugly it was, a round face with an angry, triangular, screaming mouth.

"A girl." Maggie beamed. "Fat as an autumn hen. Deborah has a fine daughter."

"Is that the way a baby should look?" Marilee asked, wondering if anything so red and splotched could ever bleach to a proper color.

"She is beautiful," Maggie said angrily. "What's the matter with you, woman? She is the most beautiful baby I have ever seen."

When the child lay at Deborah's side and they both slept, Marilee was allowed to look in on them for a brief moment. Then, in the bossiest possible way, Maggie pulled the door shut and insisted that the young mother must be left alone to rest.

The kettle had boiled dry a dozen times over, but there was hot sassafras tea ready with thick slices of buttered bread. Maggie, leaning her elbows on the kitchen table, smiled. "Beautiful," she kept saying between deep drafts of the fragrant tea. "Simply beautiful."

When her hunger was satisfied, she looked at Marilee. "Did I tell you what news I heard in the street when I went to tend my cows? A boater came downriver reporting that the marchers were within a half-day of the fort."

"Willum," Marilee breathed.

"Pray God," Maggie cautioned. "He said that fewer return than marched away."

Dawn came golden. Maggie left to milk her cows, and Marilee, yawning like a child, was setting a fresh kettle over the fire when the cannon sounded. Marilee raced to Deborah's side, fearing that the sound would frighten her.

Maybe Maggie had remembered to give her the news earlier. Maybe some wisdom beyond understanding informed Deborah's heart. She looked up weakly at Marilee and smiled.

"Willum," she said. "Willum has come."

Within minutes he was there, kneeling by her side, his great bulk taking up all the space in the room. He did not touch the child but only stared at her as he gripped his wife's hands. When he buried his head in the coverlet beside them, Marilee slipped away to make warm food for him.

Willie, soggy with sleep, was in his father's arms when Willum came to the kitchen door.

"We have a question, Marilee," he said in a voice of such tenderness that tears sprang to Marilee's eyes. "My good Debbie and I need counsel from you. What is the name for a woman that is closest to the name of Matthew?"

There was no fighting the tears. Marilee set down the pot and wiped her streaming eyes with her apron. Willie wriggled down and came to hug her tight around the legs.

"Mathilda," she finally whispered. "Of all I know, Mathilda is the nearest."

"Then so she be, our daughter," he said. "Mathilda." He repeated the name, smiling. "That has a proper ring." He turned and went back to announce this name to his wife.

Chapter Nineteen

DURING their first visit together, before
Marilee even met Willum Yarrow, Deborah
had told Marilee that while Willum might
not be the man she would have chosen to
marry if she were to live in London or Sussex, he was the proper husband here in
Virginia.

Marilee had puzzled a little over her
friend's words at the time. Through the following months Marilee hadn't really gotten
to know Willum a whole lot better. It had
been plain from the first that Willum loved
Deborah with a deep, respectful devotion.
And with his great size and strength Willum
was certainly well fitted for the building of
a plantation. She had seen his stubborn courage during the days after the attack, and his
readiness to risk his life on the march
against the Indians. But the whole of what
Deborah had meant by her words only be-

came clear to Marilee that first day of young Mathilda Yarrow's life.

Willum was thin from the long march, and fatigue had smudged dark circles beneath his eyes. He looked like a man who needed to pile on a bed and sleep soundly for a day and a night at least. Yet, instead of giving into his exhaustion, Willum summoned both strength and tenderness for the needs of his household. By the time Marilee had Willie dressed for the day, Willum had wood stacked by the hearth and water in the pail. He had sliced cured meat and set it to fry and carried a hot mug of tea to his wife before Marilee even got Willie's porridge ready.

The most astonishing thing was the skill and ease with which this giant of a man handled the newborn baby. Marilee watched him hold the child down for Willie to inspect. The whole length of the little girl's body did not reach from Willum's hand to the bend of his elbow. Yet he held the child with more tender confidence than Marilee was able to manage.

Willum was a man for all tasks, she decided, and certainly Virginia was a place where a man (and a woman, she added to herself ruefully) needed to be able to do everything.

As soon as they had finished breakfast Willum smiled over at Marilee, shaking his head. "You are a wonder, girl," he told her. "Maybe that beautiful face of yours can trick a man, but there you are, after the strains of the weeks past and a night with no sleep, still delighting a man's eye and sporting a smile as lively as a cricket's song. This must be a show you put on. You have to be worn to the bone, a creature no bigger than you are. But never you mind. The boy and I can manage here. You get yourself home and sleep this day away and be rested."

Marilee laughed softly. "I was thinking the same about you, Willum." Then she dropped her eyes. "I really appreciate your concern," she told him, "but I don't want to go back to my brother's house if I can help it." She was too upset by Abigail's engagement to say the words right out. She stammered a little. "A change is happening there," she finally said.

"A change?" he asked. "What kind of a change? You must remember that I have been gone a long time with no word from anyone. What change do you refer to?"

"Just yesterday I was told that Abigail is marrying again," Marilee told him, angry at herself that her voice sounded so weak and quavery.

He frowned thoughtfully. "That might have been expected," he said. "She's a fair woman to look at, for all that she is useless. I know it must be hard for you to see some other man replace Matthew. Who is to be the bridegegroom this time?"

"I haven't even heard his name," Marilee admitted.

Willum grew thoughtful. "I will be interested to see what man tries to fill Matthew Fordham's shoes. But I would guess that woman was much sought after."

"Much sought after," Marilee agreed. She was relieved to have this conversation interrupted by the arrival of the first of the Deborah's friends. Deborah might as well have announced an open house for the number of village women that came that morning. Smiling and excited, they brought good wishes and treats for the table and vied for the first glimpse of this newly born Virginian.

The news of Abigail's decision had obviously been passed as swiftly as the news of the new baby. Marilee caught angled glances of curious sympathy from every visitor. She saw in their faces the unspoken question that Deborah had asked her with her morning greeting.

"What are you going to do?"

Marilee herself had no answer. She didn't know what she could do. She only knew what she could not do. She could not live in her brother's house with another man sharing his widow's bed. And she certainly could not continue to creep in and out of a sleeping house, avoiding any reasonable decision about her own future.

What had she been waiting for, anyway? For Philip to return to advise her? For Michael Braden to commit himself to more than words of love and tender caring? Philip was still on the high seas, and Michael was held back from speaking to her because of her grief over Matthew's death.

Willum was at the door, greeting another caller. Briny, upset by the events of the night before and the steady traffic into the house, had gone from one spasm of barking to another all morning. Marilee fought a rising sense of desperation. Not only was all this disturbance tiring to Deborah, but also she, herself, couldn't think in such a hubbub. Yet every hour that passed brought her nearer to having to face Abigail.

When the idea first came to Marilee, she gasped at its recklessness. She felt her face turn scarlet to think how her father or Matthew would react to the daring plan she was considering. But even as she trembled at her own boldness at even coming up with the idea, she remembered a saying from the village at home: "Desperate situations demand desperate remedies."

She was desperate. And being so, she would put the question to Michael Braden herself. She would ask him if he wished to marry her. If he did, her problem would be neatly solved. If he did not? She shuddered to think of the humiliation of that event. She would not even think of it at all, she decided, for fear she'd lose heart and not ask the question at all.

When the idea came to her, it was with great force. Yet it seemed that her courage had begun to diminish at the same moment.

She could feel the coldness of fear pushing her courage farther and farther back into a corner. She feared that if she waited, even an hour more, she would not be able to say the words that she must say.

When another knock came at the door, setting Briny into a fresh explosion of barking, she took this as a sign. Lifting Briny's leash from the shelf and fastening it around his neck, she went to Willum.

"I have decided to take this noisy fellow for a walk," she told him. "The house will not only be quieter, but I will also enjoy the fresh outside air."

Willum nodded, adding only a word of warning about the men from the tavern ships in the harbor.

"I cannot think that any man will risk Briny's jaws," she told him.

He smiled in agreement as she let herself out the door.

Marilee had not seen so many people crowding the streets since the days just after the Indian attack. Fortunately these were happy people. Wives who had endured the loneliness and fear of their husbands' absence smiled up at the men at their sides. As for these men, they were in their glory. They stood about, telling great tales of their adventures to all who would listen.

Marilee smiled and nodded and accepted good wishes for Deborah all along the street. All this time she watched for Michael

Braden. How strange it was not to be able to find him. In the old days when Timothy Reeves watched over her while Matthew was still alive, she could not put her foot outside the door without Michael appearing within minutes. And certainly Michael was not a man she would miss even in this crowd, not with that glorious pale head of hair and his bright clothing.

When she finally did see him, he was a long way off at the other end of the street. She had never seen him looking so business-like. He was bending his head in such a sober conversation that she hesitated even to approach. She knew the other gentleman only as a planter whose land, like Michael's, lay near the fort. She started to turn away, feeling her courage still dwindling. Maybe this was a sign. Maybe it was a sign that she should not even try her desperate plan. But even as she stood in indecision, he glanced up, saw her, and began to make his way toward her along the street.

Even from a distance she realized that he looked different. His face was tense and his lips unsmiling. He looked older than she had ever seen him look, and sadder. Her heart went out to him. It made sense that he would be sad about Abigail's decision. She suddenly understood the urgency in his voice the day before, when she had been unable to join him. That, too, made sense. He had been try-ing to be the first to tell her of Abigail's decision. It would be like him to want to spare her the agony of hearing this news from strangers.

When he was at her side, her instinct was to take his arm. Instead of inviting this gesture, he spoke to her urgently. "Come, Marilee. Let's walk along the beach. I need to talk to you."

"Oh, but I need to talk to you," she said, skipping a little to keep up with his rapid pace. "Please, Michael, listen while I can still speak."

"Marilee," he insisted, "just hear me out first."

"No," she said firmly. She stopped abruptly in the sand so that he was a few paces beyond her before he realized she had left his side. "I must say what I need to say, Michael. If I hesitate I will most certainly lose heart. After that, I will listen to you willingly."

He looked back, frowning. "And that is a solemn promise?" he asked. "That you will listen fairly all the way until I am through?"

"I promise, Michael," she told him. He had come back to stand very close to her, looking at her in that intense way that always made her quite edgy. She wished he would stand a little farther away so that she could think more clearly.

How had she ever thought she could do this reckless and terrifying thing? She wanted to turn and run, go pelting across the sand, and never let anyone know what she had planned. She had even forgotten the words she meant to use.

"Well," he said. "What is this important thing that you had to say to me?"

Pressed by the difficulty of what she had to do, she became the old Marilee, the Marilee who had been her father's jester to Matthew's prince, the Marilee who always made jokes because life was too serious to be sober about.

Looking up into Michael's face, she smiled and teased him, borrowing the expression that he so often used. "I wager that this will be the most impertinent thing that any woman will say to you today."

"Wagering, is she now?" he asked, breaking into a broad smile. "Very well. Let us see how impertinent you can be to a dear friend. Out with your impudence."

"This is not just any light impudence that you could come by in the open market," she warned him. "This impertinence is in dead earnest."

"Dead earnest," he echoed soberly. He reached for Briny's leash and began to walk along, nodding soberly as if this were a great game that the two of them were playing.

She was glad that they were walking along side by side. It was easier not to be looking into his face when she asked that bold question. Her words did not come easily, but at least they came.

"Michael," she said quietly, "you have

been a good and dear friend to both Matthew and me. You have been kind and thoughtful and generous. My feelings toward you have steadily deepened since the day we first met. There have been times when I thought I saw the light of love in your eyes for me. I even had some girlish dreams of our being man and wife."

He stopped abruptly with a hoarse cry. He caught at her arm, but she would not be interrupted. She shook her head and twisted away from his grasp. "Hear me out," she begged. "When you seemed to find me pleasing and did not speak, I thought it was because you knew I was still grieving for my father, and then later, Matthew. That was true, and your understanding only made me appreciate you more. But now all is changed. My sister-in-law is planning to marry. I cannot live in that house with her and a new husband. I must make a new life for myself. Now comes the impertinence, Michael Braden." She saw his stricken face but forced herself to go on. "If you feel the love that I think you have for me, Michael, if you think that I would make a suitable wife for you, would you ask me now, Michael? Would you ask me to be your wife and marry me as quickly as the church will allow?"

For a moment she was terrified all over again. She could not believe the look of shock that changed his face. His eyes widened, as if he saw beyond her to something very painful. She would have turned at that moment and run away if he had not caught her by the shoulders and clasped her to his breast with a great sob.

"Oh, Marilee, Marilee," he cried, his words muffled against her throat. "You did not imagine my love for you. You were right that I only delayed my suit for fear you might turn against me as you did those others who came so heartlessly to court you in your grief."

He groaned and tightened his arms around her. "How many mornings have I kept my eyes closed when waking from sleep? I lie and imagine that glowing hair on the pillow beside me. How many times have I closed my door against the night, wishing that I were locking you inside with me? And how many times have I dreamed of this?"

Without warning he loosened his grasp on her so that his face was just above hers. With his hands tenderly cupping her head, he held his lips to hers, first gently, then more roughly until she would have cried out from pain if he had not suddenly released her.

She lifted her fingertips and touched her lips. He was at once contrite, begging her forgiveness, apologizing for letting his passion carry him away.

She shook her head. "I just didn't know that a kiss was like that," she stammered.

He stared at her. "You have never been kissed before?"

"Not like that," she replied. She remembered Philip. His lips had been warm on hers, not searching, not demanding, as Michael's had been, but gentle and giving. She realized with a start that she and Philip had kissed each other, not in passion but tenderness. Michael's has been an embrace of passion without tenderness. What a great difference that made. "Only a kiss of friendship," she whispered.

He pulled her close to his heart. "What I feel for you is a great deal more than friendship," he whispered.

"Then you are not disgusted by my impertinent question?" she asked.

"Disgusted? Never. I only grieve that you did not ask it sooner."

He still had not asked the question that hung between them. How miserable that she must ask him again herself!

"Then will you marry me, Michael?" she asked very humbly.

"God knows that there is nothing I want more in this world," he said, his voice falling almost to a groan. "We must plan. There has to be a way."

"A way?" she asked. "What can possibly stand between us?"

"Many things," he said. "Many things. Remember that I tried to talk to you yesterday, and then again when we met in the village?"

She nodded. "I remember."

"Nothing is ever as simple as it looks, Marilee. You know that I have a fancy for making wagers, for gambling, if you prefer to call it that. You must also know that luck is like a weather vane, changing with the wind and without warning. I have suffered a change of luck these months past." He laughed a short, bitter laugh. "In fact, I have wondered if that dog of yours might not have been a bad luck win for me. Since the day I wagered for that puppy, everything has gone against me."

"But luck changes, as you say," she reminded him, confused that he would think all of this was so important, in view of what they had been talking about.

"It has not changed quickly enough," he said angrily. "I stand to lose both my land and my servants if I do not pay up my debts by the first of August."

"Your land and your servants?" This seemed impossible.

He nodded. "That is the way a wagering man works, Marilee. When you are losing, you keep piling more and more on the table, knowing that one day your luck will turn and bring it all back to you. It did not turn for me."

"But surely the man who owns these debts will not see you ruined?"

"He didn't ruin me, Marilee. I have ruined myself. It is also in the nature of a wagering man to call up his debts. I have done so myself without looking at what havoc it caused. I expect him to do the same."

She was trying to sort this out in her mind.

Without knowing how much he owed she didn't know if her own resources were great enough to help him. Perhaps she could pay off these debts for him. The problem was one of timing. Philip, who managed her money, would arrive only near the time that the debt came due.

He was still talking, his voice lower now, its tone persuasive, almost apologetic. "There are only three ways that a gentleman can come by money, Marilee. He can inherit it, as Matthew did. He can earn it, as men like Willum do. Or he can marry it."

She looked up at him, waiting.

"Since it was too late for the first of those methods, it was the last that I chose, Marilee. I wanted you to understand."

"I don't understand," she told him. "What are you trying to say?"

His eyes were full on hers, pleading. "I am the man who asked Abigail Fordham to marry," he said quietly.

As she stared at him she saw his face begin to spin lazily before her eyes.

I am the man, he had said.

Her mind refused to accept the words. Her very brain spun away from what he was saying in wide, swinging arcs of light.

I am the man.

She felt her knees lose their stiffness and knew she was falling. He was calling to her from a long way away.

"Marilee. Marilee, my love."

Chapter Twenty

ALL it took was Michael's touch to bring Marilee back to her senses. As tenderly as she had clung to him the moment before, now even the warm pressure of his hands supporting her back made her feel a little ill.

"No," she cried, backing away from him. "Don't touch me. Please don't touch me." Briny was quick to hear the tone of distress in her voice. A low grumble began deep in the dog's throat, and he shouldered his powerful body in between Marilee and Michael. Once there, he pressed himself against her leg, looking up into her face and whining softly.

Michael hesitated only a moment before reaching for her hand again. A ridge of wiry hair bristled along the dog's spine as he watched Michael with vigilant eyes. "But my dear," Michael insisted, "didn't you understand me? I told you there must be a way."

"A way for us to marry when you have already pledged yourself to another woman?" Her voice rose with disbelief.

Or was it anger? The significance of what he had told her continued to unfold in her mind. He was marrying Abigail for money, for property, to save himself from ruin brought on by his own obsessive gambling. She felt humiliated that he would dare to protest his love for her in the same breath in which he had told her that he was marrying her brother's widow for her property alone.

It was clear to her at once that Michael totally misunderstood her tone. He had heard her words as a simple question. Because he had not registered the shock and outrage in her voice, he rushed to answer her question. He was so eager to give her a satisfactory answer that his words tumbled over each other.

Marilee watched him in horror. This was a man making up his course of action as he went, trying one way and another to design a way to get out of his own solemn promise to marry Abigail Fordham.

"All is not lost," he insisted. "The worst Abigail can do is to take me to court and sue me for breach of promise." He sought Marilee's eyes with his, smiling the way he knew she had never been able to resist. "Now come, love, can you imagine that? Can you imagine Abigail standing in open court and saying that I had broken a pledge to marry her? She would never do it." He shook his head, still smiling. "Abigail is too puffed up with false pride and vanity for that. Why, she is perfectly convinced that every man who sees her falls instantly in love with that shallow beauty of hers."

He paused and would have reached out to her again except for Briny's bared fangs and low, warning growl. He shot the dog a look of pure hatred but kept his voice soft and persuasive. "There's a better way to handle her. I could approach her tenderly, tell her that I still cherish her with undying love. Then I would confess that my mind cannot rest with our decision. I could say that my loyalty to Matthew kept me from her side. There would be tears, of course, maybe even an ugly scene. . . ."

Marilee felt his words swaying around her. Once she had passingly thought of Michael's effect on her as enchantment. Even the words she used to describe him in her mind were the words of magic. He was charming. And there was his extraordinary beauty, that perfectly formed face and body, that wonderful hair so pale that it dazzled her. Yet the words he spoke were cruel and heartless. They described a web he could weave to deceive Abigail. Even more sickening was Marilee's realization that he would make her, by association, a part of this ugly plot.

Her instinct was to turn and flee. She wanted to be beyond the sound of that silken voice, to have that lying face out of her sight.

But even as this thought came, she knew she didn't have the strength to run away from him. A deep sickness ached in her joints. Evil. This man was evil. And to think that she had wanted to join her life to his hardly a few minutes before.

She glanced back up the beach that she must cross to get back into the fort. Even if she clung to Briny and could make her way back to the city gate, did she dare to test this half-grown dog's valor against the drunken men that gathered on the beach?

She had never seen as many tavern boats as had ridden at anchor when she and Michael walked out there. She knew by experience that since early morning a steady flow of planters had rowed out to drink on board those ships. By the time they staggered back onto the beach, they had become dangerous men. Not even with Briny at her side to protect her did she dare pass through them alone.

Michael, although confused by her silence, was far from giving up his campaign. Falling back on his proven charm, he stood smiling, his eyes tender on her face, coaxing her. She knew that if Briny were not bristling watchfully under her hand, she would be fighting off that rough embrace. Her heart thundered under her blouse. What could she do? How was she possibly going to escape this miserable situation?

When Michael fell silent, Briny had, too. He had only stayed watchful with Marilee's hand resting lightly on his head. Suddenly Marilee realized that he had begun to tremble again and whine softly deep in his throat. Then he twisted under her hand as if he were looking for someone behind her.

Michael followed the dog's eyes at the same moment that Marilee did. Just inside the edge of the woods that lined the beach, a tall, slender figure in a blue workman's smock stood watching them. He had raised one arm and was leaning against the trunk of the tree where it rested.

His face shaded by tree limbs, Timothy Reeves's expression was unreadable. It was impossible to tell whether he had just come that moment or had stood there watching and listening for a long time.

Marilee's heart sank. How much of their conversation had he heard? In a moment of blinding pain she realized how much she desired Timothy's respect. Her face flamed to think that he might have heard her humbly proposing to this miserable, deceiving gambler. What must he think of her now, this young servant that Matthew had loved?

He had called her "the last worthless remnant of a noble line." What even uglier opinion must he have now?

Michael's reaction was instant fury. He cursed almost silently to himself and strode toward Timothy, as if to attack him. His face had emptied of all color, and that familiar white line had come around his lips. He bellowed with rage.

"Reeves," he shouted. "What rotten business is this? What are you doing here? How dare you sneak around following your betters? I'll have your skin for this on the thongs of a whip. Speak up. By whose authority have you left your labor?"

During this tirade Timothy did not flinch. He didn't even straighten up but remained standing in that relaxed position, leaning his weight against that single arm. Those strange eyes were steely as they returned Michael's gaze. Marilee looked at him with wonder. What a man this was. No wonder Matthew had cherished him so.

"Answer me, you lout," Michael shouted. "How dare you follow me?"

"Mistress Fordham called me from my work to find you and ask you to come to her," Timothy replied in the most matter-of-fact tone possible.

Michael had the grace to flush.

"One word of what you have seen and heard here, and you are a dead man," Michael said flatly. "Go and tell your mistress that I will be there very shortly."

"That won't be necessary, Michael," Marilee told him. "You should go to her at once. Our conversation is finished."

Although he looked at her with an instant expression of panic, Michael did not acknowledge hearing her words. Instead, he repeated his order to Timothy. "Do as I tell you, Reeves," he said, "and be quick about it."

Timothy looked at Marilee and then back at Michael. When he finally spoke, his voice was wholly without expression. "I do my master's bidding."

Michael was out of control with rage. "Your master is dead, you fool," he hissed at him. "Get back to your mistress."

Marilee gasped at his words. From that shock she got the strength to force Michael's attention.

"Michael," she called in a tone that not even he could ignore. As he turned, frowning, she went on calmly. "I will walk back to the fort now with Timothy Reeves."

"But, Marilee," Michael protested, moving toward her with his hands outstretched.

She shook her head firmly. "Our conversation is over," she told him. "I have nothing more to say."

She knelt and picked up Briny's leash, which Michael had dropped in his fury at seeing Timothy. Tightening it around her hand, she turned to Timothy. "Would you please walk me back to Mistress Yarrow's house?"

He nodded and stepped onto the beach beside her.

They walked in silence toward the gate of the fort. Marilee's fears about the drunken men on the beach had been correct. She was careful not to lift her eyes lest one of them make some move toward herself and Timothy. It wasn't necessary for her to look up to know that now and then Timothy glanced down at her. She kept having the feeling that he had something he wanted to say and decided that he lacked either the words or the courage to speak up. In any case he did not speak a word until they stood outside Deborah's door.

"I am here to serve you," he told her.

She had not cried there on the beach at Michael's infamous words; why should Timothy's quiet reassurance bring instant hot tears pressing behind her eyes?

"Thank you, Timothy," she managed to say. "You are very good to me."

"I do my master's bidding," he replied.

She looked up at him. The look of steel was gone from those smoky eyes. She hoped this meant that he had not used that phrase in the old, resentful way but instead that he was telling her that in his heart, too, Matthew still lived.

"My blessing on the mother and child," he added as she opened the door.

Willum was crossing the room as she entered. He stopped and stared at her, his face knotting with instant concern. "What has happened?" he asked. "You wear the face of death."

She shook her head, trying to stop her tears. "Not death but dishonor," she told him.

"Dishonor?" he said.

Debbie called fretfully from the next room. "Dishonor? Who is in dishonor? Come in where I can hear you. I can't stand this business of only hearing things around the edges."

Hastily wiping her eyes, Marilee went to the bedroom door. With her sleeping baby at her side Deborah sat back against every goose-down pillow in the house. She looked like a tired and rumpled queen propped up there.

Willum followed Marilee, bringing a stool for her to sit by the bed.

One glance at Marilee's face was all Deborah needed to make her flare with anger. "You've heard then. Poor child. Look at her, Willum. Go draw her a cup of ale to set her blood running again."

"The ale I'll bring soon enough," Willum said, "but first, what is this news that can turn this rosy girl as pale as buttermilk?"

"Michael Braden," Deborah said angrily. "It's that Michael Braden who is planning to marry Abigail Fordham."

Willum stood silent a long moment before turning to leave the room.

Deborah reached for Marilee's hands. "You know that I feared it from the first. They were shelled from the same kind of pod, those two peas."

"It's money," Marilee blurted out. "Michael is marrying Abigail to get the money to pay off his gambling debts. And to think that I thought of marrying such a man."

"He's a handsome man to look at," Willum said, as if forgiving Marilee this lapse. He handed a brimming mug of ale to Marilee and a second one to his wife.

Deborah said, "Abigail must be buying that peacock at a fancy price. He has gambled himself into holes before and has always been able to get out without taking on a woman to marry. How deep must he have gone to be driven to such a measure?"

"His land and servants," Marilee said numbly.

Willum whistled softly.

The ale must have made Marilee reckless. There, with those loving people giving her their sympathy and attention, she spilled it all out.

"I went looking for Michael Braden," she admitted. "I asked him to marry me because I could not stay with Abigail's new husband. It was then that he told me."

Willum groaned.

"He must have wanted to bite his tongue out for having asked Abigail," Deborah said. "It has been plain from the first that he favored you. But there's no way out of it for him now."

Marilee's anger came back swiftly. "Well, he's doing his best to find a way. He suggested breaking his pledge to Abigail and marrying me," Marilee told them. "How many times has he heard me say that I would wed no man to make him rich? Does he think that I find him any different from any other planter who sees a wife as a way to make his fortune? He had the gall to tell me that a gentleman has only three ways of getting money. Inheriting it, earning it, or marrying it."

"He should know. With this marriage he will have come by money in all three ways."

"All three?" Marilee asked.

"It is a common story that he gamed away a fortune in England before his family shipped him over here with land and servants for a new start," Willum explained. "And any man who marries a woman for her money will earn every farthing of it before it is through."

Deborah, who had fallen silent, then asked again the question that Marilee had tried so unsuccessfully to answer. "What will you do?"

"Do?" Willum asked. "She'll be a member of this household for as long as she wants. That's what she will do."

"That we know," Deborah agreed. "But she needs better prospects than sharing her life with our Willie snuffling across the room. She needs a home of her own."

A home of her own. Marilee thought of Maggie and her simple rooms above the stable with the breath of her cows warming the air on winter nights. Simple but her own.

"You are welcome here," Willum reminded her, "as is your dog and all your trappings."

"Trappings!" Marilee cried. She hadn't for a minute thought of her things still stored in the back room with Hannah. Her mother's china, the fine crystal, and her clothing and household goods. "I must get all my things from that house before the wedding."

At the thought she rose with a rueful smile. "Do you know how much I dread going back into that house even for my things?"

"You needn't be in a hurry," Willum told her. "I would wait until I had the stomach for it. The banns must be cried in the chapel for three Sabbaths running before that pair can wed."

Marilee dropped back onto her stool and smiled up at Willum. "Three weeks," she said. "By that time Philip could be here and help me plan."

Chapter
Twenty-one

MARILEE had not seen Timothy since that day on the beach. Neither had she summoned the strength nor the courage to return to Abigail's house. After all, there was time.

The baby was eight days old on the night Willum came quietly to the room Marilee shared with Willie. Marilee wakened at once to his touch, thinking that Deborah must need her.

Instead, Willum whispering hoarsely, told her that there was someone there to see her. When she had hastily pulled on her dress without even unbraiding her hair, she found Willum by the hearth with Timothy Reeves. Although the room was dark except for the low flickering of the hearth flame, Willum did not suggest a candle.

Timothy rose as Marilee entered, a slender shadow beyond the light.

"Reeves, here, came with news," Willum

293

said tiredly. "It seemed best that you hear it from him."

"Forgive the hour," Timothy said from his place in the shadows. "I have no time during the workday. There has been a change of plans in the master's house."

Marilee waited, trying to read his expression without success.

"There will be no more waiting for the banns to be read," Willum blurted out. "The marriage is to take place at once."

"At once," Marilee echoed bleakly.

"Timothy, here, felt you would want to know."

Marilee nodded. "I thank you for that, Timothy," she said. "Then I must go at once and pack my possessions."

"And more than that," Willum said. "Timothy here has been up to some business that you should know of."

Timothy spoke quietly, almost as if he dreaded to hear Marilee's reaction to his words.

"Your brother had many friends," he told her. "They are still his friends, and yours. This has been a busy time with the marches and the crop to be put in and transplanted, but they have been working on your land."

Marilee stared at him with such astonishment that Willum leaned to touch her arm soothingly.

"Hear him out," he cautioned.

"Strong palisades have been built around the house there, and the house itself made larger and stronger." A note of pride came into his voice. "The chimney is of brick, and the hearth draws well even in wind."

"Timothy," Marilee breathed, "what can I say? I am overwhelmed."

"There is still the matter of servants to work the crop and tend the land," Willum reminded her. "And you cannot plan to live there until this trouble with the Indians is resolved and you have dependable companions to protect you. But you have money." Willum's voice rose. "With money you can buy the time of servants even as Matthew bought Timothy's time."

"I am truly overwhelmed," Marilee repeated. "I cannot thank you enough, Timothy."

Timothy's laugh was short and bitter. "Thank your brother's friends," he said. "I have had little time to give to this, given the way my mistress drives her men."

"Is there something I should do?" Marilee asked, wondering why this news had been brought to her at such a peculiar midnight hour.

"I only wanted to be sure that you knew what had been done," Timothy said. "As for your possessions, if you could have them packed into that cart I would bring them here after my day's work is through."

A moment of lame silence followed. Something was being left unsaid. But Timothy was moving toward the door with Willum following to fasten the latch behind him. Inside the door, Timothy paused and leaned to pat Briny, who had followed him.

"Timothy," Marilee said, feeling strangely helpless, "thank you again for all your kindnesses to me."

He rose and looked back across the room toward her. Even in the dark she imagined she could see that haunting color of his eyes.

"I do my master's bidding," he reminded her.

She waited until Willum came back and bent to cover the coals again for the night. More strangeness. Willum did not meet her eyes, and he moved in a jerky, awkward way, as if he were fighting his own anger.

"Tell me about all that," Marilee said.

"You heard the young man," Willum said shortly.

"Willum," Marilee cried, stepping toward him in appeal. "Indeed I heard him and am deeply grateful. Yet why do I think that you are angry at me? Have I done something?"

Willum slumped with the poker in his hand, staring at the covered coals. "No, lass. It was not what you did. It was what you did not do that worries me."

"Then what did I not do that I should have?" she asked.

He turned to look her full in the face. His expression was not so much angry as it was sick and defeated.

"You did not tell me that Timothy Reeves heard Michael Braden try to break his engagement to that Fordham woman. Timothy is not safe while that young man lives."

Marilee stared at him, remembering Michael on the beach shouting at Timothy. "I will have your life for this."

Willum's tone was that same one of tired patience that Maggie had so often used with Marilee. "You are too innocent by half," he said. "A man only trusts as long as he is trustworthy himself. Michael knows he could not keep such a secret if there was profit in telling it. He judges other men the same."

"But what can he do to Timothy?" Marilee asked, frightened as much by Willum's tone as by his words.

"He is a servant," he reminded her. "A servant belongs to his master for the length of his indenture. He cannot even testify against his master. And once that marriage is done, Braden is Timothy's master."

At least the sun could have shone that day. Instead, Marilee walked to her brother's house under a gray, curdled sky that pressed against the earth with moist heat. She delayed her trip until midmorning to give Abigail plenty of time to be up and dressed.

As she waited for an answer to her rap on the door, she looked at her once-lovely garden. A few hardy herbs had managed to survive among the rank and ugly weeds. In the door of the stable stood the cart that Timothy had put out.

She looked away from the cart quickly, remembering without wanting to, that ridiculous way Timothy had wheeled the cart after her and Michael Braden when they walked along the beach.

Hannah opened the door, only to step back and stare at her as if frightened. Then the maid turned away and called out, "It's her, mistress. She's come."

Abigail emerged from her room and walked toward Marilee with a taunting smile on her face. In spite of the hour she was not dressed but was wearing that blue wrapper that matched her eyes. Her hair had been done up in elaborate golden coils.

"It has taken you long enough to come to congratulate me," Abigail said. "How hard it must have been to admit that all your flirting didn't interest Michael Braden."

"I now congratulate you," Marilee said, determined to control her temper and get away from this place.

"How gracious!" Abigail sneered. "I see that your manners have not improved since I saw you." She paused. "Is that all you came for? That single grudging sentence?"

"I came to get my trunks," Marilee said.

"Aha. Then have you managed to snare a husband after all?"

Marilee shook her head. "No, I simply do not want to stay when you bring another man into my brother's house."

Abigail colored with anger. "Dead men have no houses," she said bluntly. "Go and get your things. I shall be glad to have my house rid of you and them."

Marilee was astonished that Hannah slipped into the small back room behind her and shut the door firmly. While Marilee lifted her things from the shelves and set them into her trunks, Hannah plucked at her sleeve and whispered in a fierce, harried tone.

"Take me with you," she pleaded. "Don't leave me at the mercy of that woman. I swear to you that my health has come back. Mercy on me, mistress." She spread her work reddened hands out for Marilee to see. "Look at me. I am a nurse and a maid, not a charwoman. Here I labor all day long, baking and scrubbing. You brought me here, don't desert me now."

Marilee turned to her. "*You* were the one who deserted *me*, Hannah. You lied and took sides against me. Stay with the mistress you chose."

Hannah let out a great wail, which brought a quick banging on the door.

"Stop that noise, Hannah," Abigail called. "What are you doing in there, anyway? Get out here and to your work."

As Hannah left, weeping, Marilee followed, dragging the first of her trunks.

"Be sure that you have nothing of mine in there," Abigail said.

More than anything Marilee was tempted to tell her that she had nothing that Marilee wanted. She held her tongue and got the trunks safely stacked on the cart.

As Marilee set off toward Deborah's she

could hear Abigail inside the house, still shouting at Hannah. The overcast sky had begun to deliver its threatened rain. A few raindrops splashed here and there, bringing a sudden scent of wet dust to the air.

"I never have to go back there again," Marilee realized as she picked up her pace. "I never ever in my whole life have to walk back into that place again." Until the voice spoke she didn't know that her happiness was spread across her face in a wide smile.

"How good to see joy on your lovely face," Michael Braden said, his own expression sad and wistful.

"I have reason for joy," Marilee told him, pulling her arm from his grasp. "And so should you. May I congratulate you on your almost instant marriage."

He flushed with color. "It was a special permission," he explained. "My debtor was not willing to wait. Listen, Marilee, it still need not be too late."

She lifted her hands and pulled her hood around her ears. "Don't insult my hearing with such talk, Michael Braden," she told him, "and please don't walk by my side for fear your jealous wife blame the wrong one of us."

At her words he glanced around nervously, as if in fear that Abigail could see them together.

Before he recovered his poise, she had turned down the street and left him.

* * *

In her absorption with Deborah's household and her distraction with her own concerns, Marilee had paid little attention to what was going on in the village.

By the time she reached Maggie's stable she realized that something was definitely afoot. The fort gate stood open, and along the street groups of women huddled, crying.

Maggie, looking fresher and prettier than Marilee ever remembered, came out to stand by Marilee's side.

"The men left on the march early today," she said. "It is always like this when the men go away."

In a moment Maggie spoke again, quietly. "Our friend the scribe was here this morning. Many of the men wanted testaments left, and he did the writing."

"He writes a beautiful hand." Marilee nodded, remembering.

"And you can read it?" Maggie asked.

Marilee looked at her. "It is wonderfully clear," she told Maggie.

Maggie flushed with that old anger. "Clear is nothing if you do not know what the lines mean," she said crossly. "If I were to show you some lines, could you read them to me?"

It was Marilee's turn to be embarrassed. Why did she always presume that because her father was a great believer in learning that all people had her advantages?

"I would be happy to read them to you," Marilee said humbly.

Maggie withdrew a folded piece of paper

from her apron pocket and handed it to Marilee. "Just give me the sense of it," she said. "That will be fine."

Marilee's eyes skimmed the page swiftly, and she drew a quick, deep breath. "You don't just want the sense of this, Maggie," she said gently. "Come and sit and listen to the words."

Maggie hesitated before plumping down on her milking stool to look up at Marilee.

Never had Marilee read such lovely words of praise. Without resorting to the common phrases of gallantry, the scribe had poured his love for Maggie out on this paper.

"I would have the sun of your smile in all my mornings," he wrote her. "Tell me only if I can dream that one day you will be my wife and all clouds will pass from my sky."

For the first few minutes Maggie had stared at Marilee as if she had been turned to stone. At these last words she leaped up and ran off into the stable, crying helplessly.

"Maggie, Maggie," Marilee called, running after her. "Why do you weep? Why does the love of a fine, gentle man make you cry?"

"He doesn't want me, really," Maggie stormed. "He'll despise me, see if he doesn't."

"For what reason?" Marilee asked. "You have heard his words of love. How can a man love and despise with the same breath?"

"I can't read," Maggie wailed. "How can I tell him that I had to have a friend read my own proposal to me? And if we should wed, how can I keep him from knowing that the scratch of a pen and the print of a chicken are all the same to me."

Marilee touched her shoulder gently. "I will make a wager with you," she said gently. "I will wager that he cares not a whit for whether you read or no. He cares for *you* and wants you as his wife."

Maggie stared at her from a tearstained face. "But how do I tell him this?"

Marilee frowned a minute and then giggled. "Do it all at once," she suggested. "Go to him with his own letter in your hand. Tell him that you cannot read or write but have an important message you want to understand."

"How will that help?" Maggie asked.

Marilee smiled at her. "If he loves you as I think he does, he will read this letter as I have read it to you except with much more feeling. If, on the other hand, he is put off by your lack of skill, he can change the words as he goes and think that you will never be the wiser."

Maggie stared at her a long minute before bursting into laughter. "I like you better as friend than I would as an enemy," she decided aloud. Then, with a fearful face, "If you should love a man and he could not read or write, would it matter to you?"

Marilee studied her a moment. Why did she remember Timothy Reeves standing to have a letter written to be sent back on the *Pryde of Gravesend?* "It wouldn't matter at all," she said after a moment.

Chapter Twenty-two

IT rained all the next day.

The long day finally dripped to an end and brought Willum home for dinner. He seemed quieter than usual, which Marilee credited to his having been soaked to the skin through a long day of work. The candles were lit early because of the darkness, and Marilee fought a growing restlessness that Timothy had not come with the cart. When at last there was a rattle outside and a rap on the door, she was on her feet in an instant with Willum right behind her.

Between the traces of the cart stood a thick-bodied man with fair hair and a wide, genial face.

"These are the trunks for Mistress Marilee," he told Willum. "Want a hand with them?"

"I would appreciate that," Willum told

him, lifting the first dripping trunk and setting it inside the door.

"Timothy Reeves," Marilee asked. "I thought that Timothy . . ."

The man's broad face lifted to hers as he shook his head. "You didn't know then?" he asked. "Reeves left with the marchers. Today at dawn it was. Out to look for Indians."

Marilee caught a deep, astonished breath and stepped back. Timothy among the marchers. She looked at Willum, but he would not meet her eyes. He had to know. That, then, had been why he had come in the middle of the night. That was why he needed her to know what was happening and what had been done.

The door was barely closed behind the servant before she challenged him. "Willum" was all it took to make him duck his head and avoid her eyes. "You knew, Willum," she cried. "You knew and you said nothing."

"Don't be hard on him," Deborah put in firmly. "He was bound by promises before he knew what promises he had made."

"Promises?" Marilee asked, already feeling bad about the hangdog look she had brought to Willum's face.

"Timothy, himself," he mumbled. "The lad gave me no choice. He came after dark," Willum reminded her. "You know yourself, it was near midnight. He came and asked me to make two promises on my honor as a man and a friend of Matthew Fordham's."

Marilee sighed. How could she fault Willum for doing what she knew he must do?

"The first of the promises was that I would do nothing to keep him from being taken on the march. He had learned that it was I who had him pulled from the first one on account of lameness."

"Then he wanted to go?" Marilee asked, incredulous.

Strangely, Willum did not meet her eyes.

"He made me pledge that I would not try to keep him from going," Willum replied. Then he went on swiftly, as if hoping she wouldn't notice the difference between Timothy wanting to go and having Willum pledge not to stop him. "Then he asked that he have a chance to see you, to talk to you about the work that has been done, so that you would know."

"In case he doesn't come back from the march," Marilee said bitterly.

This time Willum met her eyes. "No man goes on the open sea or into the deep woods without having his affairs in order," he reminded her. "Don't you think I left a testament willing all I owned to Debbie here before I marched out those gates? It is the same."

"Promises," Marilee remembered aloud. "What other promises?"

Willum shook his head. "The other promise will not tell itself like the marching did."

Marilee looked at him, suddenly feeling a little weak. How coud she bear knowing that

Timothy was out there in the danger that faced men in the wild during an Indian war? "I cannot bear it," she whispered to herself. "I cannot bear to have Timothy in danger."

For a moment there was silence in the room, then Deborah's bench scraped as she rose. "I made no promises," she said angrily. "I made no promises to Timothy or any man as I lay there in the dark listening around the corner. It was not that Timothy wanted to march. He simply wanted to live.

"Did you ask yourself why Willum lit no candle? Did you ask yourself why Timothy stood back in darkness that he not be seen? He has been beaten, beaten by whip within an inch of his life by Michael Braden's foreman with his mistress not raising a finger to save him."

Abigail's words came back to Marilee. "Timothy's time will come, wait and see." And Michael Braden's, "He has needed putting down for a long time."

"But he can't march against the Indians in that condition," Marilee wailed.

"He has marched," Willum told her. "He thinks that by his return, his time will be up and he could be free. It was his only chance."

"Summer," Marilee said. "His indenture was to be up in summer. Summer is well spent. What was the date of that release?"

Willum ducked his head again and sighed. "There seems to be some disagreement on that," he conceded. "When Timothy asked for the paper, his mistress took it from the strongbox and showed it to him."

"But, Willum," Marilee cried. "How does he know? He can look at a million papers and have them read to him by a million lying mouths. Timothy cannot read or write."

They both stared at her openmouthed. "You know that?" Willum challenged her.

She dropped her eyes. "I know he cannot write."

Later, as she lay stiff and sleepless in her bed, Deborah came to lay her hand on her shoulder. "You cannot carry the grief of every soul in your heart, Marilee," she said.

"Only Timothy," Marilee whispered, seizing her hand. "I only carry Timothy Reeves."

Abigail and Michael Braden were married with much feasting. Marilee did not attend the wedding; neither did Willum and Deborah Yarrow. But the gossips wore the air out talking of how beautiful Abigail had looked and how her handsome husband had worn silks the same color as Abigail's eyes.

A week passed before Maggie stopped Marilee with a furtive whisper and a glance along the street to see who might be listening.

"You won your wager," she said, smiling like a child.

"My wager," Marilee repeated. Too many thoughts had passed through her mind since that day for her to remember instantly.

"My Patrick swears he likes it better that I do not read or write," Maggie confided.

"He says it gives us something interesting to do on cold winter nights. He can teach me. And if I have no great skill for reading my Patrick says that will only give him someone to listen to him when he reads. He loves to read, you know, both read and write." The pride glowed in her face.

"When will we hear banns being cried?" Marilee asked.

"When it is settled between us where we will live."

"Didn't you say he had a tight house again?" Marilee asked.

Maggie flushed. "There you go, sounding the same as my Patrick. A tight house he does have, and good fields. But what is to become of my beasts who listen for my breath at night?"

Then quickly, as if to stop Marilee's protest, she added, "And don't go suggesting that I move them there, where they might be killed in one of those Indian raids. I'll not have that."

"What of her husband and herself being killed out there?" Deborah asked when Marilee reported the conversation.

"Is it possible that she is hiding behind her beasts to get him safely inside the fort?" Marilee asked with a laugh.

I would do the same, she admitted silently to herself. To keep Timothy safe I would claim bird or beast or whatever excuse fell to my tongue.

* * *

Word of the ambush was brought back to the fort during that last week in July. The marchers had been going through a narrow file with trees on either side. At the end of that stretch of road ran a swift river. They had forded the river with great difficulty. Many of the men had slipped and lost weapons or had their gunpowder dampened by the stream.

Once the marchers reached the far side of the river, the Indians had attacked in force. Many were wounded and died before the Indians were driven back.

The men had been buried where they fell.

Marilee listened to this with a heart heavy with horror. At night, with Willie snuffling across the room and Briny sighing in his sleep, she wept.

This, then, was what love was, not tenderness as with Philip, not enchantment as with Michael, but pain. He couldn't be dead, she told herself. But if he were, she wished to be the same. How could she face a world where no Timothy Reeves would come walking, those smoky eyes on hers.

The single and solitary thread of hope that ran through those days came from Maggie.

Being in love had made Maggie a talker. She was never so happy as when she talked of her husband-to-be.

"These are hard days for my love," she confided to Marilee. "He knew all those men, knew them as customers and friends."

"I don't understand," Marilee admitted. "How did that come about?"

"I am not alone in not having letters under my control," Maggie reminded her. "Before the march, they went to my Patrick and had their testaments written. They left their documents in his keeping with the addresses of their families back in England. Now, as the names come back to him, he has those sad letters to send by the next ship going home."

Marilee stared at her a long moment. If Timothy's name was in that number, she could not bear it. If it was not, she could only be teasing herself with false hope.

"Have we lost a friend?" she asked quietly, hoping that Maggie would understand.

Maggie frowned. "I don't know who your friends are," she said finally. "I do know how thankful I am that Timothy Reeves's name has not been listed among the dead yet."

Chapter
Twenty-three

As she had during her first days in Jamestown, Marilee began to leave the house as early as she could each morning to do the daily errands. The difference was that instead of leaving to escape an uncomfortable condition, she was unable to settle to a day until she had the latest word of the marchers from Maggie.

The names of the dead had continued to trickle in for days. Although Maggie was clearly curious about Marilee's avid interest in this news, she reported the list to Marilee as Patrick Hiller had recited it to her.

"If there is a particular person you have concern about, you should just come out and ask me," Maggie finally said in her old cross manner.

Marilee hesitated for a long moment, not trusting herself to speak Timothy's name. "My brother's servant," she finally said, fearful that even then her voice betrayed too much emotion.

"Timothy Reeves," Maggie cried. "Why didn't you say that in the first? Not only was he not among those felled, but the word came that his bravery was something for a man to see."

"There's more news," Maggie went on, watching Marilee's face. "They are said to be marching back ahead of schedule. They make slow progress because of the wounded and because they must take special precautions, being so few."

"When are they expected?" Marilee asked, unable to bear the sudden, high excitement of this news.

Maggie grinned. "Come now. I am neither witch nor seer. I only know what my Patrick tells me, and he says they have started back. Now, did you come for milk or only news?"

Marilee laughed. "Milk and news," she said. "And I thank you for both."

Full summer lay on the river, white-hot days that shimmered with light. Out of sight of the gate Marilee would loosen her bonnet to let the sun warm her glowing hair. Briny's great strength and Willie's young energy made a good match. They ran back and forth along the beach until Willie collapsed in a giggling heap at Marilee's feet. It was a game with them to see who could last the longest.

Marilee had a game of her own. It was not

so much a game as a daydream that she played in her mind. She had made up a dream, a foolish, romantic, waking dream. She knew it was not a dream that could ever come true, but just thinking it eased her loneliness.

She would be walking along the river with Briny at her side, and he would twist under her hand as he had that other time. She would turn and see Timothy Reeves watching. This time he would be smiling. He would walk to her in that light tread and take both of her hands. All their past differences would have been swept away like the flotsam carried by the swift river. He would tease again and laugh, like he had in those early days before they had both lost Matthew.

Lunch was over, and Marilee was wiping crumbs from the table when Willie, who had bolted his food to get back outside to play, burst in at the door.

"Marilee," he said in a breathless way. "There's a man for you just outside."

Marilee turned, smiling, only to feel herself grow suddenly weak. There in the sunshine on the stoop stood Philip Soames. For a minute she thought this must be another waking dream. She had been watching too closely for the coming of the *Pryde* to have missed its arrival. But there he was, his fine eyes smiling and his arms stretched out to her. Without even dropping the cloth in her hand she ran to him.

Only when she ran into his arms did Briny relax and begin to beat the air with his great tail.

"Philip," she cried, tight against him. "How can this be? Where did you come from?"

"Norfolk," he replied. "Once we were in port, I could not rest until I saw you. I came by the first small boat that I could find for hire. Oh, Marilee, you know my great grief for Matthew."

"I know," she whispered. "I know."

He turned and smiled at Marilee. "For a while I thought, having come so far, that I would never find you."

"You must have gone to Matthew's house," Marilee said.

He nodded, his face hardening. "Abigail seems little changed by her great loss. She took great pleasure in telling me that you had become a woman without prospects who had cast herself on the charity of friends. She was vague enough about who these friends were that I had to ask the milkmaid."

Deborah snorted. "I don't suppose that Abigail bothered to tell you that she is newly married."

He turned to stare at her. "Married? To whom?"

"No stranger to you, Philip. She is wed to Michael Braden."

He shook his head and sighed. "I should have guessed. But as much as it grieves me to see Matthew so soon forgotten, if ever a woman deserved Michael Braden, it is Abigail. And Michael deserves such a woman as she is."

There was such extraordinary pain in his face that Marilee leaned to lay her hand on his arm. "I know you are no friend to Michael Braden," she told him, "and neither am I."

"I am sure that Deborah has told you why I dislike that man so deeply."

"Indeed I have not," Deborah said tartly. "This Marilee of ours is a sister to Matthew in more than her fine looks. Being no gossip herself, I hold my tongue with both hands in her presence."

Philip looked at her with surprise and then laughed. "Good girl, Deborah. It is not so much a story as a tragedy anyway." He paused. "My Dulcie," he said gently.

My Dulcie. How astonishing it was to hear Philip Soames speak a woman's name with that same tenderness that Maggie spoke of "my Patrick."

"I have never heard that name," Marilee confessed.

He laid his hand over hers and stared blindly at the hearth. "Dulcie was on the ship with Abigail and Deborah and the others. She was not the most beautiful of those maidens but the gentlest." He shook his head distractedly. "I still cannot believe how quickly we fell in love. When our eyes first met across that room, we both laughed, knowing that we were destined for each other. We spent the whole of that passage making plans. I would give up the sea, the sea that I left the university for to satisfy my mother's wish. I would be a planter and she would be my wife. Then we were at Jamestown."

Marilee dropped her eyes, embarrassed that she could guess the rest of that story. She remembered her own reaction when she had first seen Michael Braden, smiling and making his way through the crowd toward the *Pryde of Gravesend*.

"Enter Michael Braden," she said dully.

"He put a spell on her," Deborah said hotly. "Mark my words, that is how it happened."

Philip nodded. "Deborah is right. Without a tear in her eye she told me that her promises made at the ship's rail were the stuff of idle dreams. Even the words she used were not phrases that would usually fall from her lips. She and Michael Braden were married before my ship left port, even as Matthew and Abigail were. By the time I returned she was dead of fever."

"Michael reported it as fever," Deborah corrected him. "What killed her was heartbreak and neglect. Left alone on that dreary plantation, heavy with child and treated unkindly, she simply did not love life enough to cling to it."

"Oh, Philip," Marilee said softly. "Is any life what we would ask it to be?"

He shook his head. "What did Abigail

mean when she said you were a woman without prospects?"

"She means that I will not marry a man simply to make him rich or to pay off his gambling debts. Until I am able to live on my own land, Deborah and Willum have taken me in."

Philip turned to her, his voice suddenly urgent. "The *Early Lark* got here before the Indians struck. Did you and Matthew get my letters?"

Instant tears filled Marilee's eyes. For a moment she could not even find her voice. "We did," she said finally. "Thank God we did, Philip, or I could not have borne what happened later."

He looked at her, confused, then went on. "Did he talk to you about what I reported in that letter?"

She couldn't meet his eyes. "He said your letter was interesting," she began.

"Whatever you said in that letter opened Matthew's eyes to what was happening in his own house," Deborah put in. "He died knowing that while his wife was not the angel she pretended to be, his sister indeed was."

Philip studied Marilee's face a long moment, then sighed. "But the other thing, my trip to your village. Did he tell you about that?"

Marilee shook her head. "Our village back home? Nothing."

"Ah," he said, "then I have great news for

you." He spread his hands on the table and smiled broadly.

"I carried two letters from here to your village, Marilee. You are missed there, sorely missed. Every villager asked for you and sent their prayers." He paused to smile. "What I did in your village is not over," Philip told her. "Matthew had decided that you might be slow to find a man you wished to marry. In any case, he knew you would need servants you could trust. Matthew wrote to the mayor of your village telling of this need and that you would pay for the transport of those villagers who wanted to come here under your care. The second letter was from Timothy Reeves to his own family, asking which of those men wished to be a part of your plantation and earn their land as he was earning his."

"And did that work?" Marilee asked. "Will any of those men come?"

"Four," Philip said proudly. "Four are with me on the *Pryde*, and finer men than these Virginia has never brought to her shores. One man, Edward, is a brother of Timothy Reeves, and the other three are cousins: John, Jeremy, and Chad Barker."

"Edward Reeves," Marilee cried, smiling. "What a jolly boy he always was."

Philip nodded. "And Chad Barker, whom you may not know since that family lived a good distance from your village, is a miller. The others are yeomen with all the skills of their station."

"Such a great bounty, Marilee. Even without a husband you will be safe with such men around you. Philip, you are a wonder," Deborah said.

"The wonder was Matthew," he corrected her. "I grieved for Marilee's condition, but he took steps to correct it."

Marilee rose. "Both of us have tasks to do, Philip," she told him. "Deborah must feed her child, and I must exercise Briny. How would you like a walk along the beach with us?"

Philip rose swiftly. "What a wonderful idea. We will see you later, then, Deborah."

There were sails in the distance, coming from Norfolk. "That will be the *Pryde*," Philip said thoughtfully. "It has occurred to me in these last minutes that perhaps you may not want to stay here and be a planter. There is still England, Marilee, and a man who would find deep joy in having you as his own."

"But, love, Philip?" she asked quietly.

"A kind of love," he said carefully.

She took his hand and lifted it to her lips. "I know that phrase. I have for you a kind of love that will not change or fade or be worn by the friction of time. But that would not be enough for either of us. We are both too romantic."

He smiled and drew her arm close against him. "How well you put it. The difference between us is that I will never love again, not like I did Dulcie, for all that I saw her weakness kill her. What about you, Marilee? I pray that you have no such hopeless love."

His words caught her off guard. Looking up at him, she began to weep helplessly. "Oh, but I do, Philip. I love a man who loathes me, who blames me for all the joylessness of his life."

"What kind of a man is this?" he asked.

"The finest of men," she whispered. "Timothy. Timothy Reeves."

Chapter
Twenty-four

As they talked, the *Pryde of Gravesend*, riding with the tide and favored by a steady wind, had moved upriver. Now she was abreast of them, her sails being trimmed to drop anchor at Jamestown. From the dock upstream the gathering crowd already had begun to shout at the passengers and crew aboard the ship.

Marilee, with Philip's hands tight on her arms, fought helpless tears.

"Then he is mad," Philip said firmly. "If he does not love you for the likeness you bear to Matthew, if he does not love you for your own joy and strength, then he is a man whose mind has fled."

"No," she insisted, explaining how Matthew had tried to protect her and, in the act, earned Timothy's hatred for her.

"Sad," Philip said. "That is so sad. I know

how deep a love your brother bore this young man. I wondered at his devotion until I met the young man myself and discovered how great a soul hides behind those strange, laughing eyes. Where is he now? Prospering as a planter?"

She shook her head. "He is supposed to be returning from a march against the Indians."

Philip stared at her. "What does that mean?"

"It is the governor's plan," she explained. "Since the massacre, he has sent groups of marchers out to drive the Indians from the area where Englishmen are living. Every man must go one time or another or send a man in his place. Timothy Reeves was sent by Abigail Fordham. She tried to send him before, when he was still lame from an injury, but Willum Yarrow got his name pulled out."

"I wonder that he is not a free man to go for himself by now," Philip said thoughtfully.

"I wondered the same, but his mistress claims his time was not yet at an end."

"It is strange that his brother was so sure that he was now free," Philip mused.

"In any case, he is gone, and I have word that he survived an ambush with great courage. Now I only pray that he is not among those wounded who are slowing the return of the group."

"This will be hard news to break to the

men aboard the *Pryde*," he told her. "They have counted the waves in their eagerness to rejoin Timothy."

She smiled ruefully. She had no waves to count but certainly had done the same with days. Calling Briny to her side, Marilee looked up the beach. "You need to be there, Philip," she said. "They are letting down the boats."

"You need to be there, too, my dear," he reminded her. "You will want to greet the men who will be your stout right arms in the days to come."

It was Edward she saw first; Edward, who was Timothy's older brother and as fair as Timothy was dark. He grinned like a boy at the sight of her and nudged his companions roughly.

"The heavy man on the left is Chad," Philip told her. "John is the taller of the other two, and there's Jeremy."

"Where shall I put them?" she asked in sudden panic. "What will I do?"

"Did you tell me there was a house on your land now?"

She nodded. "I have not seen it since it was rebuilt, but Timothy claims it is firm and strong."

He nodded comfortably. "There is only the matter of the night, then. We will find pallets for them." He laughed. "Farmers who have been this long at sea would sleep on a stone if it had earth beneath it."

Once the boat was ashore, Marilee felt as if she stood inside a forest of men. Their greetings were shy but eager, and Edward asked at once for his brother Timothy.

Bless Philip. He repeated Marilee's report as she had given it to him. Edward's face darkened as he listened, assuming that heaviness of anger that she had seen so often on Timothy's face.

"There is something wrong," he said at once. "Say what you will, his time is past. By now he should have his land and money and be all for himself."

"But are you sure, Edward?" Philip asked.

"I am sure," the young man said angrily. "I know the date like my own because it *was* my own. His service began on my birthday many years ago."

Marilee turned to Philip. "Then he was sent out only two days before his indenture was up. Abigail owes him money over and above the fact that she risked his life without any right to do so."

Philip nodded. "Let's be calm for now and find these friends a place to sleep tonight."

Marilee laughed. "I have filled the Yarrow house to its seams, but wait." She paused. "I have a friend with a warm stable floor. For a night, would that do?"

Edward grinned at her. "A cold stable loft would do, the hard earth outside the stall would do, a rock by the roadside. We are in Virginia, men, and a new life." His laughter came so like Timothy's that she had to turn away to hide her tears.

Willum Yarrow, having returned from his land to find the ship in port, came to Marilee's side. He gave a Virginian's welcome to each of the men and teased Marilee. "You thought yourself put upon by men courting you to wed," he reminded her. "Three planters have stopped me on the way to ask if you would sell the indenture of even one of these men."

The way their faces fell brought a whoop of laughter from Philip. Before he could speak, Marilee answered for herself. "Tell all who ask that these are friends of Matthew Fordham's and mine. None among them is for sale."

Willum's welcome carried them along the village street to his own house. Philip had them followed with a lad from the ship with food and drink.

Only when they had eaten and leaned back did Edward again bring up the subject of Timothy's absence.

"There seems little justice that a man is sent to march when the people who send him know that he will be a free man before the march ends. In our village we would have a place to complain about such treatment."

Philip nodded. "And so do we here. If Timothy is not at once repaid for his service and freed on his return with extra for this marching, I will take it to the governor. As you heard from Willum's report there is a great shortage in Virginia of good workers. The governor knows that such men must be protected."

"And what if the ship must leave before the marchers return?" Edward asked.

Philip frowned. "I will ask an audience with the governor before I go, to be sure that he knows about this offense."

Willie was too tired even to snuffle in his sleep by the time the men were bedded in Maggie's stable. Although Marilee was no less exhausted, she sat a long time with her arms around her knees, staring into the darkness. What great changes had come in one day. Not even the sight of Michael Braden with Abigail on his arm had been able to lower her spirits . Only Timothy haunted her. How he would have loved greeting his kinsmen at the edge of the river. How he would have joined in their stories around Willum's table. Why did it have to hurt so much to love him as she did?

Marilee had traveled upriver to her land in the winter. Philip had been at her side then, as he was now. She shut her eyes tight to press back her tears. Matthew had been along, too, with Timothy's fine, strong arms pulling at the oars. Now the woods that had been barren were rich with summer green. Nut trees hung with a promised harvest, and wild fruit glistened in the brush.

Edward Reeves, behind her in the boat, fell speechless at the richness of this country.

His cousins could not point out enough things that were rare and wonderful.

"There is a fortune in wood alone," Jeremy said, awed. "Poplar and walnut, cedar and ash."

Timothy had been too modest about the house. It was large enough for a young family and tight against the wind and rain. He had not mentioned that a garden had been set and fenced against the rooting of the hogs.

When they had looked their fill, entered the house, and set a fire in the hearth to freshen the air of the room, Philip looked around at these men.

"When we contracted to come to this place, we all thought we would have Matthew Fordham's counsel. Lacking that, we would have Timothy's guidance. Neither man is here. How do we deal with this?"

There was much scraping of feet on the floor and glances back and forth. The eyes stopped at Edward's face.

He cleared his throat and reddened at the speech he was forced to make. "We have been kinsmen and friends for all our years. Now we are together in this new land. If the body must have a head, let it be by the drawing of straws until Timothy comes."

Given the choice of staying the night or having more supplies brought in the next day, all four men chose to stay. "There is enough to eat and drink to last a day or two, anyway," Edward pointed out. "For myself

I am ready to see the next building go up so that our mistress will have this house for her own comfort. The sooner my hands are on a tool, the better I'll know myself."

Returning down to Jamestown on the tide, Philip chided Marilee for her silence.

"I am overwhelmed," she admitted. "Suddenly I can see a life for myself, a life rich with work and good friends and laughter."

"They are good men. I'll miss them on the passage home. But alone, Marilee? You are too young and beautiful, too much a woman to face even so rich a life alone."

She met his eyes with hers. "I hope I am also too wise to make bad compromises."

The next few days should have gone on wings. Marilee was busy enough, buying and assembling the supplies and tools that were rowed upstream to her men. True to his promise, Philip sought and received an audience with the governor, telling him of Timothy's plight and the poor example it offered for Englishmen who might take their lives in their hands and sell their labor to become Virginians. Abigail Fordham Braden, as contractor of Timothy Reeves, was called to explain this act to the governor himself. Philip returned from that meeting blazing with fury.

"I should have known," he cried. "I forget that governors, too, are mortal men in a far country with few handsome women." He paced Deborah's kitchen in swift, angry steps, turning on Marilee. "You can imagine it. You probably saw enough of these shows to imagine every cunning trick. She dimpled and wept and drew deep breaths that put a strain on the bodice of her well-cut gown. She melted him like a candle in the noonday sun."

"But what did she say? How did she explain what she did?"

"She didn't explain, she offered excuses. I thought I heard the fine hand of that devious Michael Braden behind her words. She told of still being a little giddy from the loss of her husband. She pleaded that she was poor at counting, being a simple woman of domestic taste."

"Domestic taste," Deborah exploded. "She only accepted Matthew's proposal on the condition that she never be required to do menial tasks of any kind, such as baking or wiping a pan. Briny is more domestic than she. At least he can be depended on to lick a plate clean."

Philip sighed and slumped down on the bench beside Marilee. "Well, in the end she was admonished and told not to make such an error again and let off scot-free."

"But what of Timothy?" Marilee wailed.

"Timothy has neither dimples nor a fetching cleavage," Deborah said crossly. Then she added, "I almost forgot. Maggie was here. She had made the cheese you asked for and has it ready to send to the plantation by boat tomorrow."

Philip rose and offered his hand to Marilee. "I could use a stretch in the night air to cool my temper. Shall we get the cheese now and have it ready to send with the other things? I'd like a chance to thank her again for her kindness to our men, anyway."

Briny whined to be taken along, but Marilee shut the door against him. "He terrifies Maggie's cows," she explained.

The stable was quiet, with the cattle on their knees drowsing. "I think our friend has company," Marilee whispered, hearing the muffled sound of voices from the room over the stable.

Philip held up his hand and frowned. Then he turned to Marilee with pure delight on his face. "Upon my word, Marilee, someone is reading from *A Midsummer Night's Dream*."

"That will be Patrick Hiller," she told him.

"Hiller," he repeated. "From where do I know that name?"

"He is a planter who adds to his income by serving as a scribe."

"Of course," Philip nodded. "His name was on the letter Timothy Reeves wrote to the men of his family."

After a mutual nod of agreement Philip rapped at the door. Maggie came down the stairs carrying a candle. The warm light gave her complexion a becoming rosy tint and lit the pale halo of her loose hair. Patrick stood protectively watching her from the landing above.

"We came for the cheese," Marilee told

her, "but my friend Philip Soames would like to meet Patrick Hiller."

"I heard you reading," Philip called up in explanation. "How well you do it!"

Patrick, flushing with pleasure, started down the stairs, only to have Maggie shake her head. "Come up, both of you. We would enjoy your company."

An hour passed in lively talk between the men on the subject of their favorite reading.

"The *Pryde* must be leaving very soon," Patrick said. "I have been busy writing letters that will go with her."

"Too soon, I fear," Philip said, his face hardening in anger again. "I have not done all that I wished to for our friend Timothy Reeves, and the time grows short."

"Another friend of Timothy's," Maggie said, smiling at Patrick. "That lad has many good friends."

"And at least one clever enemy," Philip grumbled.

Marilee did not interrupt his telling of that whole sad scene of Abigail and the governor. It seemed to make him feel better to get his anger out in words.

"At least she proved she had his indenture," Patrick said.

"She proved nothing. She came without so much as a piece of paper," Philip said. "It was all her charm against my charges."

"People have been known to impose on servants whose memories are poor and who can't read," Patrick said quietly.

"I can believe that, seeing what I saw to-day." He rose and smiled at Marilee. "I must be taking this lady and the cheese home before Willum sends the dog after us."

It seemed to Marilee that Patrick said good night with a very distracted air.

The urgent rap on the Yarrow door surprised the family at breakfast.

"Philip," Marilee cried, rising, "is the boat leaving so soon?" Her mouth dropped to see Patrick Hiller at Philip's side.

"Never mind the boat," he said, entering with barely a nod at his host. He was almost dragging Patrick behind him, the scribe flushing with embarrassment and hanging back a little at this rude entry.

"We have them," he told Willum in an excited rush of words. "We have them cold and hot and in between. We have them by land and sea and air. Let her flirt her way out of this one."

"Philip," Marilee wailed, "tell us what you are talking about."

"Timothy," Philip said. "Timothy Reeves and that widow of Matthew Fordham's." He seized Patrick's arm with such force that the man wavered a little as he stood.

"Tell them. Tell them, Patrick, what has come about."

Patrick Hiller, with a wary eye on Philip, told his story. "It bothered me that my friend here said no copy of the indenture was shown to the governor. Back home I got out the papers that Reeves left with me." He flushed. "They were marked and sealed to be opened if he didn't come back." He glanced up defensively. "Well, he's not back, is he?"

At Deborah's confused shake of the head he nodded a couple of times. "That being the case, I opened them."

He fanned the papers out on the table in front of him. "Now, the first is a will leaving all his land and payment at end of service to his brother Edward in England. That soiled paper there is his baptism sheet from the church at home. The one with the seal is his indenture paper, signed by Matthew Fordham."

Willum reached for it, only to have Patrick nod. "Never mind, it is as she said. Timothy was a free man two days after he left on the march. That last paper is the one that set me on my horse riding to see Mr. Soames here, when the dawn finally came."

"Read it," Philip prodded. "Read it to them."

Patrick Hiller cleared his throat and held the paper well away from his eyes. His voice took on a deep and legal tone.

Hearing the words, Marilee felt a chill raise her flesh. Never had stiff and careful phrases such as those brought such a thrill of happiness to every inch of her body.

"I, Matthew Fordham, being sound of body and mind and in full control of my faculties, do make this signed and sealed declaration of intent. If I should die or be

334

lost at sea or disappear from the world of men and not be found, my valued friend and indentured servant, Timothy Reeves, is declared free of his indenture at that moment. He is to be given his rightful release money and tools with my blessings. No service or penalty shall be exacted of him by my heirs or assigns. This before God and these sworn witnesses."

Even Willum's face flowed with tears.

"Oh, Matthew, Matthew," Marilee whispered, almost to herself.

"Wait," Philip cried, "you haven't looked at the signatures. See who signed as witnesses."

Deborah leaned to look at the names. Marilee saw them at the same time and groped for the edge of the table. The first name she had never seen before, a man's name in a bold scrawl. The second name drawn in a feathery script she knew well was Abigail Fordham's.

Marilee, along with Philip and Patrick, had waited a long time in the governor's outer chamber before a portly man came out of the governor's office and approached them. Philip rose, smiling. The man shook his head.

"Mr. Soames, the governor asks me to remind you that he spared time for you in the case of Mrs. Matthew Fordham only yesterday. In view of other urgent problems waiting his decision, he regrets that he cannot see you."

335

Marilee, without thinking, was on her feet. "Oh, but, sir, that was not Mrs. Matthew Fordham but his widow. She is now Mrs. Michael Braden."

"Braden?" the man asked, his voice rising a little.

"Miss Fordham is correct," Philip put in swiftly. "I would ask you to submit our plea again. And, sir, it is not Mr. Soames but Officer Soames of the *Pryde of Gravesend.*" He flushed as he added, "The grandson of Admiral Soames of Her Majesty Queen Elizabeth's fleet."

The man stared at Philip, then at Marilee, before turning and hastening back into the governor's private room.

"Philip," Marilee breathed, staring at him in disbelief.

He shrugged. "I have never done that before in my life," he confessed. "I didn't even mean to do it then. I was just so afraid that we wouldn't get justice for Timothy."

"It is nothing to be ashamed of," Patrick Hiller said in a tone of awe.

Philip shook his head. "It's not that I'm ashamed. It is just that I am not a seafaring man by nature. I was a second son and a scholar. When my brother was lost at sea with my father, I had no choice. There has been a seafaring man in our family for five generations." Then he winked at Marilee. "Maybe today I get my money's worth."

The courier sent by the governor to bring

Abigail Braden had to wait for her to dress. Hannah's hands must have trembled during the arrangement of those gleaming coils of hair. Abigail either lacked the luster that usually distinguished her grooming, or the governor was, as Philip said later, also normal enough not to like having been made a fool of.

In the crowded Yarrow kitchen they all toasted the heavy monetary penalties levied against the Bradens. They toasted the fact that Abigail Braden would have to apologize to Timothy Reeves in church before her neighbors. They toasted Philip's cleverness in bringing up his grandfather and Marilee's mention of Abigail's proper name.

Chapter
Twenty-five

MARILEE had been hearing but not really listening. She had heard the growing sense of urgency behind Philip's attempts to provide her servants with all the supplies and tools they needed to get her plantation into operation. She had heard Patrick Hiller report on the number of letters he had written to be carried to England on the *Pryde*. She had not faced the fact that Philip's ship could possibly sail before the marchers returned, Timothy Reeves among them.

The day came, but the marchers did not. They had been reported within a day's march but moving slowly. Nothing altered the change in the tide of the James River. The *Pryde of Gravesend* readied to sail.

Philip himself suggested that they part on the beach so that she could wave him good-bye as long as his sails were in view. This was the reason he gave for asking her to go there.

She knew that he wanted to spare her the public show of her grief at their parting.

She clung to him in love and gratitude as he whispered, "I never say good-bye, you know that. But God's blessing on you and your Timothy."

She shook her head, protesting. "I have told you a thousand times, Philip, the man despises me."

Philip laughed softly and touched her cheek with his hand. "And I have told you that if he is such a madman as that, he is not the Timothy Reeves that your brother loved." Then he leaned and pressed his lips to hers. "God willing, I will spend Christmas at your hearth, Marilee."

With Briny at her side, she watched from the beach as the *Pryde of Gravesend* moved with the outgoing tide down the James toward the sea. As the ship passed that stretch of beach where she waited, she could see Philip clearly, his wide and loving smile, the intense darkness of his eyes. He dwindled to a spot of color on a toy ship. Finally even the white of the sails passed from view, and there was only that fused line where the blue sky met the moving darkness that was the face of the river.

Twice Philip had asked her to marry him, and twice she had sent him away. This time he had held his life out to her as a port against the storm. She couldn't argue the logic of his words. She still had no protector in the colony and had moved from being, as

Abigail had so tactlessly put it, "dependent on the charity of friends," to being dependent on the health and goodness of her servants. Her future depended on so many factors beyond her control. If her house could be finished by the onset of winter. If the men from the village thrived there and made a success of her plantation. If the trouble with Indians was brought under control so she dared live so far from the palisades of the fort. If. If. *If.*

One thing alone had not changed. When she had come here from England, there had been nothing there to return to. Here she had at least had the unfinished business of Timothy Reeves. While Philip had done much toward undoing the harm that Abigail and Michael had caused him, she could not leave Virginia until she saw him settled into the life he had paid so dearly to achieve.

"This could be another starving winter, you know," Philip had warned her. "There is little Indian corn to buy, and your own crops have been burned. Fields that should have been used to grow food have been set in tobacco. The ships that should have brought provisions have carried only fancy clothes for the newly rich planters, and liquor to make them poor again."

"There is more than one kind of hunger," she reminded him, hoping he would understand.

He did. He pressed her hand and touched his lips briefly to her cheek. "Either Timothy

Reeves is a fool or you are no reader of men," he told her.

Briny, restless at Marilee's inactivity as she stared at that line of sky where the ship had been, whimpered and tugged at the leash. She sighed and took up her basket. The sour red plums that grew in the woods beside the beach were turning red. She had promised a basket to Deborah to make the thick tart conserve that Willum liked with his meat. With Briny snuffling at her side, she walked from bush to bush, selecting the ripest ones for her basket.

There so close to the ground, she not only heard the blast of the cannon, she also felt it tremble through the soles of her slippers. She sat back, fighting sudden tears. Now, at least, she would know. When the word had come down the river that the marchers were so near the fort, Philip threw a great fit.

"One day," he fumed. "One more day and I would be able to watch for myself as Timothy Reeves taste the sweet nectar of revenge."

Willum had said nothing. His eyes were everywhere but on Marilee's face. "Timothy will be with the marchers, won't he?" she had asked him.

"Like as not," he had replied. "Like as not."

At least an hour had passed before the red plums were level with the top of Deborah's basket. Walking back to the beach, she set the basket down, released Briny from his leash, and said, "Now run, my patient friend."

The dog went wild with excitement, dancing around her while she chose the stick, backing up with his eyes intent on it as she drew it back to throw for him. She laughed merrily as he raced after the stick.

The winning of Briny might well have been, as it had turned out, a piece of bad luck for Michael Braden. But Marilee was sure that the wolfhound had brought her only good fortune. At seven months he was still not full-grown but stood a full thirty inches at the shoulder and weighed well over a hundred pounds. His long, narrow head and strong teeth were enough to make any man hesitate to approach him. His dark, intelligent eyes showed spirit to match the strength of his great, sturdy body.

During these last days even Willum, who had shared Matthew's fears for her safety, did not complain when she went about by herself. "With that dog at your side you have a personal army," he told her.

"Here, love," Marilee called to Briny. "I will find you a better stick."

Although he pricked his ears at her words, he stood stiff, those strong front legs braced as he stared past her. Then, unlike his usually protective manner, he ducked his head briefly and began to wag that golden plume of a tail. He whimpered softly, making the same gentle sound that he made when he greeted Willie.

"Briny," she called, half-afraid to turn without him firmly under her hand. The dog padded to her silently, bracing his shoulder against her leg as he whined up at her beseechingly.

Only then did she turn and see Timothy Reeves.

Timothy's garments were streaked with the dust of miles. His face was darkened by the sun, throwing the slender line of his scar into high relief. Dark curls hung long on his neck, and his smoky eyes held hers across that distance. The thinness that had looked to be weakness when he left had turned to solid wire. There was no sign of a smile on his face. He only looked at her, not seeming to breathe.

"Mistress Marilee," he said quietly, "I am back to do my master's bidding."

She wanted to speak to him but could not find her voice. She wanted to approach him, but the sudden weakness of her knees made her afraid to try even that first step. She reached out to him instead, with both hands, whispering, "Timothy."

Briny took the word as a signal. He leaped forward and threw himself against his old friend, whimpering with delight. "Stay there, lad," Timothy said laughing. "You will have me down at this rate."

He crossed the space between them swiftly and caught her hands in his. Only then did he smile. Marilee couldn't remember such a smile on his face since that Good Friday when both of them had lost so much.

"You are here, then," he said with relief. "Still here."

His words confused her. "Where did you think you would find me?"

"I feared I might not," he admitted. "When we were a day out, we met hunters who had news of the fort." He paused and shook his head. "I asked for news of Mistress Fordham. He told me there was no Mistress Fordham in this place anymore. He said that the pale one was now Mrs. Braden, and if he be not mistaken, the other one was now Mrs. Soames."

"Soames," she echoed in amazement. "How did he come by that?"

He shrugged. "He told of how you had spent every hour with Soames as long as the *Pryde* stood in port. He said there was much talk of you and Soames closeted with the governor on some mysterious private business. He told of your traveling up to your plantation with him, not once but over and over, of solid men you had placed there for its management."

His eyes searched her face as if asking that all this be denied.

How wonderful that he had not been told that his brother and cousins were those "solid men." How happy he would be to learn all that had happened in his absence. "All that is true," she began, "but —"

"But there was more," he went on, still

gripping her hands hard. "Then I was in the streets of the town with the cannon being fired and every man having a friend to greet him. I dared not to go to Mrs. Braden's house for fear I might be held there and not get to see you. I went to Willum Yarrow's but the house was empty with them off somewhere. I asked everyone. Every answer came the same. That you had not been seen since the sailing of the *Pryde*."

"Oh, Timothy," she said softly, "I am sorry."

He shook his head. "Sorry is too small and weak a word for what I felt. You see, all through that march I was getting my words ready. We had gone so far, were away so long." Then he smiled, that wide smile lighting his face while his eyes shone. "Sorry doesn't handle how my heart might have died if you had gone."

He shook his head as if to shake off memories. "When the rain turned the path to mud under my feet and the sun baked me red with flame, I marched on for only one thing. I had words to say, Mistress Marilee. I had words to say to you, and knew I could not rest until they were spoken. I could not even die without those words said, they were that important to me."

"Timothy," she said softly, "the important thing is that now you are home and all will go well."

"Not enough," he said. "The words have to be taken back, the wicked, evil words I spoke to you ... words of blame. I blamed you for Matthew's death. I blamed you that you kept me from death. Then, when death came for me, anyway, I blamed you for healing the wound that would have killed me. Most of all I blamed you for things you could not control, for the fact that Michael Braden was smitten with love for you and fawned over you like a sick whelp."

"That's over, Timothy," she told him, unable to bear the pain that his words brought him. "It's all over."

"Not the worst of it," he said dully. Then, releasing her hands, he turned and took a few steps away so that she could not see his face. That lean, strong back slumped with discouragement. "But I must say the words that are burned into my mind. In all these things you were blameless. I struck at you with hate because I was in such pain myself."

"Please don't do this to yourself, Timothy," she begged. "I understand. I really do." In a couple of steps she caught up with him and laid her hand on his arm.

At her touch he whirled, the old darkness back on his face, and his tone was angry.

"You think you understand, do you? Oh, Mistress Marilee, how far you fail of understanding. Didn't you see the old light flame up afresh when you first put your small foot on this shore? Didn't you know that I had loved you since you were a laughing child at Matthew's side? How I cherished you, your wonderful fears, your playful games, the sight of you dancing more like the thistle spun by the wind than a human creature. The one hard thing in coming here with my master was that I left you there. But I am like a coin pressed the same on both sides. They both spell love for Fordham. One side was Matthew, the other you. Now tell me that you understood that."

"Timothy, Timothy," she whispered as he tried to pull his arm from her grasp.

"There," he said roughly, "I have said the words. Now I will be gone."

"Wait, Timothy," she begged, seizing his arm again.

"Mistress," he said urgently, "let me go, or what happens will be no fault of mine."

When she did not release him at once, he whirled and caught her by the shoulders, holding her painfully tight for a long moment. Then he lifted her chin with his finger. "No fault of mine," he whispered, and bent to place his lips on hers.

Never had she felt such warmth. It was as if all the pain and fear and terror was wiped away by that warm, urgent pressure on her lips. She clung to him, not ever wanting him to go away.

In the end he loosened her hands and turned away with a sigh. "There, it is out. The words are spoken. If you never say my name again or meet my eyes, I shall have earned it."

"Timothy," she whispered, "would you be a Michael Braden? Would you pledge a wo-

347

man your love as he did Abigail and then turn and change your favor?"

He whirled on her in anger, only to see the teasing smile on her mouth.

"Never call a man such a name unless you want to fight him," he warned, easing into a smile himself.

"Well, I do want to fight you," she told him. "I will fight you if you try to leave me, and I will fight as I fought for your life in the chapel and for fairness to you in the chambers of the governor."

He frowned, studying her.

"What is this?" he asked. "I don't understand you."

"Timothy," she said, "when was your indenture up?"

He flushed with sudden anger. "There be some difference on that between the mistress and me. I had remembered it as summer, but she swore I was still hers when she sent me on the march." He flushed that deep color again. "Not being a reading man, I had no way to prove her wrong."

"Do you remember another paper that Matthew gave you, that you left with the scribe Patrick Hiller?"

He frowned. "A long time ago that was, right after he was married."

She nodded. "That paper gave you your freedom in the event of Matthew's death. Since she herself signed it, she knew she had no right to your service. That was why Philip and I were at the governor's." She smiled. "She is in debt to you for all that time you should have been a free man."

Those smoky eyes studied her intently. "And now I am to be free?"

"You *are* free," she told him again. Then, forgetting his warning, she seized his arms. "This is all true, Timothy. You are a free man, and Michael and Abigail Braden must pay you damages for the freedom they took from you, for the labor you did for them, and for the marching you did in Michael Braden's place."

He shook his head. "Free," he repeated. "With pay besides. All this from the papers I left with the scribe?"

She watched the idea of freedom unfold in his glorious face. She saw the swelling of his chest and the way he seemed to grow a full inch taller even as he stood there. Then, as quickly as this transformation came, he grew sad again and turned away.

"No man could fail to rejoice at such news," he said dully.

"Then rejoice," she ordered. "You have your freedom, your land, some money." When he still stood listlessly, she went on. "You could even have a wife if you had sense enough to propose to her."

She had finished the sentence in the same tone in which she had begun it. Her words registered slowly. Then he turned.

"I am a servant," he told her. "You are a lady."

She shook her head. "We are both Virginians."

He stared a long minute at the ground. "What would my master say?" he asked. "If I should dare think of such a thing, what would our Matthew say?"

Marilee sighed. It seemed to be her destiny to have to propose to every man twice. She shrugged. Well, in the case of Timothy she would do it a hundred times if that was what it took.

"Matthew would say something very original, like 'Blessings on you both.' "

He raised his eyes to hers, and the smile came slowly. "Blessings on you both," he repeated, taking her into his arms. Then, carefully, he said, "Marilee, love of my whole life, will you be my wife that I may love and protect you forever?"

"Yes, yes, yes," she whispered until his lips closed on her own.

There against him she realized how much more there was to tell him. He must be told that the house stood ready and that a second dwelling for his brother and his cousins was already half-raised. Most joyful of all, he must be told that these kinsmen whom he cherished waited for him only a brief boat ride away. She curled closer, smelling the sun on his cheek against hers. There was time for all those words later. For now, the warmth of his embrace was too wonderful to leave.

This then, was love, not magic, not concerned caring, but finding yourself in someone's arms so comfortable that it was almost as if you had been born to end up there.

* * *

An exciting excerpt from the first chapter of LAURA follows.

LAURA

by Vivian Schurfranz

Chapter One

LAURA Mitchell gazed out the classroom window at the snow-laden branches and the spirals of gray smoke that drifted upward from the brick chimney across the roof and into the bright blue sky. A few wet snowflakes gently descended on the iron fire escape. Laura's thoughts strayed from Mr. Blair's droning lecture to Joe Menotti, darling Joe, the love of her life. To think he didn't even know she was alive! How she yearned for him to see her as a mature young woman instead of a freckle-faced child. After all, on March 10, 1918, she would be sixteen, and next fall a senior at Jefferson High.

With a pang she wondered if the war would still be raging and if Joe would be drafted and sent overseas. She knew that his enrollment in medical school would help, but more and more young men were being sent overseas to fight the Germans. The war, which had been going on for four years, surely couldn't last much longer.

Suddenly Joe's handsome image danced across the frosty windowpane. In the lacy pattern she could trace his dark head and his finely chiseled profile with the strong chin and straight nose. Gradually her own face materialized. All at once his head moved down to touch her lips. As she visualized his sparkling dark eyes and his slow grin, she smiled, and delight swept over her. Yes, she *knew* she was a woman, but now she had to convince Joe of that fact!

Well, she had Friday night at the movies to look forward to. Every Friday night since she had been nine, and Joe thirteen, he had faithfully taken her to the movies. One of these Friday nights he would see her in a new light. After all, she was beginning to notice that a transformation was taking place in her. Only last night she had stood before the mirror and examined her changing features. She was growing up! Her big green eyes had taken on a deep, rich emerald glow, especially when contrasted with her shining brown hair surrounding her pure oval face. Her figure, too, she realized, was maturing.

Her mother, a pillar of the war effort,

would have thought Laura frivolous. She would no doubt have laid stronger guidelines for Laura to follow, so her excess energy would have a more proper focus. It seemed that Laura, rather than her older sister, Sarah, received the brunt of the new guidelines and ground rules in the Mitchell household.

Laura's thoughts returned to her new look and the way it could help her gain Joe's attention. She promised herself that at one of these Friday night movies he would see a new Laura Mitchell. She tucked an unruly curl into the depths of her abundant hair, pondering how she could accomplish this mission without appearing like a flirt. Quietly she tapped her pen against the inkwell. There must be some sort of solution to this problem.

"Laura?"

"Y-yes?" she stammered, pulling her thoughts back into the chalky classroom atmosphere.

"We'd like an answer," said Mr. Blair, her history instructor. He was a young man in his thirties. With arched eyebrows he now waited, holding the map pointer against his left leg, much as a Prussian general might hold his swagger stick. His ice-blue eyes bore into hers.

"I-I'm sorry, but I didn't hear the question." Laura felt the warmth creep into her cheeks. No matter what she had done this semester, she had never been able to please Mr. Blair.

"Of course you didn't," he said softly. "You've been daydreaming again. I asked you to describe Pickett's Charge for the Confederacy." His smile was smug, certain she wouldn't be able to answer.

Just last night, however, Laura had read about the charge of the South as they tried to break the Union line at Gettysburg. She vividly recalled every detail as she cleared her throat and began to recite, accurately. She ended her response with a sweet smile at her teacher.

Running his fingers up and down his watch chain, which dangled between two vest pockets, Mr. Blair observed her for a moment. Reluctantly he nodded and muttered, "Not bad for a girl."

Laura supposed she should have been pleased at his backhanded compliment, but she only flushed angrily. Why was he always surprised that a girl could grasp history as well as any boy? Seething, she watched as he turned and drew a map of the battlefield on the blackboard, showing the various positions of the generals.

She wished he would discuss current news and what was happening along the western front. Thousands of Americans were pouring into France and filling the gaps in the Allied line. How many of General "Black Jack" Pershing's troops, including her brother, Michael, were in France? Oh, if only this wretched war would end and Michael would come home again. Her older sister, Sarah, had a double reason to wish the war was over, for besides Michael, she had Frank, her fiancé, in northeastern France to worry about. Frank was a flyer with the Lafayette Escadrille. Poor Sarah. She didn't talk much about Frank . . . but the experts predicted that the average life of a pilot was only three weeks. Frank had been a flyer in France for three months, one of the lucky ones. But luck had a way of running out. He wrote to Sarah often, and she knew their letters were filled with wedding plans. As soon as he came back to Washington, they would marry. Please, God, she prayed, let Frank come back safe and sound.

"Cassandra," Mr. Blair rapped out the name of Laura's closest friend. "What was the result of Lee's retreat at Gettysburg? Did General Meade pursue him?"

Laura glanced over at Cassie, whose large brown eyes stared at Mr. Blair, then Cassie lowered her long lashes and studied her folded hands. It was obvious she didn't know.

"Have you read the material, Cassandra?" he asked with a resigned expression on his chiseled features.

Cassie looked up. Her delicate face was impassive as she said quietly, "No, sir, I didn't have time for my schoolwork last night."

"You didn't have *time*?" he mused. "How very odd!" His lopsided smile mocked his unsmiling eyes.

Cassandra said nothing, but her cheeks

reddened. Mr. Blair continued. "You had more pressing matters to attend to rather than your history?"

"Yes, sir, I did," she said as her lovely chin rose a notch and she looked straight into Mr. Blair's eyes.

Mr. Blair was obviously enjoying this confrontation, knowing he had the upper hand. Laura was astonished at Cassie's bold reply. What was she thinking of?

Mr. Blair tapped the pointer against his leg. "What may I ask was this urgent matter?"

"I'd rather not say," Cassandra answered calmly.

Laura studied Cassandra's perfectly formed nose and mouth, envying her friend's beauty. Her gentle, but firm, stand against Mr. Blair reminded Laura of Joan of Arc facing her inquisitors.

"Very well," Mr. Blair snapped. "Come in before school in the morning for additional work."

When the bell shrilled, Laura gathered her books and hurried to Cassandra, who was already halfway down the hall. Breathless, she came alongside her best friend. "What made you say that, Cassie? Mr. Blair will loathe you forever."

Cassie shrugged her slim shoulders and looked over at Laura, giving her an enigmatic smile.

"Well?" Laura questioned, consumed with curiosity. Even though she was of medium height, she still had to look up to Cassie. "Are you going to tell me about your mysterious doings last night?"

Cassie hesitated. "Not yet, but perhaps one day soon, Laura." Her expensive gray-and-plaid dress was cinched at her small waist with a wide black belt, and she moved so gracefully. Everytime Laura walked beside her she felt like an energetic, disheveled child with her long hair in disarray and jacket flung over her shoulder.

"All right," she said, respecting Cassie's secret. "When you're ready to confide in me, I know you will. I just hope you don't antagonize Mr. Blair any further. I know how vindictive he can be. No matter what I do, he pokes fun at me or drips sarcasm." Her tone was one of bewilderment as she tried to fathom Mr. Blair's reason for his dislike of her.

"Don't you see?" Cassie said soberly. "He's upset by women and what they are doing now. You're a threat to him, Laura Mitchell. You dare stand up to him. A man like Mr. Blair can't tolerate that!"

"I'd say you were pretty defiant, too." She looked at Cassandra in amazement, though, for in a few sentences she had analyzed Mr. Blair's treatment of women, his female students in particular. "Just be careful you don't push him too far," she warned.

"Oh, I won't," Cassie promised.

Later, going home from school, as Laura approached Washington Circle she could see a crowd with several mounted policemen shouting and yelling as they tried to hold their rearing horses in check.

When Laura came closer, she could see that they were disbanding a group of women. She caught and held her breath. What was happening?

All at once a patrol wagon, with siren blaring, pulled up and came to a screeching halt in the center of the melee. Several policemen leaped out and pushed their way into the crowd, hitting women at random. One man knocked a thin woman to the ground, while another officer stood over her with his billy club raised. Laura stifled a scream. She wanted to run to help the prostrate woman, but her knees shook beneath her. Three policemen surrounded the poor woman, yanked her to her feet, and half-dragged, half-carried her semiconscious form over to the closed van. It was horrible, and all Laura could do was to stand and tremble.

The sound of neighing horses, cursing police, and screaming women unnerved Laura. She was so helpless, almost paralyzed, as she watched a woman, who had chained herself to a lamp post, being taunted by a policeman attempting to spring the padlock.

The women began to flee, scattering in every direction, so that the whistle-blowing officers, both afoot and on horseback, couldn't grab them.

A small woman in black with a yellow ribbon across her chest darted in Laura's direction. Her hat was askew, and one long braid dangled free.

Instinctively Laura ducked behind a hedge but peered at the scene through the branches. The woman hoisted a placard high in the air —GIVE US THE VOTE — and dashed to a statue. Her hat flew off, and she spun around to fling her sign at the pursuing horseman. As the policeman dismounted she huddled at the base of the statue of George Washington, and although she tried to scramble away, the policeman grabbed her by the loose braid. With his nightstick waving above her, he pulled her along. Despite the woman's frantic struggle, she was hustled to the waiting van, handcuffed and relentlessly thrust inside.

Terrified that she might be arrested, too, Laura watched in agony as each of the women was captured and forcibly thrown into the van. One suffragist fought with her attacker, beating him about the head with her sign, but he furiously jerked it from her hands, threw it in the gutter and stomped on it.

Laura placed her fist against her mouth, not daring to utter the moan that threatened to escape. What had these women done? She knew they were suffragists by the yellow ribbons across their chests, and she knew they were demanding the right to vote, but what terrible deeds had they really done?

The woman chained to the lamp post spoke softly to one of the officers, but he paid no attention. Several others joined him, and they roughly pried her loose from the tangled links of chain.

"Oh, no, no," Laura whispered, seeing the woman's bloody wrists. Her stomach heaved, and her hands were clammy.

After the van had been jammed to capacity, it rattled away with its horn honking triumphantly. The mounted police followed while Laura stood numbly watching them leave the violent scene.

Washington Circle, deserted and tranquil, appeared as if nothing had happened.

The moonlight cast a silver glow over the emptiness, except for a marble George Washington who perused all before him with a calm, but resolute, face.

Strewn over the ground were pamphlets and tiny American flags, which fluttered in the wind like dead butterflies. Laura, tears filling her eyes, slowly gathered several pamphlets, all the while thinking of the suffragists and their cause. She stooped for a tiny flag and stuck it in her lapel.

SUNFIRE™ ROMANCES

Spirited historical romances about the lives and times of young women who boldly faced their world and dared to be different.

From the people who brought you WILDFIRE®...

An exciting look at a NEW romance line!

Imagine a turbulent time long ago when America was young and bursting with energy and passion...

When daring young women defied traditions to live their own lives...

When heart-stirring romance and thrilling adventure went hand in hand...

When the world was lit by *SUNFIRE*...

JOANNA by Jane Claypool Miner $2.95

After her sweetheart has shipped out to sea, lovely JOANNA
leaves her farm to find mill work in Lowell, Massachusetts.
What she really finds are dangerous working conditions, a
romance with the mill owner's nephew Theo, and the challenge to join other women at the mill in a strike that could
cost JOANNA everything she has gained.

JESSICA by Mary Francis Shura $2.95

Set in the harsh Kansas prairie of 1873, this is one of the most
romantic Sunfires. Jessica Findlay, while caring for the child of
a young widower, is caught in a ravaging flood. A young
Cheyenne brave saves them, and so begins a secret, forbidden
romance between star-crossed lovers.

CAROLINE by Willo Davis Roberts $2.95

When Caroline's brothers leave Missouri to join the California
Gold Rush, their adventurous sister decides to set off after
them. Lopping off her long blond hair and donning a pair of
britches, she disguises herself as a boy for the long, dangerous
journey. But how can she keep from revealing her identity to
her travelling companion... attractive Will Riddle?

KATHLEEN by Candice F. Ransom $2.95

It's Boston; the year is 1847. Kathleen has just arrived in
America after a long and torturous journey across the
Atlantic, and every member of her family is dead. But her
proud Irish heritage and a yearning to return home again
compel her to take a job with the wealthy Thornley family...
where she falls in love with her rich employer's son.